Blood

American Vampires #2

BROTHERS

NEW YORK TIMES BESTSELLING AUTHOR

JA HUSS

Edited by RJ Locksley
Cover Design by JA Huss

About the Book

For thousands of years, the Darkness has chosen its champions—granting power, feeding ambition, and demanding sacrifice to those it favored.

The Vampire Paul is not this champion.
He is, however, cunning and patient.

Ryet, cursed by his demonic transformation, is bound by blood to Syrsee, a witch whose very existence fuels his hunger and his torment. Each drop of her blood brings him closer to becoming the monster he fears, even as their connection grows intoxicatingly intimate. Is it love between them? Or just an addiction?

Paul, the creator, sees Ryet as his masterpiece, the key to his salvation—and his undoing. Driven by ambition and the promise of a legacy, Paul will stop at nothing to see his vision realized, even as it fractures the fragile bonds of love and loyalty he's earned with Ryet.

But it is Josep, favored and chosen by the Darkness itself, who holds the true power. As he wields his gifts to shape the future, his arrogance blinds him to forces conspiring for control.

The Darkness always demands more—and the battle for eternity is only beginning.

Two Weeks Ago
We are the Darkness and the Darkness is us.

I walk towards **Paul** and place my hands on his shoulders, looking him in the eyes. They are red these days, like the anger inside him. "This is it?"

Paul nods his head, searching my eyes or maybe getting lost in them. "Ryet's not here yet, but he will be shortly. The girl is being bled out right now. You will have your share in a matter of hours."

A long exhale comes out and I release Paul's shoulders. I turn, then walk across the smooth rock cave floor and over to the little pool of cool water that is collecting underneath my trickling waterfall.

I look down into the water—it's black. Black and shiny. Like a mirror. Like a portal to the Darkness that lives deep below the earth. I can see it on the other side of the water, though this is not how I physically make contact with it.

The Darkness undulates with slow, gentle movements. Like ink. But it's not ink. It can rise up and be whatever it wants to be. It could be me, or Paul, or anyone. It has been me, many times over. It was Paul too, once upon a time.

I turn back to Paul, smiling now. Because this little witch's blood will change everything from this day forward. Nothing will ever be the same after tonight.

We are making a new kind of Darkness. Something that

hasn't been attempted since... well. Since the Darkness came to be, I imagine.

"We did it," I say.

Paul is looking handsome, as usual. Especially surrounded in the misty lavender light of my cave. "We did."

I can hardly believe it. "He's going to be born tonight?"

Paul nods. "Absolutely."

"And how long—"

"I don't know. A week, perhaps? You know how slow things move across the ocean. Regardless, the Obscurati will know what's happening soon enough."

"Yeah." It almost comes out as a chuckle. But I turn just in time to hide my smile. The lavender mist cooling my body and filling the cave is making everything glow.

Paul and I met after he tried to kill his maker, as one occasionally does. It's not a heinous crime, per se, but the Obscurati look down on cheaters. And Paul is nothing if not a cheater. He takes shortcuts.

Well, he did. That was his real crime. Not the killing of the maker. Evolution must be done stepwise—slowly and carefully, over many hundreds of years—so when a talented newborn skips ahead, well. He must be put in his place and forced to slow down.

That's all that happened back in the Old World. Of course, it's very easy to see the complete picture from a distance. But in the moment, it didn't feel like a slap on the hand. It felt very personal. Paul's banishment to the wild lands of America was only meant to be a timeout. He didn't understand that and, of course, I didn't bother filling him in. Punishment is a cure for tarnished character and Paul's character was in desperate need of polishing.

Paul was energetic, and ambitious, and eager. I was tired, and bored, and apathetic.

I was never a talented newborn, but I had favor with the Darkness. I was singled out in this way. The Darkness has liked me since my birth. It would visit often when I was a scion, following me like an ink-stained shadow through the years. Guiding me forward. Giving me little hints about how to proceed when the ambition to figure it out on my own eluded me.

It had me make terrible, terrible things. Of course, these terrible things were for the Darkness itself, not me. But I was the one responsible for them and the Darkness did not interfere with my punishment from the elder brothers in the Obscurati. They didn't like the fact that I was favored. That I could, theoretically, get the Darkness to do my bidding by simply asking.

I wasn't interested in asking for gifts from the Darkness. Not then, not even now. There is a high price to pay when you are blessed with success without earning it. Nothing is free, after all. There is always a cost.

The brotherhood couldn't force me to use my gift. But they could make my life very uncomfortable if I didn't.

So that's what they did.

My life, from the moment I was second-born as a scion, was a series of torturous events at the hands of these brothers, so when Paul came to me with this offer—a vial of dead blood to kill myself in exchange for a blessing from the Darkness so he could complete his project—of course I agreed.

I never wanted to be this thing that I am.

I never asked for the Dark blessing.

I didn't kill myself. Obviously. It's funny how it happens

like that. You get what you want, your greatest desire, and then… it's just not as sweet as you thought it would be.

I still have that jar of dead blood around here somewhere.

When Paul was banished, he said, "Come with me." He wasn't as congenial back then. He was rather dark, actually. His voice always had a tinge of anger in it.

And of course, I went with him. Because the Darkness wanted to go as well.

It came with me, you see. Like an ink-stained burden on my back. Heavy with anticipation and weighted with expectations.

And now, here we are. After all these failures, success in the form of a scion called Ryet.

"Did you have your visit with the Darkness?" Paul's voice is different. Angry again. He's been playing the part of a congenial asshole for centuries and I suppose he's tired of it. Just like I was tired back in the Old World.

These days I almost never think about killing myself. I think about what's coming instead. It's enough. Especially now that we're so close. But even just the dream of it was enough. If there was a chance we could succeed, I could push on.

I turn to Paul and nod, answering his question. "Weeks ago." I point to my neck, even though the puncture marks healed almost the moment they were made. "But it's still in there, of course. All you have to do is bite."

He stares at my neck, perhaps searching for those puncture marks. Then he goes still for several moments.

I watch him as his mind wanders. Perhaps imagining the news and the faces of the brothers when they hear of our success. Perhaps he is imagining the weight of the crown he will soon be wearing.

Beautiful Paul. He was favored always, as well. In his own way. Not by the Darkness, though. By everyone else *but* the Darkness.

They had high expectations of him. And did he ever deliver. Certainly not in the way they figured, but he did deliver. Hideous, awful things. All from a single drop of blood in the dark.

Just one drop. That's all the Darkness gave him.

But what he did with it, my God. Spectacular. It truly was. Even I was impressed and I have made many a hideous thing in my day.

"Yes. Right." Paul's stillness breaks and he walks towards me.

There is a moment of awkwardness as he considers how he would like to take my blood, which is not for himself, but a gift to pass on to Ryet and the little Black witch.

It's been a very long time since he's bitten me. There's no point unless I have something to give him. The last time that happened was when we made Ryet. It was Paul's idea to genetically engineer a witch for him.

But while it was his idea, I was the one who made it happen.

Teamwork makes the dream work.

Paul is suddenly right up against me, pressing himself into my body, his hard chest against mine. I press back, as one does when they are about to be fed on. There's no way to stop the arousal. I gave up trying thousands of years ago.

Then I look Paul in the eyes and bite my lip. He smiles when the blood trickles out and this smile pleases me. My eyes brighten the room with light in response.

Paul inhales, like he's gathering up my scent, and then my

hands slide over his hips and his grab my head, preparing for the kiss.

And then he's kissing me. Taking my blood into his mouth. He sucks on my lip until it heals and then, tipping my head back to expose my throat, he bites.

I don't know what it's like to bite me. I only know what it's like to be bitten.

It's a walk in the woods for me. Snow under my feet, lavender mist filling the air around me. It's a place Paul and I made together over the centuries. This is how we manifest the passing of the blood. It's just our minds walking in this forest. Nothing more. My body, I know from past experience, is unconscious back in the cave.

Losing time isn't anything to be worried about though. And soon enough, I'm opening my eyes in the cave and I am drinking Paul. I take the blood back, relishing the newness of it. Closing my eyes and letting images flash past. They do not make sense to me, but I don't care about the images. All I want is that blood.

When I've had enough, I bite my lip and he drinks me again.

We do this over.

And over.

And over.

Until we are the Darkness and the Darkness is us.

Right Now.
Welcome home, Syrsee.

J'm hungry and the cravings have started again. But I just fed two hours ago and even though I know it's getting worse—it's *all* getting worse—giving in to the craving right now just feels like acceptance. Which is the best way forward for me. Acceptance. Because there's no way out of this. There's no way back.

"Wow." Syrsee blows out a breath, making a little mist of steam in the cab of the truck. She's smiling. "They're nice people."

I'm smiling too. On the outside, at least. "Yeah." I put the truck in gear and we move forward up my driveway, leaving the little welcoming committee—my neighbors who live along this holler with me—behind us in the rear view. "They are nice. I mean, they weren't always like this. When I first showed up here, they didn't like me at all. It was as if they knew there was something wrong with me."

"They didn't act that way today." Syrsee is leaning forward as we go up my hill, anxious to see what's at the top. Which is my house and my land. Our new home, I guess.

For now, at least.

"No. This generation is pretty cool about the whole thing. I don't even think they're afraid of me anymore."

Syrsee chuckles. "Should they be?"

Maybe not before—I've never had any urges to hurt

humans. It's been a long time since I've taken any notice of humans—but I'm definitely not the same guy anymore. "No. Of course not." I say this with a confidence I don't actually feel. But it must come off genuine enough because Syrsee is barely paying attention to my answer. She's too busy looking around. "It's not much"—I mean the house, which has just come into view—"but I built it myself."

Syrsee leans back in her seat as I park the truck in the gravel driveway in front of the cabin, still looking around. "Seriously?"

"Yep." I turn the engine off, but neither of us makes to get out. "About... fifty years ago, I guess. Cut down all the trees myself and everything. There were a few teenagers around back then who weren't afraid of me. They helped."

"Are they still alive?" She's looking at me now.

"Yeah. Billy Mark and Robby Corten." I smile, thinking about them. "They were eighteen or nineteen. Something like that. Which was old enough to drink at the time, so they would bring me beer. Try to get me drunk so I would talk. It didn't really work, but they hung around and helped out, so I painted them a little picture about the devil I worked for."

"You told them about Paul?"

"I didn't tell them his name. I just tried to explain that monsters weren't what they thought."

I'm looking at her when these words come out of my mouth. Her green eyes are flashing. Bright and curious. She was so mad at me back in the desert when she threw that fit on the side of the road. She was tired, and confused, and scared, too.

After I took over and started handling things, she changed. Her stress level dropped, she took a nap, and she was relieved,

I think, that she didn't have to make all the decisions anymore. Then she stopped being afraid of me.

It's probably the wrong move for her. I mean, I don't *want* to hurt her. I have no plans or desires to hurt her. But I didn't have any plans or desires to be turned into a vampire, either.

Yet here we are.

Syrsee is still looking at me. Reading my mind, I guess. "I'm not afraid of you."

"Don't you think you should be?"

She lifts one shoulder up in a shrug. "We'll see." Then she opens her door and gets out of the truck.

I stay where I am. Allowing myself another moment to shake off the feeling that my future, which is tied to her future, will be a disaster.

It doesn't have to be that way, Ryet. You don't have to turn into a cliché.

No. That's true, I guess. I don't. But I haven't been in control of anything in a very long time. I'm fairly certain that whatever is coming has nothing to do with my wants or choices.

I take a deep breath, let it out, then get out of the truck and try to see my ninety-three-acre West Virginia hilltop through Syrsee's eyes.

It's a lot of forest. Really thick with trees. But there are dozens of trails going through it, so it's good for hiking, which is good for thinking. And I kinda need that right now.

The drive was nice, but most of the time over the past few days my situation didn't really feel real. Now, though, the wings are starting to itch. I can feel them pushing up against the skin of my back. Stretching it. And one day, probably one day very soon, they're gonna break through the skin and just the thought of that is enough to make my heart race.

JA HUSS

Syrsee is standing on the stone pavers that lead up to a nice-size front porch, but she's turning in a circle, trying to get a three-hundred-and-sixty view to start things off.

I shake off the sense of foreboding, then walk up to her, place a hand on her hip, and point a finger in the direction she's facing. "There's a trail through there that leads to a lake." We turn a little to the right as I continue to point. "That clearing keeps going over that drop, and into the valley below." We turn again. "There's an old cabin that way. I lived there while I was building this place." And our final turn brings us face to face with the house. "Two bedrooms, two baths. Nothing fancy, but every bit of wood that you'll see—inside and out—was cut from the trees in these forests."

She turns a little so she can see my face. "You're very handy, Ryet."

"Well, I started out as a mechanic and when you have sixty-five years of youth, that's a lot of opportunity to learn things."

"Hmm. Probably right. But I doubt Paul spent his youth learning how to build cabins and remodel bathrooms."

"No." Then I laugh. "I can't even picture that." This is when I realize we haven't talked about Paul yet. She hasn't said anything about what happened up in the tower room of Paul's compound. I don't remember much about that night, and most of what I do remember was just Syrsee yelling at me to hold myself up and walk as we made our way through the house to Paul's bedroom so we could escape through his secret tunnel to the garage. I don't know what happened in that tower. Obviously, we—Paul and I both—were drinking her. We were drinking each other too.

Blood. That's really all I remember. There was a lot of blood.

14

But this is not the time to talk about Paul. She must feel it too because when I take her hand and start leading her up the stone pavers as an excuse to change the subject, she doesn't protest.

The porch is very nice. I like porches, so whenever I'm building a place I always put one on. But everything about this cabin is nice, actually. I spent about five years building it. Five years, near the beginning of my second life, where I mostly lived like a normal man. I took my time—no reason not to— and lived in the small cabin in the woods.

Syrsee and I walk up the porch stairs and then I realize I don't have my keys. We didn't take my truck, just some random truck from the Montana compound's underground garage. I put up a finger. "Hold on. I need to break in."

Syrsee chuckles. "Need any help?"

"Nah. There's a root cellar over there." I point to the right side of the house. "It's got a back entrance."

"Well, that's not creepy."

"I'll be right back." I hop over the porch railing and go around to the back of the house and down a little embankment. At the bottom I find a stacked-stone wall built into the side of the hill. There is a heavy wooden door leading to the space inside.

The root cellar is not locked and when I enter the first thing I notice is how well I can see in the dark. The second thing is that I can smell *everything*. The earth, water from a recent rain, half a dozen small animals with completely different scent profiles, dried leaves, sticks, the wood I used to build the shelves and even the nails holding the shelves together.

I squint into the darkness, fascinated by my new vision

skills. Not like it's daylight. Not like it's moonlight, either. Something else. There's a bit of color. Silver. No. *Lavender*.

And there's something in there, because the mist is moving and undulating.

"Paul?" I peer into the shadows. "Is that you?" Which is kind of a dumb thing to assume, but I associate him with the ground. The dirt. Him and Josep, both. I haven't read a lot of vampire lore so I'm not sure how common this urge to bury one's self in the ground is, but Josep lives underground full time and Paul stays buried for extended periods as well.

Of course, there is no Paul in here. And a moment later, there is no mist, either. My ability to see in the dark fades and even the scents that were just a moment ago so clear and distinct are gone. All I smell now are mice. And you don't need any kind of supernatural powers to smell mice.

"Well." I sigh. "Was that a tease or a threat?" Hard to tell, but it doesn't matter. Because there's no one here to answer back.

It's just me. Alone in the dark under the earth.

＊＊＊

WHEN I OPEN the front door for Syrsee I find her sitting on the porch in an old rocking chair. She gets to her feet quickly, like I scared her, then lets out a breath, confirming it to be true.

I raise an eyebrow at her. "You OK?"

"Sure. Yeah. Why?"

"You look… spooked."

She swallows, shaking her head at the same time. "No. I mean, it was a little quiet. And you were gone longer than I thought you would be. Was there a problem with the root cellar?"

"No." I shrug. "I mean, the tunnel was a little muddy." I point to my boots, which have evidence of this. "But it's still a good root cellar. It's holding up."

Syrsee leans to the side a little, trying to see past me. "Tunnel? Where does it come in? To the house, I mean."

"Oh. The basement." I wave a hand at the door. "Come on. Come inside."

"That's double creepy, Ryet."

"Unsurprisingly, it was Paul's idea. I just… put it in. But it does come in handy."

Syrsee is about to step past me and enter the cabin, but then she pauses, looking at me. "Have these people around here ever met Paul?"

I think back for a moment. Trying to remember a time when Paul might've been here when the humans were hanging about. "Yeah, they have. The boys who helped me, at least. But they didn't realize what he was."

"I don't understand." Syrsee makes a face. "They would not be able to tell that he's evil? They wouldn't *feel* it, Ryet? Because even if I was blind, I would be able to feel his wrongness in a crowded room."

"Well, you're a Black witch, Syrsee. You can probably do a lot of things regular humans have no clue about. They couldn't really see him."

"Was he a ghost or something? An apparition? Only half there?"

"No. He wasn't a ghost. Mirage is maybe a better word. They could see him, but they didn't pay any attention to him. I think he was going through something—a phase, or some kind of vampire maturation point, maybe. Because he would spend years at a time in the earth back then."

Syrsee and I both look at the side of the house that leads to the root cellar and come to the same conclusion in pretty much the same instant. She's the one who says it out loud. "That's why he needed the root cellar?"

"Maybe. Anyway." I let out a breath, wanting to change the subject. I'm hungry. I don't care about Paul and his mysteries. I just want to *feed*. I invite her in with a wave of my hand. "Welcome home, Syrsee."

She hesitates for a moment, perhaps wondering if a vampire inviting you into his home might come with conditions. Kind of like that myth humans have been perpetuating for the last hundred years about inviting a vampire into a human home.

But if these conditions do exist, I'm not aware of them. And she, being a Black witch—albeit a baby one—can probably feel my honesty the same way she can feel Paul's evil. So she steps past me and goes inside. I follow and close the door behind us.

2 - Syrsee

Nothing but a hen.

He's hungry. I can see it now. I've spent the last two weeks feeding him and there is definitely a pattern of behavior that only occurs when he needs my blood. It's nothing as obvious as bloodshot eyes or pale skin. It's more like an energy coming off him. A vibration, almost. It's always there, but when he's hungry the velocity of the wave increases.

Wow. Velocity. Not a word typically found in my vocabulary. I know what it means. Speed. But it's a very specific kind of speed that pertains to waves and…

I shake my head to stop this train of thought. *What the hell, Syrsee? No one cares.*

Anyway. When he's hungry this wave vibration is more urgent. I can't explain it, but I can feel it and it's happening right now.

It comes with colors too. Like the purple letters that came with the phrase 'blood lovers' back when I was first turning into… well, whatever it is I am now.

I haven't had much time to think about the changes happening inside me. I can feel them. But I can't explain them. I just know I'm not the same person who walked into my grandma's cabin on New Year's Eve. The moment I walked out, and she was dead, everything about me changed.

And that's just the beginning. Who the hell knows what

was done to me while the blood orgy happened up in that tower room at Paul's compound.

I close my eyes in this moment when Ryet's back is to me and he's closing the cabin door. Then I take a quick breath, give myself a speedy pep talk—which amounts to nothing more than *Don't think about it, Syrsee*—and force myself to smile so when Ryet turns back to me I don't come off as resentful.

Even though I feel some resentment about this whole situation.

The little neighbor welcome wagon down the hill was a nice distraction. And it's all been fine since Ryet woke up and we started heading to West Virginia. It was a relief, actually. For him to take over and start making decisions so I didn't have to.

But reality won't wait forever. And my pep talks suck.

Bright side—Ryet's hunger is distracting and imminent, so I don't really have the luxury of dwelling on my insecurities. The color of the wave coming off Ryet is not purple. It's yellow. Kind of gold, actually. Which is good. Because I've got enough purple going on these days and having a separate color for this particular event—or behavior, or whatever you want to call it—should make it easier to determine which state of insanity I'm currently residing in.

Purple equals past, present, future. Also sex dreams. Which aren't dreams, but kind of are... so... yeah. I've got way more purple than I need.

And now, gold equals food. As in *I* am the food.

"So." Ryet is smiling and walking towards me. He pans his arms out, presenting his cabin. "What do you think?"

"It's really nice." I look around. Turning in a slow circle to take it all in. And it *is* nice. It's very log cabin-y on the inside.

Wide-plank wood floors, cotton-rag rugs, couches that don't have drink holders, and an entire color wheel of neutral colors. Browns, and warm grays, and off-whites.

Even though we've only known each other a couple of weeks, it's the kind of work I've come to expect from him. Lots of wood paneling, and logs, and it's clearly been made with care.

Care is a good word for Ryet. He's careful. Very careful. He likes details. Not just in the craftsmanship of his woodwork or bathroom renovations, but in his choice of words, the way he approaches people, and how he, even now, keeps a certain distance from me.

I look back at him and that gold wave is coming right at me with an ever-increasing intensity. "You're hungry." I don't ask it as a question. I already know and I don't feel like wasting time with words that don't matter.

He doesn't say anything, just shrugs up his shoulders while looking me in the eyes.

"It's OK. I get it. You need to eat."

"I'm sorry. I really am. I wish it wasn't like this."

"But it is." I offer him a smile. It comes out small, so I make it bigger. None of this is his fault. It's not my fault, either. It's just... reality now. He needs to eat and I am his food. "Where should we do it?"

Ryet looks around, then offers up the couch. "How about right there?"

It's as good a place as any, so I walk over and sit down as Ryet crosses the room and joins me. Feeding him was different in the truck. When he was asleep, he would wake up just enough to grab at me. He wasn't strong enough to force me to feed him. So he didn't... like... pull me out of my seat, or anything. I just leaned over, and he just latched on to my neck. The feedings were quick, too. Painful, as well. But it was a minute or two of sucking and then he'd be full, or whatever, and he'd slump back into his seat, falling back into unconsciousness.

But since he woke up the feedings have been different. They're still short. He doesn't take a lot. And if he hadn't been doing that all along, I'd assume that he was cutting them short on purpose for my benefit. But they've always been quick, so I don't think he needs much blood. He just needs it frequently. They're less painful, at least. In fact, sometimes it's a little bit erotic. The feeling of blood being pulled out of me... I dunno. It's a trigger, I think. Something hormonal, maybe. Because it makes me want him. It makes me *want* to feed him.

There's a bit of awkwardness as we look at each other, neither of us really sure how to make this less uncomfortable.

Ryet tries a smile. "Hi."

Which makes me smile. "Hi."

"I'm sorry—"

I put up a hand. "Just... don't. There's no point in apologizing. It's not your fault. It's not my fault. And there's nothing we can do about it. You can feed off me or... take your chances on what happens if you don't. I'm not recommending that, by the way. Whatever those consequences are, I'm absolutely sure it will be much worse than... this." I make a little gesture to the two of us. "And I guess I could refuse to feed you. But you must have it, Ryet. And if I say no, then..."

I don't finish. I don't need to. If I don't feed him willingly, he'll just take it from me.

I am his *food*.

It's not personal, it's just nature. It's survival. If I were starving and saw a hen, for instance, I could catch it, and keep it as a pet, and eat the eggs. We could be friends. Companions. But if it stopped laying eggs, what choice would I have? I would kill it. And then consume it. It's just survival.

Ryet sighs. "I don't understand it all yet. But I'm going to figure it out. And part of that is figuring out how to free you from this."

It takes a real effort not to scoff at his *proclamation*, or whatever it is. But I manage. And I force a smile too. "Here." I lean towards him, moving my hair aside so he can have access to my neck. "Go ahead."

"Come on, now. We can do better than this." He says this easily. Lightly. Like feeding him my blood can be fun.

"What do you mean?" My tone is the opposite of fun.

He reaches for my hip and pulls me towards him, then grabs my legs and pulls them over his lap. One arm sliding behind me, the other hand reaching for my breast.

I stop breathing. Conflicted. Because the feeding is already a little bit sexual and this is just adding to it. I'm not sure I want to associate drinking my blood with sexual arousal.

But I can't deny that I like this switch in position. I like the feel of his body next to mine and his hand on my breast. It's not like I want to stop all this closeness and touching, it's just disconcerting that I find it enjoyable, given that he's literally eating me.

I don't have time to ponder this further, though, because that hunger of his is coming at me like a wave and my whole body picks up on his cravings. There doesn't seem to be any way forward except for surrender. So I let out a breath and lean my head to the side. Closing my eyes as he presses his mouth to the soft, tender skin just below my jaw.

I expected a little more hesitation. A few more awkward moments. More effort, on his part, to protest the unfairness of it all. But almost immediately I feel the sharp twinge of his teeth piercing my skin. It's like two needle pricks. Jolting, a little bit painful, but over quickly.

He pauses here. This has been his little ritual since he woke up. When he was mostly unconscious, he didn't pause. He sank them in deep and took. So the pause is his conscious effort to make it easier on me. I'm not sure it does, though. It might just prolong it. I might just prefer he be rougher and get it over with.

There is a little bit of pressure now. And this is what triggers the hormonal response, I think. Because new feelings rush through me. And the slower he goes, the more I feel them.

His hand is on my breast, gently squeezing it, when he takes the first pull.

I almost come undone from the warmth that floods through my body. His lips on my neck, the pulling of the blood, his hand on my breast—it's more than just a little bit sexual, it's erotic and I'm getting turned on. My breath is coming faster, my heart beating quicker, and for a moment, I think I might come.

Then I'm sure of it, but just before I do, he stops. Pulls back. Sighs.

And all the feelings inside me go with him.

I let out a long breath, feeling very embarrassed at what almost happened, and then open my eyes. Ryet's head is resting back on the couch cushions, his eyes closed, his lips smiling. Like he just came as well.

I bite my lip and squirm until I'm off his lap and back in my own space. "Feel better?"

"Mmmm-hmmm." He can barely talk. "Much better."

I watch him for a few moments, captivated by the

expression of bliss on his face. Picturing myself with that same feeling if he had just fed on me for a few more moments. The most confusing part of this is that I'm not sure if I'm upset that he's feeling this way and I'm not, or I'm just resentful that it's so enjoyable for him.

Ryet sighs, then opens his eyes. "Thanks. I really do feel much, *much* better."

"How come you don't feed longer, Ryet? I mean, instead of taking frequent little sips, couldn't you just… take a lot and need it less often?"

He sinks into the cushions a little. Like he's getting comfortable. His eyes are lazy and low. Like he might sleep. "I don't really have control of it."

"What do you mean?"

"I need it. I get it. And the moment my teeth sink into you and the blood flows, I lose control. The need goes away and then… I don't even make a decision to be done. I just pull away when I am."

I'm not sure if I should be horrified about this or… no. Actually, horrified is the only appropriate response to what he just said. "What if you…" I can't finish. I don't want to have this conversation and I'm instantly sorry for asking the question.

"What if I kill you?"

I shrug up one shoulder. Might as well get the answer to this now, rather than later. "What if?"

He forces himself to sit up straighter and open his eyes wider, looking at me. "I don't think that's how your death works, Syrsee. Maybe, before you fed me, you could die like other people. But now?" He shakes his head. "You need the long drink. That's when you feed on me, and then I feed on you, and we pass the blood back and forth until…" He gives up on the explanation. "It's not an easy thing to do. It's not quick, either."

My head turns away from him automatically. I don't mean to do it, but I'm glad it happens. Because I don't want him to see the look on my face. I can't hide it anymore. I can't hide the resentment and the horror.

I don't want to resent this. I don't. I like Ryet. I don't want to be anywhere else right now. I want to be with him.

But how will this relationship ever be about anything other than *his* needs?

We will stay together. But it won't have anything to do with liking each other, let alone loving each other one day. We will stay together because of my blood and there is no way to change that.

I resent that I am the only way he gets to stay alive and I resent that I am nothing but a hen to him. Feeding him eggs. Until one day, I'm too old to do that. And on that day, he will give me something called the long drink. And that's when I will be released.

That's when I will go to Hell.

All the way over.

It is decidedly unfair. I understand this. I'm not a mind reader, but I don't need to be. It's very clear that this relationship Syrsee and I have is unbalanced and one-sided. Not because I don't like her—I do. But she will never believe that my feelings for her have nothing to do with the blood.

I'm not even going to try to convince her that this is the case, even though it is. Because if I were her, I wouldn't believe me either.

I need her. Not in a traditional lovesick way. I physically need her to... well, I don't really know what would happen to me if I stopped drinking, but I imagine it's not really up to me if it gets to that point. I imagine that it would be instincts. I imagine I would hunt her, then put her in a prison that I would call a bedroom, and then I'd feed on her for the rest of her life.

This is what Paul did.

And I'm becoming Paul.

Maybe not in the literal sense. But I am becoming a vampire. I can feel the fucking wings on my back. The sharp bones pushing against my skin. Soon, they will break through that skin and once that happens there will be no way for either of us to deny what's going on here.

It's easy to pretend we're still those people we were a

couple weeks ago when we were in White River. Bantering, smiling, eating food, making plans.

But we're not those people. Me, for sure. Obviously.

But her too. She has changed as well. She hasn't told me about it, but I can taste the magic inside her. Something is different. And it's changing. Every time I feed, I taste something new in her.

Syrsee has already wriggled out of my lap and positioned herself across to the other end of the couch. She stretches her long legs out, her feet pressing against the side of my thigh. Touching me from a distance.

I don't want to look at her face. I'm afraid of what I'll see there. But it's better to just confront it now. Better to get it over with so we can try to move on.

My head turns in her direction, but my eyes take another moment to catch up. When we finally look at each other, she looks as conflicted as I do. "I know what you're thinking," I say.

Syrsee doesn't say anything, just slowly shakes her head. Then gets up and walks over to the window.

I get up and follow her. Stand directly behind her. "You're thinking… *He needs me now. And there is no way I could ever trust him.*"

"Ryet—" She turns to face me.

But I put up a hand to stop her. "It's normal. I mean, if I was the food and you were the monster, I'd resent you too."

She bites her lip and frowns. "I don't want to feel this way about you. I like you."

"I like you too. And not just because I need your blood. We were… hitting it off, right? Before all this vampire shit happened?"

She nods. "We were."

"It doesn't have to change." She doesn't believe me. Hell, I don't even believe me. But I push on, anyway. "That should be our goal, Syrsee."

She raises one eyebrow at me. "To… convince each other we're in love?"

"No." I let out a frustrated breath. "Not in love. I mean, I like you. But I don't know if I love you. And you definitely don't love me. I don't want to pretend. I want you to believe me about this part especially. I don't want to pretend. I want it to be easy."

"Which part, Ryet? The part where you drink me a dozen times a day?"

I just stare at her, a little bit taken aback. I deserve that remark, I do. But she could try a little harder. Of course, it would be a very bad idea to say that out loud. "The part where we… spend time together. Not feeding. Doing other things."

"What other things?"

"I dunno. Walking in the woods. Grocery shopping. Going out to dinner. Cooking and shit like that. Normal things. Like we started doing before—"

"Before you started drinking me?"

"*You* fed *me*, Syrsee." It comes out harsh. "I didn't ask you to do that."

"Well…" She falters. Or perhaps she was going to cut me again with more words, but loses her nerve. Regardless, she takes a breath. "Paul told me you were gonna die. What was I supposed to do? I didn't want you to die. It was probably a lie—"

"It wasn't." I say it sternly so she knows I mean this. "It wasn't a lie, Syrsee. I would've died. I think he's killed many, *many* men like me over his lifetime and I think I'm the first who *didn't* die."

I let out a breath and try to relax. I'm not mad at her. There's nothing to be mad at her about. She's allowed to have doubts. Hell, I'd have doubts too. But she's wrong about this and if I don't tell her she's wrong, then who will?

So I continue in a lower, calmer voice. "And the reason I didn't die is because of you, Syrsee. So… thank you. I mean that. Thank you. And now that's out of the way, I won't blame you if you hate me. Because I don't want to pretend that we like each other. I'd rather you openly hate me than pretend to be my friend. So if you hate me… OK. I'll accept it, I'll leave you alone, I'll give you whatever you need to get you through the feedings. You can live somewhere else if you want. You can… see people. Whatever it takes to make it up to you, I'll do it."

She scoffs a little. "Trust me when I say this, Ryet—dating is the last thing on my mind."

"Well, the offer stands. You don't have to live here—"

"If you could eat once a day, maybe that would be an option. But I feel your need, Ryet. And I know you've been trying to go for longer periods, but you won't be able to fight these cravings all the time. And what is the point of moving out if I just have to feed you every few hours?"

I want to say it will get better. That the cravings are only strong and feedings so frequent because I'm new. But I don't know that. And now that Paul is gone, I don't have anyone to ask. I can't even ask Lucia, not that I would. But if she were still alive, it would at least be an option.

So I just shrug with my hands and sigh. "I don't know what I'm doing. I don't know what's happening to me. I have bones coming out of my back, Syrsee. And I don't know what they are, or what they're gonna look like, or what else is gonna change about me."

She swallows hard and turns to look back out the window. She probably can't stand the sight of me. And I just went and reminded her that I'm literally turning into a monster and it's going to happen right in front of her eyes.

Syrsee's voice is also low and soft when she speaks again. "I don't want to... hate you, Ryet. I don't hate you." She turns to face me again. "I want to love you. I want to... sleep next to you. And kiss you, and laugh, and have fun. I don't want to just be your *food*."

"Is that what you think?" I point to myself. "That I see you as food?"

She huffs a little. "Well, I get that it's kind of crude, but that's what I am. I'm literally feeding the monster inside you."

"I don't think you're food, Syrsee."

"What if that's the only reason you like me? And what if you don't even know that? What if your cravings—"

I don't let her finish. "Let me make this very clear." She stares up at me with wide, green eyes. "You are not food. Your blood is not *you*. And it's not the reason I like you. I like you because you're funny, and smart, and beautiful. And you're the one person in this whole world who I can be myself with. That's it. That's why I like you. And it's the same reason any man likes any woman, Syrsee. That part is not different and that part has not changed."

She pauses, taking a moment to internalize this statement, I guess. Then she lets out a sigh. "Well." A forced smile appears. "OK. That's why I like you too." Now she bites her lip, like she's holding something back and nervous about it. "It just feels a little..." She pauses. Stares at me.

"What?"

"It's gonna sound..." She makes a face and shakes her head. "It's not gonna paint me in a good light."

"What isn't?"

"The truth."

"Should I… promise not to hold it against you?"

"Are you that evolved? Because most people aren't. You might say you won't hold it against me, but then one day you'll be mad at me."

"What did you do?"

"To make you mad?" She raises an eyebrow.

"Yeah. What did you do to make me so mad that I would hold this truth against you in the future?"

"I… shrank your jeans." She tries not to smile, but fails.

"Anything else?"

"I… didn't put the cap back on the toothpaste, I'm a horrible housekeeper, maybe I even cheated on you."

Now I raise an eyebrow.

"I'm not saying I would, I'm just saying you could be mad at me for anything. It could be small, and annoying, and unimportant. Or it could be big and life-changing. The point is, you can't know how you will feel about me in the future and if I admit these feelings to you, one day you're gonna look at me and that's all you're gonna hear inside your head."

I reach for her, placing my hands on her hips, smiling down at her as she sighs. "It's not fair. That's your truth, isn't it? This relationship we have, it's unequal. You're thinking… *What do I get?* And this isn't the kind of person you usually are. You maybe even hate yourself a little for thinking this. But it's true." I shake my head and shrug my shoulders. "There's no way around it. I'm definitely getting more out of this than you are. Not only that, I have more to lose, too. So how could you ever trust me?"

She sighs and looks down at her feet. "That's exactly what

I'm thinking." But she takes a breath and looks back up at me. "This isn't who I am."

"Well, ya know what?" I hike a thumb over my shoulder to indicate whatever is happening on my back. "This isn't who I am either."

"And yet we are these people, Ryet. We are. And I don't want us to start keeping score. I don't want to constantly think about how I'm giving more than you are."

"Well"—I kinda laugh a little—"I don't want to constantly be thinking about how you're always getting less. So… I guess I will just need to work on this."

"You'll work on what? Making me feel *loved*?"

"I get it. It's not a perfect solution. But…" I take her hands and hold them in mine. "It's worth a try. Maybe one day you'll believe me. I guess that's all I can hope for. I mean, what other choice do we have, Syrsee? If you've got a solution, let's hear it. I'm sorry it turned out this way. I'm sorry you're stuck with me. I'm sorry for all of it. But I need you. And that will never change."

She nods, pressing her lips together. Her words come out even and clear. Like she's given this some thought. "Well, I cannot give you my heart like this. So. I think we need to separate things until we can sort through all the feelings."

"Separate things *how*?"

"I think we should just be friends."

"Oh." I turn and pace the living room, scrubbing my hands down my face as I look out another window facing the opposite side of the house. "So you want to *withhold* something." I turn back to face her. "Is that what you're saying?"

She doesn't deny it. In fact, she nods her head. Then she

confirms it out loud. "Yes. I want to withhold something. I want there to be a very clear line of what we are right now."

"Which is what? Friends?"

She shakes her head no. "We need to start over. All the way over."

"So you *want* to be food."

"At least it's the truth. I need this truth right now. When you feed, it can't be intimate. It's... a transaction, Ryet. And it has nothing to do with how we *feel* about each other."

I'm actually speechless. But what can I do but agree? "OK."

"So I'll need my own room, and a car, and..."

"Whatever you want. That's all fine. There are two bedrooms here. You can have your pick. We'll go shop for a car, I'll set up a bank account, and..." I mean, what else is there to say?

I just stop talking and shrug. Then I turn, without looking at her again, and I walk out.

4 - Syrsee

It was definitely a plan.

I watch Ryet through the window. He doesn't go far, just over to the truck where he starts gathering things up from the back cab—our road trip mess. Then he's slinging a backpack over his shoulder and heading back towards the house.

I move to the kitchen and start opening cupboards so he doesn't think I was watching him. I'm still doing this when he comes through the door and sets the backpacks down on a chair.

His gaze lands on me and he frowns. "Shit. We don't have any food, do we?"

I realize this is something he's going to take personally. Ryet eats, but I don't think he needs to. He could go without food in the cupboards and fridge because my blood is his food.

But I can't go without food. So it's proof that we are very different and this relationship we both seem to want is going to be a lot of work.

Months, at least. Years. Who knows, it might take decades to figure it all out. I might be an old, dying woman before we finally come to terms with it.

"We could go into town," Ryet offers.

I *do* want to go into town, but I want to go alone. "I think I'll go by myself."

Ryet looks hurt for a moment, but reins it in quickly. "If that's what you want."

"Do you need anything?"

He's about to say no. I'm almost positive. But then he pauses to think. "A razor." He rubs his hand over his scruffy cheeks.

"Anything else?" I want him to say food. Steaks. Sandwich meat. Cheese. A donut, maybe. Something, anything, that will prove to me that blood isn't his only nutritional requirement.

But he just shrugs. "Nah. I'm good."

"OK." I press my lips together and then walk over to him and hold out my hand.

He reaches into his pocket and then drops the truck key into my palm. "Do you need directions?"

"No. We passed the town on the way in. I think I can find it."

And with nothing left to say, he gives in. "OK. Be careful. See you in a bit."

I nod and leave, taking in a deep breath of fresh air as I close the front door behind me.

IT ONLY TAKES ABOUT **ten minutes** to get back to the town of Mount Royal, West Virginia. The green sign that welcomes me as I pass by the city limits says 'Population 435.' It's about ten blocks long but only two blocks wide because it's situated between a major highway and a river—the Tygart Valley

River, to be specific. It's cute. Looks like something you'd see in a movie. You have to pass through a covered bridge to get into town, then go over some railroad tracks, and after you do that the first thing you see is a church. A very stately Romanesque church made of red bricks, a dramatic semicircular arch front and center, and symmetrical towers on either side.

I'm not gonna lie, the church gives me a queasy feeling in my stomach. Though it doesn't look anything like it, I can't help but be reminded of the church in White River, which I am now convinced was a cult, and I feel lucky that we got out of there alive.

I shake my head and roll my eyes at my stupid thoughts. They were Paul's people, obviously. They weren't gonna hurt us. They were... gonna watch us, maybe. Make sure everything went to plan, I think.

It was definitely a plan.

The Guild sent me to White River so that I would bump into Ryet and he would get to feed.

That's probably ninety-nine percent of the truth, but something about that town and those people still bothers me. Specifically, that herbal tea that Emily gave me for Ryet's fever.

We didn't drink it, of course. I ended up feeding him and he got better. But Emily had a look on her face at the pancake breakfast when I said we didn't drink it.

I was distracted at the time. And not very suspicious yet, so I didn't pay much attention to this look of hers. But remembering back, I think she might've been trying to poison us or something.

A laugh bursts out of me. "Syrsee, get a hold of yourself. No one is trying to—"

I almost slam on the brakes, that's how shocked I am when I spy the sign over the general store. It says 'Mount Royal General Store,' but that's not the shocking part. The shocking part is the horse and rider symbol on both sides of the name.

I'm already passing that store—heading towards the bigger, regional supermarket that's straight in front of me—when I see the symbols. Luckily, I do not slam on the brakes. I keep cool and make a U-turn at the next cross street. Then I go back the way I came and ease the truck into the parking lot, settling right underneath the sign.

I get out and look up at it, pondering the message of the symbols. The one at the front of the word has the horse pointing right and the one at the end of the word has the horse pointing left.

Which can only mean one thing.

There is a Guild Lounge inside this general store.

My heart thumps wildly inside my chest as I internalize what is happening.

There is a *Guild Lounge* inside this store.

What does it mean? Are they following us? Have they always been here? Watching Ryet?

Then I look around at the quaint little town with its covered bridge, and picturesque church, and general store.

Sure, just up ahead there are more modern buildings. The regional grocery store. A bank. A library. None of them built recently, but none of them exhibiting nostalgia for days gone by like this side of town is.

This side of town that is clearly being controlled by the Guild.

What should I do? Go in? Say hello? Ask if they have room for me on the mani-pedi schedule?

Or go back home to Ryet and tell him we need to get the fuck out of here?

And go where?

Besides, what's the point?

If there's a Guild Lounge in this town, is there any possibility at all that they don't know exactly where Ryet lives? And given the fact that ten people were standing at the bottom of his driveway when we pulled up to it, is there any possibility at all that they don't already know we're here?

They know.

And if they left this symbol up, then they meant for me to see it. And if I was meant to see it, then I was meant to go inside.

I pull the door open—making a bell jingle over my head—and then scoot past a line of customers who are waiting to check out.

"Hello!" someone calls out. "Welcome to Mount Royal General Store!" It doesn't come from the person running the register, he's too busy checking out the line of customers. It comes from one of the interior aisles, a well-practiced greeting from an employee who is trained to the sound of the jingling bell over the door.

I scan the interior of the store and immediately, I see the next clue. Another horse and rider on the back wall. The horse is pointing left, so I turn that way and find another pointing down a hallway.

I draw in a long breath, then slowly let it out, trying to calm myself. I don't have Zusi's card anymore. It was in my purse and I don't even remember the last time I saw that purse.

But I'm here. What else am I gonna do but try to go inside? Just go home and pretend I never saw it?

Not a chance.

I walk towards the hallway where the horse is pointing, and then, when I get there, I look over my shoulder to see if anyone is watching. If someone was, I could maybe talk myself out of this. But no one is.

So I turn into the hallway and stop, staring at the door just ten feet away. It's a glass door, but it's not transparent glass. It's frosted, so while I can see shadows on the other side, I can't make out anything specific. It looks very modern with the stainless-steel accents and the card reader near the doorknob.

Very out of place. So out of place I start to wonder if anyone else can see it.

'Probably not' is my guess, but there's no real way to check my theory.

I *can* see it, though. And even though I don't have a card to enter, I'm going to try anyway.

I walk down the hall, stop at the door, and I'm just about to knock on it when it is pulled open.

Suddenly, there is a man in front of me. I'm literally eye level with his neck. And when I look up, my mouth opens in shock. "Tristin?"

He doesn't smile. That's not Tristin's style. He doesn't frown either. He just narrows his eyes at me, then grabs me by the arm and pulls me inside, closing the door behind me.

5 - Ryet

They're Josep's problem now.

It's hard for me to watch Syrsee go. There is a weird feeling inside me, an urge to go after her and bring her back. It's almost painful. It starts out as hollowness in my stomach and then progresses to a pressure in my chest as I watch the truck disappear back down the driveway.

I don't take anything about myself for granted right now. I don't know if this urge and these feelings are just emotional because we just made a major decision about our relationship —one I'm not necessarily happy with—or if it's some kind of reaction to my food source being too far away.

Food source. It's crude, but it's accurate.

Of course, Syrsee is much more than food to me. And I *thought* I was much more than an emergent vampire to her, but maybe not.

I don't know. But here is what I do know—making big decisions about anything right now would be a mistake. There's too much going on. There are too many new things to decipher. There are too many confusing feelings. So I'm trying to let it all slide down my back. Trying not to get caught up in the sense of loss, which isn't even real. I haven't lost her yet.

Yet.

That word sticks in my mind for far too many seconds.

Is it inevitable? That she will hate me one day? Is it

inevitable that she will become just another feeder in a bedroom being fed on by me?

I wish I had people to ask. In human lore like movies and TV shows, vampires come in groups. There is always a leader, a bunch of minions, and an older, wiser father or mother vampire who knows all the secrets and doles them out, little by little, on a need-to-know basis.

And even though all that shit is fiction, I'm starting to feel a little cheated. Because I have no one and nothing to guide me through this. I'm a blind man crawling around on my knees in the dark.

I turn and find myself looking at the door to the basement that leads to the root cellar. And before I know what I'm doing, I'm heading towards it. I pull open the door and stare down into the darkness, my new, better eyes adjusting automatically, focusing on the hidden shapes in the black. Steps. That's all they are.

Then the smells are all back. I can smell everything in the cabin individually. The floorboards, the curtains, the gas in the lines feeding the stove. They are separate and distinct.

But then I smell what's in the basement. And it is not separate and distinct. It is a bouquet of scents that all mix together perfectly. Dirt, and insects, and water, and rust, and iron, and tree roots.

It is the scent of earth and the moment I get to the bottom of the stairs and my feet touch the ground, a wave of relief floods through me. The pressure in my chest eases and the hollowed-out feeling in my stomach evens out. I sit down on the bottom step, take off my boots, and then stand back up, my toes wriggling in the wet dirt.

A breath comes out. I relax.

This relaxation is so immediate, I take off my jacket, then my shirt, and a minute later I've stripped naked and the scents all around me are something new now. They are a mist of lavender and it coats my body like rain.

I forget what my problem was.

I forget why I'm here.

I almost forget everything as I pull open a door and walk forward into the tunnel that leads to the root cellar. The mud squishing under my feet—even that feels good.

Syrsee wouldn't like this. I would not want her to find me like this. I would not want her to know that I am a thing that lives underground. That I am a thing that needs it. Because only gross things live underground. Only gross things don't need the light can survive in the darkness. And I can already feel it inside me. The idea that I don't just live here, I *belong* here.

The door to the root cellar appears and I open it and step inside, looking around with my new, vampire eyes. The shelves are not empty, but everything on them has rotted into a petrified version of its former self or just deteriorated away into bits and pieces. There are about a dozen glass jars on one shelf, the size of baby food jars, and next to those are vials.

Vials? I blink a few times, wondering when the hell I would've put vials in here.

Never, that's when.

Come to think of it, when did I ever can up baby food?

Again, it never happened.

So where did these jars and vials come from?

I walk over to the shelf and pick up the first jar. It's covered in a thick layer of dust and I have to wipe this all off for several seconds before I can see the label. It's faded and old, obviously, but it's also fancy. Vintage might be the right word. I read it out loud. "Thirst." Which tells me nothing. So I pick up the next one, perform the same actions, and read it out loud as well. "Hunger." I repeat this for all the jars. "Gasping. Purging. Chills. Sweats. Fatigue."

I think about these words for a moment and realize that they are symptoms. Not of diseases, but the lack of basic requirements. I set the last jar back down and start picking up the vials, cleaning them off, and setting them on the shelf in a neat line. Then I read the labels. "Despair. Loneliness. Regret. Contempt. Estrangement. Fear. Shame. Guilt."

I let out a long breath. Because I think this is like a medicine chest. Cures for what ails me. Which means I have all these things to look forward to.

With this realization, I sober up. The last bit of magical haziness that came from feeding on Syrsee evaporates and I suddenly feel like a man who woke up after a bender.

This makes me huff out a laugh. Because maybe I should drink the vial filled with the cure for guilt. And shame. And regret.

Fucking hell, I should just drink them all.

I don't, though. I just turn around and go back down the tunnel, pick up my boots and clothes, and then go back up the stairs. Once the basement door has been shut behind me, I wash my feet in the bathtub and put my clothes and boots back on, feeling a little stupid for taking them off in the first place. Then pick up our backpacks and put one in each of the two bedrooms.

I give Syrsee the one with the private bathroom and I take the other.

I unpack the meager things I have collected since being

reborn. Three pairs of jeans, two thermal shirts, four t-shirts, and some socks and underwear. I put all these things in a dresser that is mostly empty—the top drawer is filled with towels. Then I put my toothbrush in the hallway bathroom.

This is it. This is what my life has become. A backpack of clothes and a toothbrush. I don't even have a phone.

But just as I'm thinking this, I look over at the one hanging on the wall in the kitchen. I walk over there and pick it up, then smile when I hear a dial tone.

Too bad I don't have anyone to call. But I feel five percent less isolated than I did thirty seconds ago and I'll take it.

I'm just turning my back to it with the intention of heading outside when it rings.

I turn back, staring at it. "Really?" I ask the phone.

It responds by ringing again.

I pick it up. "Yeah."

"Ryet! Oh. My. God! *Ryet*! I've been calling you for weeks!"

"Echo?"

"Are you OK? Where are you? Is Paul there?"

"Yes, I'm OK. You called me, so you know where I am. And no. Paul's not here."

I have never hated Echo. I actually kinda like her. She's a little brown-noser when it comes to Paul, but she's just a halfbreed. It's kinda her job to do that. She takes a moment to actually internalize my answers, then huffs out a laugh. "Right. I called you. I forgot, it's a landline. So you're at your place?"

"Obviously." Though I don't hate Echo, this is enough to make me tired of her. "What do you want?" It occurs to me here—only after I've said these words in the rudest way possible—that I should possibly, maybe be nicer to her since she is… well, all I've got in terms of friends and family at the moment. Sad as that is.

"Paul is gone. Do you know where he is? I mean, I'm sure he's fine. Underground or something. But the halfbreeds, Ryet. They're taking advantage of everything. They're going a little crazy too." She lowers her voice here. "I found Lucia up in that tower room. Paul cut off her head, Ryet. Her *head*!"

"Right. Yeah. I was there." Sort of. "So. Why are you calling?"

"The halfbreeds. What are they supposed to *eat*?"

"I'm sorry?"

"They… we… *we* have to eat. And the feeder died. What happened to the Black witch you and Paul brought home for us? Do you know where she is? We're… *hungry*."

"First of all, I didn't bring her 'home' for you. I didn't bring her there at all. Second, you're a halfbreed. Order a pizza if you're hungry."

"Well"—she scoffs here—"duh. We have eaten. We just… haven't… *eaten*. If you know what I mean."

She means blood, of course. "Listen, Echo, I'm sorry it's turned out this way, but the blood is gone."

"*What*? What do you mean?"

"The blood. Is gone." Even if I was in the mood to share, I would never share with the halfbreeds. There is no way in hell that Syrsee will end up feeding halfbreeds. She's mine. She was made for me. And the sooner these tweakers get past this little truth, the better. "You need to go back to eating like humans. For every meal. There are no more Black witches in your future. Is there anything else?"

Echo is speechless on the other end of the line.

"Echo?"

"Right. Um. Are you *sure?*"

"Am I sure there is no more blood for you? Yes, Echo. I'm sure."

"But where is Paul?"

"I don't actually know. In the ground, probably."

"The ground."

"Yep. Are we good?"

"Last time he went to ground he stayed away for two years. Is that what we can expect?"

"Probably."

"O... K." She pauses. Like she's picking and choosing her words very carefully. "But who's in charge here? I mean, we've never been left alone before. We always had Lucia."

"Josep, I presume."

"I'm sorry?"

"Jo-sep."

"Who the hell is Josep?"

"The vampire who lives under the house. Good luck with that, by the way. I've gotta go. Bye."

I hang up the phone, smiling, feeling a bit satisfied, actually. It's not nice to confuse her. I mean, she probably is feeling the effects of no blood. I've never been a halfbreed, obviously, so I can't be sure. But even if it's just psychological, it's an addiction at this point.

I would not want to be her, that's for sure.

They're probably gonna go crazy out there in the mountains. But whatever. They're Josep's problem now, not mine. I grab my jacket and step outside.

It's only then, when I'm standing on the porch with the cold air swirling around me, that I realize I was way too warm.

It's back. It's been thirty minutes—maybe forty-five—and the hunger is back.

I take a seat in a short-back rocking chair that I made forty years back, and I settle in to wait for Syrsee. Telling myself, over and over again as I close my eyes and breathe deeply, that I will not attack her when she gets here.

6 - Syrsee

Tell her goodbye.

*T*ristin is still gripping my arm very tightly even after the door closes behind me. I wriggle free—try to, anyway—and spit up at him, "Let go of me."

"Calm down, Syrsee." Tristin says this in his low, monotone, unaffected voice. And even if I wasn't already pissed off, this tone of his would be enough to set me off.

"Calm down?" My eyes are wide, my voice too shrill. "Calm. *Down*? You fuckers set me up. 'You need to take a ten-day trip, Syrsee. So you'll be safe, Syrsee. You need to be very careful. We're trying to keep you safe, Syrsee!' Any of that ringing a fucking bell, Tristin?"

He puts his hands up and backs off. "I know, we lied to you. I get it. But we didn't know we were lying. We take orders too, Syrsee."

I narrow my eyes, so angry I start to tremble. And this is when I realize that the feelings inside me are so much more than anger. I seethe my words out. "You. *Betrayed* me."

"We didn't."

"We?" I look around. "Where is the rest of this 'we?' Where is Zusi?"

"She couldn't come—"

"How convenient for her. She betrayed her best friend—and you know what?" I pause my rant to laugh here. "I get it. She was never my friend. They were paying her. She was on scholarship. I was just her job—"

"That's not true, and you know it."

"I *know* it?" I scoff. "How would I know any different, Tristin? What I just said is a fact. A *fact*." I point my finger in his face. "She was assigned to me."

He lets out a long breath. "I understand that." And now he's getting angry too. His eyes are narrowing and he's clenching his jaw as he talks. "She was assigned to you. Just like I was assigned to you. But it doesn't mean I'm not your friend."

"My—" I can't even finish. The nerve. The fucking nerve of him. "I'm food, Tristin. I'm the scion's *food*. He drank me thirty minutes ago."

Tristin recoils from this statement. Like it's a real, physical thing that just tried to attack him.

"And he's not a scion anymore, by the way." Everything in that sentence is snark. "He's a vampire now. That was the plan all along. And the Guild was the one who made it happen because they—you!" I point at his face again. "You and Zusi are the ones who made that happen. I'm going to be turned into my grandmother. I'm going to spend the next few weeks trying to come to terms with it, but I'm going to fail. And then I'm gonna run, or something, and he's going to hunt me down, chain me up, and keep me in a bedroom that's nothing more than a refrigerator to hold his food. And that's where I'm gonna die, Tristin. Dirty, and old, and wasted away in a bedroom that stinks like death."

He's shaking his head the whole time I'm talking. "It's not gonna happen that way."

"Really?" I sneer this word out. "How the hell do you figure?"

"Because he's not a vampire. Not *yet*."

"Well, there are wings growing out of his back, Tristin. He feeds on me every couple of hours. And it's getting worse."

Tristin crosses his arms and shoots me a smug look. "If he's so fucking dangerous, then how did you get away alone? Hmm? If he's so fucking dangerous, and he's so fucking worried about you escaping, or whatever, where is he? Why isn't he here?"

"Are you trying to insinuate that you *know* him? That you understand him? That I have no idea what I'm talking about even though I'm the one who spent the past month with the man?"

"No. I'm saying you don't have the full story."

"The full story?" The arrogance of him stuns me. "Do you know why I don't have the full story, Tristin? Because they never let me read the fucking books, that's why."

"It was for your own good."

Now I actually laugh. It's a big one too. One that echoes off the ceiling. I turn, ready to walk out, but he puts a hand on my shoulder.

It's not a grip. It's a very light touch. And when he speaks, his words are softer too. "Zusi was forbidden from coming here to the lounge to meet you. But... since when does Zusi follow the rules?"

I stop. Inhale. Then turn to him again. "She's here?"

"Not here. But close by." He pulls out his phone, taps the screen, and then takes a deep breath. I can hear it ring just once. Then Zusi's voice. "Is she there?"

My heart hurts so bad in this moment, I just want to cry. She betrayed me. They all betrayed me. But it's Zusi's deception that hurts, not the Guild's and not Tristin's. I trusted her with my life and she sent me to the vampire to be food.

"Can I talk to her?" Zusi says. It's not on speaker, so this is just a low, tinny sound coming from Tristin's hand.

He offers me the phone, but I shake my head. "I don't have anything to say to her."

"Syrsee!" Zusi is talking louder now. "You have to listen to me. I didn't know. They didn't tell us anything. I would've never, ever sent you to that town if I had known. That's why they didn't tell me."

"I'm not having this discussion over the phone." I'm talking to Tristin when I say this. "If Zusi wants to explain herself, she will do it to my face."

Then I cross the reception room, sit down in a tufted chair made out of leather so soft it feels like butter, and sigh as I fold my arms across my chest in defiance.

Tristin puts the phone back up to his ear. "I'll call you back." Then he ends the call without waiting for Zusi's response.

He looks at the room for a moment, trying to figure out where to sit, I think. There are no chairs, just two couches on opposite sides of the room. It's not an intimate set-up—the distance between the two couches is ten feet, at least. It's not meant to encourage conversation between Guild members as they wait for their pamper sessions. It's meant to separate them. Give them space.

So his choices are to sit next to me or take the couch across the room.

He takes the couch across the room.

Part of me knows that this is just Tristin. He's... kind of a cold guy. Not in any way touchy-feely. And I could accept that as the reason he doesn't want to sit next to me, but I don't. I think he chooses the couch across the room because he doesn't want to get too close because I'm really not in the mood to give him the benefit of the doubt.

Once seated he leans forward, resting his elbows on his knees and propping his chin up with his hands. Then he just stares at me.

"What?" I snap.

"I understand how you feel."

"Don't patronize me, Tristin. You have no idea how I feel."

"You're wrong. Do you think you're the only one who was ever betrayed by the Guild?"

I scoff and shrug. "Probably not. But this is about me. Not everyone else."

"So you don't want to hear my story?"

"What story? You were a privileged Guild kid, everyone knows that."

"They do not know that because I was not a privileged Guild kid. I was on scholarship, just like Zusi. Just like you."

"Just like me? You're crazy. You're nothing like me. Being too poor to afford Guild School tuition isn't even close to being a Black Witch."

"That's not how the scholarships work, Syrsee. Scholarships are for outsiders."

"And I guess you're gonna tell me you're one of those now, huh? Save it, Tristin. You're a Guardian. I was a glorified librarian. I was never allowed into the classes that Zusi took."

"Zusi, sure. But I'm not Zusi. Zusi's family *is* Guild. They were outsiders because she is the first in her family to be a Guardian. They are poor—dirt poor, actually. I've met them. I've seen how they live. But they do have some Guild blood in them. It's all very mixed..." He sighs. "Anyway. I don't come from the Guild. I come from the Obscurati."

As soon as this word comes out of his mouth I'm back in

the purple mist of the wooded clearing with Paul as he tried to explain what would happen to me.

"My promise is that you and Ryet can be together. And the two of you can have a baby, Syrsee. I'll show you how it can be done. This baby would be the new breed of Black witch. And trust me when I tell you this, the Guild will want her. They will be girls. And there is a good reason to take them to the Guild. Because the Guild will do everything in their power to protect them from the Obscurati."

The Obscurati, he said, were his bosses.

"You are the new mother of all demons. You are the dark now too, Syrsee. And from here... we rule the world."

"What does that even mean?" I ask Tristin. "Who are these Obscurati people? Where are they?"

"They're... everywhere. Well, except for America."

"Why not here? What's so special about America?"

"It belongs to Paul. And he was cast out. He made abominations back in the Old World. Sick things. And he was punished for it."

"Is that what he wants me to make with Ryet? Sick things?"

Tristin shrugs. "I don't know. I am not privy to the ambitions of Paul. I doubt it, since the last time resulted in a very severe banishment. But the important thing here is that whatever happens next, it must not happen in the presence of the Obscurati. They must not get a hold of you, or any children you have. They must not get Ryet, either. He's under our protection too."

"Since *when?*"

"Always. He's always been under our protection."

"So you were lying to me the whole time. You were never trying to keep me safe."

"I was lying." He shrugs with his hands.

And this throws me. Because I was really expecting him to tell me no, he didn't know. He was lied to as well. We were all lied to. That we're still a team. Still on the same side.

But instead, he gave me the truth.

It's a big letdown.

Tristin continues. "Paul and the Guild have a deal."

"Me."

"You're only a small part of it, Syrsee."

"He said I would be the mother of demons. I don't want to be the mother of demons, Tristin. I don't want to do any of this."

"Well," Tristin sighs—it's nearly a scoff—"that's like me saying I don't want to be a rogue. But here I am."

"What the hell is a rogue?"

"It's a type of vampire."

I blink at him. *"You're* a vampire?"

"No. I'm a rogue."

"What's the difference?"

"I was cut when I was born. More accurately, I was burned. They cauterized my wing buds so they never formed. Then they took out my heart and put it back in."

"What?" Just when I think this world cannot get any more horrifying, there's more. "Why would they do something like that?"

"This stops the blood thirst because it interrupts the maturation process of the filtering in my lungs. It makes me 'other'. They consider me... a eunuch. But..." He closes his eyes, sighing. "Not the way you think."

I look down between his legs, but then quickly look back up again.

Tristin smiles. "All of that is still very much intact. I'm just missing wings and the blood thirst. I am a low creature to the

Obscurati. A… servant. They send the rogues to the Guild as representatives."

"Representatives of…?"

"They rule the world, Syrsee. The Guild and the Obscurati. With the Darkness, of course, which acts like a judge."

"I don't understand. If the Guild and the Obscurati are working together—"

"Since when do two hands of a three-handed government work together?"

"I don't know."

"Never. It never works that way. It's all in the Guild library."

"Well, that explains my ignorance, I guess. They never let me read the books."

"They couldn't, you see. Because they didn't know if you were the true match for Ryet. They really didn't think it was going to work. But now that it has—"

I stop listening because I remember more of what Paul said that day we were in the purple and he was trying to explain what would happen next. *"If you take your girls to the Guild, they will be safe and so will you. And not only that, Syrsee, they will reward you for coming home to them and let you read the books."*

I finish for Tristin. "They will let me read the books."

"They will want you to know everything."

"So that's why you're here? To take me back to the Guild?"

"Not just you. Ryet must come as well."

A little pain stabs my heart once again. Because this is the catch. I can go home. I can read those books that were forbidden to me. I can learn all the secret things. I can have all the knowledge of my history. But only if I bring Ryet with me.

It hurts, I'm not gonna lie. It hurts. Because this is just yet another trap.

"What do you think Ryet would say if I told him this story?"

Tristin gives me a small shrug. "He would... be suspicious. I would, if I were him."

"But... if he wanted to make me happy, he might relent, don't you think?"

Tristin smiles. "Probably."

I let out a long sigh. I knew it was too good to be true. They don't care about me. They don't care about Ryet. They care about power.

"Do you think he likes you?"

"Who?" I ask.

"Ryet."

"Does he like me... as a person? As his food? As his friend?"

"As his lover?"

"I'm not sure yet."

"Well, I think he does like you. And you've been gone for a while now, so..." Tristin stands up, smiling at me, his job here done. "I'll see you out."

I stand up too. "What am I supposed to do now?"

"Convince him, Syrsee."

"Why can't you just come take him? Why do you need me to deliver him?"

Tristin scoffs. "Is that a real question? He's a *vampire*, Syrsee. A baby one, but still. He's more powerful than he realizes. He has no idea what he is or what he can do. There is no way we could take him if he didn't want to come. He would just... kill us all. And he wouldn't even have to make a decision to do this. It would just happen. It would be instinct. We need him to *want* to cooperate."

"And that's where I come in." I force this to come out neutral, but that's not how I feel. I resent this entire conversation.

"Yes." Tristin smiles, happy and content that I am seeing things his way. The Guild way. He walks over to the door and opens it for me. I get up and I'm just about to walk through it when he asks one final question. "What should I tell Zusi?"

I close my eyes, forcing myself to remain calm. Then I open them and look at Tristin one final time. "Tell her... goodbye."

Then I walk out.

7 - Ryet

A pretty shitty ride so far.

There is a gold mist surrounding my feet by the time Syrsee arrives home in the truck. It's my hunger manifesting as color. I guess. I don't really know what it is, but it comes with the cravings when they get bad and right now, they're bad.

When I meet Syrsee at the truck, it's not the bags of groceries I want to grab, it's her. I want to push her up against the door and drink before we do anything else. Before I even say hello.

I force myself not to do this. I force myself to smile, remain calm, and let her load up my arms with paper grocery bags.

Then I carry it all into the cabin with her trailing behind me.

She doesn't say much, but I don't care. I am not even capable of having a conversation right now. It takes every bit of willpower to not attack her and drink.

For a moment I think she will insist on putting everything away before she feeds me. But she lets out a breath and turns to face me. "You're hungry."

I can't even speak so I just nod.

"It's weird, but I can feel it. And it's pretty overwhelming right now, isn't it?"

I nod again.

"OK." She steels herself, leaning against the counter with hands grabbing at the edges. "Do it. Quick."

I'm next to her before I even make a decision to do this. And a moment later, her blood is rushing into my mouth. I lose myself—everything goes gold and purple—but then Syrsee is grabbing my hand, pulling it off her breast.

"Ryet—"

I ease back, eyes closed, mouth dripping. "Sorry. I didn't realize—" But that's all I get out. Because I'm drinking her again.

I'm not sure how much time passes—seconds? Minutes? Years? All I know is that when I open my eyes, I'm on the couch and I can hear the shower going in the bedroom where I put Syrsee's things. I don't even know how I got here. But I don't really care, either.

It takes several more minutes before I can open my eyes and keep them open for more than a few seconds. It's like a drug, this blood. It sends me somewhere else, but not really. I've never done heroin, of course. But I've seen the addicts on the streets with needles sticking out of their arms, their eyes rolled up, their minds in some other place.

That's how I feel after I drink. But it's getting worse, not better. The more I do this, the more it affects me. It makes me slow, in both mind and body, and I don't like it. Because if I'm slow, I'm not paying attention. And I feel an overwhelming need to pay attention.

Like maybe my life depends on it?

If I could die, it might.

Can I die?

I don't know.

My back is itching like crazy so I take off my shirt and reach around, scratching. But as soon as I do that there is blood under my fingernails and the hard knobs of bone have finally broken through the skin.

I lean forward, looking over my shoulder, trying to see it. I get a little glimpse, but not much. Not enough. So I walk over to the mirror near the front door and stand with my back to it.

The little knobs are white, which surprises me for some reason. I was expecting black webs, like Paul's. But it's not that far along and I actually think this is just bone. It's good and bloody, though. Kinda gross, actually.

"Oh, my God." I turn and find Syrsee watching me from the open bedroom door. She's dressed in a pair of jeans and a maroon t-shirt that she must've picked up during her trip to town. Her long, dark hair is still wet. "Your wings."

I nod. "Yeah." To say that I am less than thrilled about this would be an understatement. "It's really happening, I guess."

"Does it hurt?" She doesn't come towards me. Doesn't come get a better look at it. Doesn't offer to clean the blood off me and dress the wounds. Something I think she would've done a couple weeks ago.

"I'm not sure if it hurts, but it's definitely uncomfortable."

She doesn't know what to say to that, so she says nothing.

I change the subject. "Feel better?" I add a lightness to my tone, trying to turn this whole thing around.

I hate that she hates me. I know she has every reason to. And hate is probably a strong word. It's not hate, it might be revulsion, which would be worse, in my opinion. I'd rather have the hate.

"Yeah. I do. Thanks." She heads towards the kitchen. "I'm going to make dinner." I watch her pull open the fridge and start gathering things, things I didn't help put away because I was in my post-feeding high, or whatever it is. She places several ingredients on the counter. "Do you want some?"

"Do I want some?" I smile at her. "Yeah. I do." She smiles back at me. "But"—her smile falls—"I don't think I could keep it down, to be honest. So I'm gonna pass."

She forces that smile again, but it's fake. "Right. I figured, but I don't want to leave you out."

"I appreciate the offer. I really do, Syrsee. And I hate that we're so distant right now. I wish it was different. Actually, I wish it was the same as before. I wish it was like it was."

"Yeah." She nods. "Me too." But then she just turns away and starts preparing her meal.

I don't know what to do next. I don't have a TV here, so I can't turn that on for background noise. I do have a radio, though. An old-timey one that takes up way too much room in one corner of the cabin. So I walk over there, turn it on, and then bend down, trying to find a station. It only takes a second to find the first one—polka music.

Which makes me laugh, and when I look over my shoulder, Syrsee is smiling as she cuts up some vegetables. "Do you polka?" I ask.

She shakes her head, still smiling.

I move the dial to another station and find classic rock. I don't ask for her opinion on this. I'm not in the mood for Ozzy. So I continue down the spectrum and land on bluegrass. When I stand up and turn, she's nodding at me. "This is kind of appropriate."

West Virginia music, for sure. "Do you know how to play an instrument, Syrsee?"

"No. I took a little piano in college. Just for fun." She scoffs. "Actually, I didn't pick that class. The Guild chose all my classes and they put me in piano for two semesters. It was a private class. Just for me. And I kinda liked it, but I didn't learn much. I didn't even know how to read music when I started. So it was a whole lot of 'Jingle Bells,' and 'Happy Birthday,' and 'Twinkle Twinkle Little Star' for a while."

"And what could you play by the end?"

She sighs, but not a tired sigh. More of a thinking-back sigh. "'Für Elise.'"

"That's impressive."

"Trust me." She's slicing a cucumber. "It was tediously slow in tempo. And it took me the whole second semester. I learned that one and 'Lean on Me.'"

"Fun."

"Do you play an instrument, Ryet?"

"Guitar and violin."

She stops cutting to look up. "Seriously?"

"Yeah. Why?"

"Hmm. Just didn't see that coming. But..." Her eyes meet mine. And we stare at each other for a moment. "You would've had a lot of time, right? To learn."

"Yeah. I had lots of time."

She sighs again. This time it is a tired one. Then she puts down her knife.

"Everything OK?" I ask.

She wipes her hands on a dish towel. A brand-new one that she must've bought today because I've never seen it before. "I have to tell you something."

"All right."

"I ran into Tristin in town." She says this in a rush, like she needs to get the words out before she loses her nerve.

"Who's Tristin?"

"A Guild member. He says he's some kind of rogue vampire?"

"A what?"

"I'm not really sure about that part. It's not important, I don't think. The important part is... they want me to bring you in."

"Bring me in?"

"To the Guild."

"They want you to betray me?"

"Kinda? But I'm not sure."

"Which part aren't you sure about?"

"I'm not sure they're... the bad guys."

I walk over to the kitchen counter that separates me from her and brace my hands on it. "I think you should start from the beginning. I didn't even know about these Guild people until right before I met you. Paul never told me, so I'm not sure what any of this means."

"Well. I grew up with them." She sighs, like it's a lot more complicated than that. "I'm not sure what they are to me, but they used to be my family. Until they sent me to White River, that is."

"Oh."

"Yeah. They set me up. They told me that they were sending me somewhere safe—"

"And they sent you straight to me."

"Yep."

"Which turns out to be the very short end of the stick as far as deals go."

She shrugs, but doesn't disagree.

"So... why are you telling me? Why not just tell them so they can come get me?"

"Oh, they know where you are." She holds up a finger. "And I didn't tell them that, by the way. There's a lounge in the general store in town." She must read my confusion because she wipes a hand through the air. "Never mind all that. The point is, they can't come get you. They're afraid of you. They want me to talk you into this."

"Is that what you're doing?"

"No. I'm not going to talk you into anything. I don't trust them and I don't think you should either. I'm just telling you what happened because we've got enough shit between us right now, ya know? We don't need secrets."

This answer actually gives me hope. "You have no idea how much I appreciate what you just said."

"Oh, I have an idea." Then she laughs, letting out a long breath. "I like you, Ryet. I want you to know that. I'm confused, and I feel cheated, and I don't know if we have a future together. But if I have to choose between you and them? I'm choosing you. I'm not going to leave you for them, even though Tristin promised that they will let me read the books."

"What books?"

"The ones in the library. I was a librarian for them for the past several years, until you got too close when my grandma was dying and they made me leave. It's filled with all kinds of information that I was never allowed to know. Things about me. Things that would explain me."

"And now they're using that to bribe you?"

"That's how it feels."

"What do they want with me?"

"I don't know, really. Something about babies, I think."

"*Our* babies?"

"Maybe? I don't know. Like I said, they didn't tell me anything all growing up. And what Tristin said to me in town was just a tease."

"Do you need this information? This history of yours?"

"I wouldn't mind having it. But I'm not going to turn—"

"Then we should go."

"What? But what if they hurt you?"

"If they could hurt me, wouldn't they do that instead of sending you to talk me into it?"

She frowns at me. "Are you doing this because it's a fair trade for the blood?"

I actually laugh. "Um. Yes. But..." I hold up a finger. "I really do want to make you happy. I like you, Syrsee. If you want to go there so you can get your history, then fuck it. Let's go. It's not like we have other plans."

"You're not afraid?"

"Of...?"

"The Guild?"

"Maybe I should be, but no. I'm not. I think it's gone too far." I point at the emerging wings on my back. "There's no going back from this. I'm a vampire. And I've spent enough time with Paul to understand what kind of power comes with this transformation. Maybe I'm not in control of it yet, but if they had a way to subdue vampires, they would've done it already."

She and I just stare at each other for a moment. Then a small smile begins to creep up her face.

This is when I realize I'm giving her something she truly, truly wants. She wants to go home and I'm the only way she can do that. It *is* a fair trade. And I don't care what these Guild people try to do to me, as long as Syrsee is happy, then I will let them do it. "Do you know the way, Syrsee?"

"Yes. It's up in New Hampshire."

"Should we leave tomorrow?"

Syrsee scoffs. "Tomorrow? *No.* We just got here, Ryet. I need a break. Don't you need a break?"

"I need what you need. I want to give you whatever it is you need. And if you need to go home, that's what we'll do."

Everything about her softens as these words of mine float through the air, drifting on some unseen current. Syrsee watches them, like they are real things that can be seen. And when her eyes meet mine again, she suddenly looks like the woman I met outside the diner that night. Someone who hadn't yet met me. Who hadn't yet been changed by me.

I want her back, that version of her. The happy one. I want her back.

She's unhappy now. And maybe, in the future, we will get more moments where we come together on an issue, like we're coming together on this one, but that's not the same as happiness. It's something far less than happiness.

"I want you to know," I say, my voice low and my eyes locked with hers, "that I really mean that. Whatever you need, Syrsee. It's yours. And while the trip is a good way to start making up for what I've turned you into—"

"What you've turned *me* into?" She's pointing at herself. "Ryet, I'm the one who did this to *you*."

But I'm shaking my head no. It wasn't her who did this, it was Paul. But I'm not in the mood to discuss Paul right now, so I just finish my sentiment. "This trip is just the start, Syrsee. If you have to be a slave to my hunger, then I have to be a slave to your happiness. Whatever you need, I will provide it."

We stare at each other for a long moment, simply looking into each other's eyes. Is she searching for truth? Is she condemning me to Hell? Is she thinking... *He's manipulating me. He's evil and so are all his promises?*

Because that's what I would be thinking if it were me in her place and Paul in mine. I would be thinking, *Lies. He is nothing but lies.*

Syrsee comes around the counter and walks right up to me until we are so close, she has to look up to meet my gaze. Her arms drape around my neck, sending chills down my spine, and then she leans up on her tiptoes and kisses me.

It's a small kiss. There's no tongue and we don't really linger. So when she pulls back I ask, "What was that for?"

"For... being patient with me this afternoon as I was freaking out."

"To be fair"—I let out a breath—"you have every reason in the world to freak out about what's happening to us."

"To *us*," she says. "That's the thing I was forgetting. It's not happening to me, it's not happening to you, it's happening to us. I like you, Ryet. And if I wasn't stuck with you for the rest of my life, that's all I would be thinking about. How I would love to be stuck with you for the rest of my life. How could I stick you to me? That's the question I would be asking myself." She pauses, like she's trying to come up with the right words to express her thoughts. "It's like... a soulmate bond. Something very romantic in the movies. Two people forced into being a team due to forces beyond their control."

"Who fall in love despite their differences," I add.

And this makes her smile. She might even, for a moment, be happy. "They fall in love despite their differences, and then overcome great challenges. Which only makes their bond stronger."

"And by the end, they're dying to die for each other."

She laughs. And it's a real laugh. "Yeah. That."

"Well, I would like to go on record that I'm truly sorry for stealing your happiness, Syrsee. If it were up to me, I would set you free. I *would* die for you."

"Please don't do that." She reaches up and places a hand on

my cheek. "For real, Ryet. Please, *please* don't die for me. Please don't leave me alone in this stupid, evil, unfair world."

Is it magic? Have I somehow... done something to influence her feelings? Because this is what I wanted. Syrsee, desperately in love with me.

And now here she is, and... I sigh. "I promise. I won't die for you unless it's absolutely necessary. But let's not romanticize this, OK? Let's keep it real. This is important to me. I need to feel like this is real because so much of my life has been a lie."

"Well, I can certainly relate to that."

"Your hesitations about me, us, all of it—they were completely justified. I'm never going to stop wanting your blood. I'm always gonna crave your blood. And this need of mine, it's a physical thing."

She sucks in a breath and presses her lips together, like she's trying to be brave. "I understand. But... what if you craved... kissing me?"

"What?"

"What if you craved... complimenting me?"

I smile down at her, feeling a new lightness in my heavy soul. And this lightness, once again, takes me back to that night outside the diner. When the snow was fresh, and her smile was new, and even though we had no idea where this was going, it was still good.

She doesn't have to do this. She doesn't have to ease my guilt. But that is what she's trying to do. And this is a gift I don't think I will be able to repay. Not because I don't want to, but because there is nothing I could give her that would compare to the blood she's giving me. There is no way for me to even out this debt I'm incurring. And she has every right to resent me for this eternal disparity that began, pretty much, the day we met. "It's a small thing, Syrsee. Craving your lips and calling you pretty."

"Maybe to you. But I would love it. You'd be the perfect boyfriend. All considerate, and polite—you really are polite." I laugh. "And traditional. Not to mention handy." She grins up at me. "If you craved me in any other way it would be amazing. So why is craving my blood so different?"

"You tell me."

"Because I am insecure, Ryet. And acting like a child about it. Blaming you, instead of coming to terms with my feelings. I want to resent you because I can't resent myself. But I'm the one who did this to you. And the hypocrisy of blaming you for my mistakes... well. It's next-level deception."

"How about we just call a do-over?"

"No. It's not enough. I'm sorry, Ryet. And I need to apologize."

I don't want to accept her apology because it's unnecessary. But it would put this quarrel to bed if I do. So I say, "I will forgive you if you forgive me."

She smirks up at me. "What do you need to apologize for?"

I laugh. "All of it."

"It's not your fault, Ryet. And you were right, earlier. *I* fed *you*. I made this decision for you. And I'm truly, truly—"

I cup her chin in my hand and press my thumb against her lips to silence her words. "It's over. Don't apologize again. You saved me, and even though it's a little bit terrifying that wings are starting to grow out of my back, I'm glad you saved me. I haven't had much happiness in my life, Syrsee. It's actually been a pretty shitty ride so far. But this time with you? It means everything to me now. And I would not trade death for this."

"OK." She exhales and nods her head. "Do-over."

I take her face in both my hands and then I lean in and kiss her properly. It's long, and lingering, and there's lots of tongue.

She pulls away first, blushing and breathy. Then she takes my hand and leads me towards the bedroom where her things are.

I follow, nearly grinning maniacally with this turn of events. "What about your dinner?"

"Ryet." She says this over her shoulder as we pass through the door. "I've got all the time in the world to eat dinners." Then she tugs me over to the bed, already taking her shirt off.

She's not wearing a bra underneath so I'm immediately presented with her spectacular breasts.

She bites her lip a little as she unbuttons her jeans. Then wriggles them down her legs along with her underwear. So just a few seconds in, there she is. Standing before me, naked.

The craving is immediate. For her blood, for her body, maybe even for her soul, though I quickly push that last thought out of my mind. I walk over to her and her hands are already popping the button on my jeans. And by the time my mouth covers her in a kiss, she's pushing them down my hips. Taking my cock in her hand. Pumping it, as if I need any priming. I want to throw her down on the bed and fuck her senseless and I'm just about to do that when the rational side of me kicks in.

I like hard, fast sex as much as anyone. But I don't want this to end. I don't want her to come to her senses. I don't want to quickly and efficiently meet her needs so she can go back to making dinner.

I want this time with Syrsee to be never-ending. I want the sex to be slow and drawn out. I want us to become prisoners of time with nothing more to think about than the wanting.

So I push her back, letting her bump into the side of the bed. I catch her with one hand around her waist before she falls backwards and gently ease her down onto the mattress. She's staring at me with half-lidded eyes. Waiting for what comes next.

I bend down, my hands on the inside of her knees as I open her legs. And then I lower my mouth down between them, and she gasps, and bucks, and moans as I lick her with my tongue. Taking my time, licking all her folds, flicking my tongue against her clit as I push a finger up inside her.

Her hands are gripping my hair as I do this, her lower legs rubbing up and down my lower back. I want to bite her—and the moment I think this she says, "Bite me, Ryet. Right here." She's pushing my head down her thigh. And I hear the blood pumping through the artery in her leg.

The bite happens so fast, the blood is already in my mouth before I can even make a conscious decision. Her orgasm is immediate, and loud, and long. She's pulling my hair, then scraping her fingernails over my back and digging them into the thick muscles of my shoulders. She comes again. And this time, I pull back, blood dripping out of my mouth. Dripping down her leg as well. I watch her until she sighs, then I lick the wound I left on her leg until the blood begins to clot.

Her eyes are closed, like she's tired and spent. But then she moans out the words, "More."

I stand up, push her up the bed until she almost hits the headboard, and crawl up her body. The blood craving has subsided now, but a new one takes its place. The urge to be inside her. This new hunger causes a vibration inside me.

I spread her knees open wide, then ease up between them, my cock so hard and engorged, I have to restrain myself when I slip inside her wet pussy.

She feels so good, but it can get better.

And it's like she's reading my mind because Syrsee turns her head to the side and offers her neck to me. But even if she wasn't offering, there would be no way in hell that I would not drink her right now. I would take it—her—I would take her blood any way I could get it.

It's a sick thought, but it's easy to push away because when I sink my teeth into her flesh, I'm not taking it. I'm giving her what she wants. As soon as I take the first pull of blood, her legs wrap around my hips and her hand is between my legs, sliding up under my balls so she can fondle them in her palm.

When I thrust forward, she throws her head back, moaning. And in this same moment I drink again.

I drink her, and I fuck her, and she comes all over me.

8 - Syrsee

I've had them both now.

*W*e *fucked and he drank* and now Ryet is tired. But I'm having trouble sleeping. And I want company. So I design a conversation to keep him awake. "Do you think I'm enchanted?"

"Hmm?"

I can tell his eyes are closed even though I can't see them. He's got his arms around me, all pulled into his chest, and all he wants right now is to sleep.

I feel his weariness. But for some reason, I'm amped up. "Did you enchant me?"

He leans into my neck, chuckling as he kisses it. I feel the sharp teeth graze lightly across my skin and for a moment, I hold my breath, wondering if he will drink again.

Part of me wants him too. It feels... good. I hate to admit that, even if it's just to myself, but it does. I like it. It makes me want him. Sexually. Which is... hot. But also... cringy. Because I *am* enchanted. I must be. That's the only possible explanation for how he makes me feel.

"You're the one with the magic, Syrsee." His words are mumbled and soft. Like he's already half asleep.

"So I enchanted myself?"

His arms loosen and then he's turning me to face him. "Hi."

"Hi yourself. Sorry to wake you. I'm just..."

"Worried?"

87

"No."

He stares at me for a moment. And there is a weird glow in his eyes. The red, which I have seen before, but which has been hiding recently. "Unsettled?"

"No."

Now he closes those eyes again, smiling in the soft light that filters in from the living room through the open door. "I enchanted you."

"You did, right?"

He nods. Eyes still closed. "Sure." And then he really does fall asleep.

But now I'm trying to pin down why my mind can't slow down.

Maybe I need a drink of blood.

It's a throwaway thought. A joke. But once I think it, I can't help but wonder if maybe I *do* need a drink of blood. Not mine, of course. His.

And then my thoughts are drifting back to that night in the tower bedroom at Paul's estate. And how I drank Paul. And how it felt. And how he's not even the man I love.

"Ryet?"

"Hmm?" His answer is far less audible than my question.

"Can I taste you?"

I feel him go stiff, then his eyes are open again. "What?" And this one word is not in any way whispered or sleepy.

"Never mind—"

"No. Do you... are you... asking me to give you my blood?"

I really don't want to say yes. But it *is* what I'm asking.

He doesn't wait for an answer. He just brings the palm of his hand up to his lips, punctures the fleshy skin below his thumb, and then presses it against my lips.

It's just a trickle. Just a taste. That's what I tell myself when I slide my tongue over the hot liquid. The sharp taste of iron, the bitterness of copper, and... something else. The sweetness of the purple.

And then I'm inside it. The lavender mist is all around me and I'm in the forest. Paul is sitting on the fallen tree trunk. But the snow is gone now. It's spring here, I think.

"Well." He looks kind of pleased with himself. "You came back. I have to admit, I wasn't expecting it to happen so soon. You're such a delightful surprise, Syrsee. Now come, sit. Tell me everything."

He pats the tree trunk, beckoning me.

But before I can take a step, I hear...

"*THAT'S ENOUGH. STOP NOW, SYRSEE.*" Ryet pulls his palm away. Then his arms are around me again, hugging me close, his lips kissing my shoulder, those sharp teeth grazing the surface of my skin like a promise.

All the unsettlement leaves me as his blood mixes with mine.

I feel the high. That's the only thing to call it. The blood is a drug, like morphine or heroin, and the whole world disappears when it's coursing through my veins.

I dream.

Not of Paul, but both of them.

Paul and Ryet.

Because I've had them both now. Paul's blood, Ryet's blood.

I'm too tired to think it through. Too tired to care, really.

All I want to do is sleep.

9 - Ryet

Bacon and dirt.

I watch *Syrsee* as she sleeps and think about what just happened. How she drank me and how it felt. It's erotic, of course. It's always been that way, even when Paul was feeding off me. The pull of blood straight from my veins is an aphrodisiac. A very powerful one. Paul explained it once. "It has to be this way, Ryet. How else could I convince men like you to drink monsters like me?"

I close my eyes, replaying that conversation back in my head and suddenly missing him and the way he used to tempt me.

It wasn't exactly sexual, but it wasn't exactly not, either.

It has been almost two weeks since I've talked to him now. We've been estranged for much longer periods. When he goes underground—and he would do this every dozen years or so —it's always for months at a time. Sometimes years. But he never *leaves* me. He would find me in my dreams and I always *felt* him. Like he was watching me from some distance away.

Something has changed, though. Something very big, because I don't feel him watching. What I do feel is his absence. I feel like I might never see him again.

He used to hover like a parent. Always asking me how I felt. Always asking me if I needed blood.

Which makes sense now. Since he literally made me.

How many times has he failed at this? How many Ryets has he gone through?

And how many more are out there?

Am I the only one?

It seems highly unlikely. I mean, there was no guarantee that Syrsee would feed me.

I'm still looking at her when I think these words. *She* fed off *me* tonight. Drank my blood, and not only was she able to keep it down, but it satiated something inside her.

She was restless and now she looks peaceful. The blood is what changed that.

Is she changing as well? No wings are growing out of her back, but is there some kind of second stage to the life of a Black witch?

Paul didn't let me read the books either. Not literally, of course, but I wouldn't know anything about the life stages of a Black witch because no one ever tells me anything.

This thought leads me down a new path and my mind drifts to the Guild and how she was approached in town. They want her back, but why? Is it because she is part of the Guild family?

Seems about as likely as there being no other scions out there, ready to transform into vampires.

The Guild is using her to get to me.

I am not afraid of these people. It might be naïve, but I just don't care about them.

I care about her.

She stirs in her sleep and a piece of hair falls over her face, obstructing my view. I casually, but carefully, push it out of the way so I can continue watching her.

Why is she drinking blood?

And why do I suddenly feel hungry?

My stomach rumbles at the thought of food, and because eating food is both something normal as well as something

Syrsee needs, I get up, hike my pants back up my legs, leaving the button open, and go out into the kitchen.

My eyes find the clock as I approach the kitchen—it's only ten-fifteen—and then I look through all the food she bought and put out on the counter and decide she was going to make chicken and pasta before she took me into the bedroom for sex.

So that's what I make. And thirty minutes later, the whole place is filled with the scent of something good. Something I haven't craved in decades. I go back into the bedroom and find Syrsee sprawled out on the bed, face down. She was naked, so she still is, of course. And the way her body is presented to me right now is enticing.

But for some reason, I'm craving that food more than I am her body.

"Syrsee." I reach down and shake her shoulder.

"Hmm?" She mumbles this, turning over and giving me a spectacular view of her breasts as she sighs. "What's up?"

"I made dinner. Come eat."

She cracks one eye open. "You made dinner?" Then she smiles and sniffs. Maybe even gets a little excited.

"Chicken fettuccini."

"Yum. And it's like you were reading my mind. That's what I was going to make."

"Yep. I figured that out. Come on, get up. Get dressed. Let's eat. I'm hungry."

She sits up, but I can tell this takes some effort. Like she would almost rather sleep until morning. "I don't want to get dressed."

My eyebrow goes up. "OK."

She laughs, then swings her legs out of bed and stands up, just a few inches from me now. She places her hands on my shoulders and leans up to kiss my mouth, just barely skimming her lips against mine so she can whisper. "Your blood, Ryet. It was... *good*." She pulls back, tipping her head up so she can look me in the eyes. "Can I have another small taste?"

She doesn't wait for me to answer, just kisses me again. This time her teeth graze over the tender skin. She doesn't bite me, but I definitely get the feeling she wants to.

And hey, if she wants blood, who am I to deny her?

I bite my lip, just like Paul used to bite his lip for me, and then I let her lick up the blood.

It's not enough. And I remember this feeling. The cravings.

But I also remember Paul being cautious. It felt like he just wanted to deny me the blood at the time. And he did. That was why he never let me drink too much. But I now realize it wasn't to be in control or to make me want it more. There was a reason for his denial. And it was probably something biological. My biology, specifically. The slow, deliberate maturation process that he was in the middle of inducing inside me.

So I don't bite my lip again once it's healed. I just kiss Syrsee until I'm hard and I start to forget about the food.

But then my stomach grumbles and Syrsee pulls back, looking down at it. "You really do want food?"

"I feel like I'm starving, Syrsee."

"I feel the same." Her head tilts up so she can, once again, look me in the eyes. "Only I seem to crave your blood all of a sudden. What do you think this means?"

"Honestly, I don't know. But it's..."

"Probably not good?" For such a serious subject, her tone is one of unconcern.

"Probably not."

She just smiles at me. Then, without getting dressed, leaves the bedroom. Throwing one last glance over her shoulder as an invitation for me to join her.

I do.

She's already looking for plates when I arrive in the kitchen. "That cupboard there." I point at the one with plates in it.

She gets two and starts putting food on them while I grab a bottle of red wine that's been chilling in the fridge since she got home.

A few minutes later, we're sitting across from each other at the small dining room table. She's naked, but unconcerned about this as she eats. Which I do find delightful, but it also worries me. It seems out of character. Granted, I haven't known her that long. I actually barely know her at all. But her willingness to just eat dinner naked feels like something new. Feels a lot like this blood craving, actually.

I finish first and I almost go back for more, but this craving for food, in combination with Syrsee's craving for blood, makes me hesitate.

What is going on now? Is this normal?

Maybe my hunger for real food is, but Syrsee shouldn't be craving blood.

Actually, how would I know that? Paul never explained anything about the Black witches to me. I was just always hunting them. This one, specifically. What if drinking blood is something she needs to do? What if symbiosis is the whole point of our relationship?

"What in the world are you thinking about?"

I look up and find Syrsee staring at me. "What?"

"You face is nothing but angst. What's up?"

"Don't you think that wanting my blood is a bit weird?"

"A *bit*?" She laughs, sitting back in her chair a little, giving me a really nice view of her breasts. "Of course I think it's weird. All of this is weird."

"Do you crave it? Or need it?"

"Hmm." She studies me as she thoughtfully considers my question. "I'm not sure."

"Do you want more right now?"

"I wasn't thinking about it." But her eyes are already looking at my lips. Then they slide up to meet my gaze. "But now that you mention it…" I get a coy smile from her here. And then she's getting up and coming around the table to me. I grin as she lifts her leg over my lap and straddles me, settling her thighs on mine and placing her forearms on my shoulders, her fingertips playing with my hair right at the nape of my neck. "That was an offer?" Her voice is sweet and a little bit teasing.

"You really want more blood?"

"If you're offering."

I have a thousand questions. But mostly, I'm thinking about fucking her while she drinks me. She is, after all, naked in my lap.

She's obviously reading my mind because her hand slips down to the zipper on my jeans. The button is still open so it's an easy thing for her to just reach in and pull out my cock. I'm already hard, but when she starts stroking me, it gets even stiffer.

Syrsee is bold tonight. She doesn't even hesitate, just lifts her hips up and presses the tip of my cock up to the entrance to her pussy. She's already wet and the next thing I know I'm slipping inside her and she's got her mouth pressed up against mine, whispering. "Let me drink. Please, let me drink."

I bite, taste the blood for just a moment, and then her

tongue licks it up. It's over too quick. And then she's asking for more. "Give me a *real* drink, Ryet. Give me what I give you." These words come out low and sultry. Almost like she's trying to seduce me into it.

I know this is a bad idea. I've spent the last sixty-five years listening to Paul tell me how drinking too much is a very bad idea. But when she starts moving on top of me, I suddenly don't care. I *want* her to drink me. And I want her to do this while we fuck.

I bite the palm of my hand, letting my new fangs sink deep into my flesh so the blood will flow easily, and then I put it up to her mouth, letting her take a good suck. And all the while she is writhing in my lap. Her hips grinding on me. I grab them, squeeze tight at the bones, urging her to move faster.

Suddenly, there is a swell of feelings inside me. Warmth, and chills, and fire, and ice. And while all this is happening a light, golden mist begins to swirl up from the floor.

We come at the same time and I'm absolutely sure the whole world can hear us. But the only thing on my mind right now is her. Her blood, specifically.

And the moment that the craving hits me, she's offering me her neck.

I don't hesitate. I'm not even capable of hesitating. I sink my teeth deep into her neck and she recoils from the pain. But I've got her arms pinned to her sides and I don't relent.

The first draw is magic. And this is when I realize what we're doing. We're drinking *each other*. We're mixing our blood. Her inside me, me inside her. Over and over.

Is this what it means to have your own personal Black witch? Someone who was made for you, and only you? Are we doing it right?

But I'm too distracted by the taste of her blood to give

these questions any more thought. It's sweeter now. More enticing than it was, if that's even possible.

Flashing red lights are going off in the part of my brain that is still capable of logic, but I ignore them. Paul's face is there too, and then suddenly his words are loud in my head. "Be careful, Ryet. This is Black magic you're doing. You're making something here."

But Syrsee is moaning in my lap and we taste too good to care about consequences.

I must pass out, because the next thing I know I'm waking up on the couch. I don't even know how I got here. Or Syrsee, either. She's lying alongside of me, her face pressed into the cushions. The euphoria of the drink is gone now and there is a feeling inside me that I can't quite place. It's not shame, exactly. It's not regret, either. But it's something like that. Something worrisome. Something that lingers in my gut like a mistake not yet realized.

I close my eyes again and start trying to make sense of things.

Syrsee is drinking blood.

I'm eating food.

She's getting visits from the Guild.

I'm growing wings.

When I woke up in the truck out in the desert, I thought it was pretty much over. I mean, I knew the wings would be coming in. But that was all I was expecting. A physical change, which the craving of food is. But I don't think it's over. Whatever's happening to me, these wings are just the beginning.

And Syrsee isn't just some feeder I need to keep around to eat. Something is happening to her too. She's sexy. I mean, she's always been sexy, but she's more than that now. She's provocative.

She reminds me of—I sit up. Blinking into the darkness. Unable—*unwilling*, really—to finish that thought.

But there's no way to deny it. Syrsee reminds me of *Lucia*.

"Holy shit." I say this out loud. Then I say it again. "Ho-lee. Shit."

I get up, button my jeans, and begin pacing the room. What if...

"No." I say this out loud too. But saying it and believing it are not, in any way, related to reality in this case.

This is how Lucia became a vampire. It has to be. It's never been a secret that Paul never considered her a true vampire. It's also never been a secret that she started her life as a witch.

Though not a Black witch.

But what does it mean? What does this mean for Syrsee?

"Don't you wish I was still here so you could ask?"

I turn, stunned, and find Paul sitting at the dining table eating a plate of food. But not pasta, like Syrsee and I had for dinner. It looks like... body parts. Bloody body parts. "You're not here."

"Does it matter, really? In the grand scheme of things?"

"I'm imagining this. You're not here."

"Where am I then, Ryet? Hmm? Do you have any ideas? Because I *feel* like I'm here." He looks down at his arm, watching it… flicker? Shimmer? Wink? I'm not sure what it's doing, except proving my point, actually.

He's *not* here.

He's in some kind of dreamwalk.

"I could answer all your questions, you know."

"How?" I ask.

"Come find me." He shrugs. Like it's just that simple.

"Go home, you mean?"

This makes him smile. "So. You *do* think of it as home." Then he starts laughing and with each passing second, he slowly disappears.

SLOWLY, **gradually**, the realization that I am asleep hits me. I'm aware that Paul was nothing but a dream, but I don't open my eyes and fully wake up until I realize I'm not in bed. I'm not on the couch. I'm not in the *house*, actually.

I'm in the earth.

The sweetness of it is almost intoxicating. And once again, like when I stepped into the root cellar, I can smell everything as individual scents.

This is when I sit up.

Because I *am* in the root cellar.

Not just lying on the ground, either. I'm in a hole. Freshly-dug earth mounded around me. Covering me. Comforting me like a blanket.

I blink, seeing everything in the darkness. I'm not actually in the cellar, but the tunnel. Which kind of pisses me off because I've fucked up the passageway with this hole I dug. And it was me who dug it. I can smell the dirt under my fingernails.

I look down at them and realize they're a little more claw-like than I remember them being last night. This is when I feel the wings. I can't see them, and they're not touching anything but air, but I know they've grown.

Sure enough, when I reach around and probe with my fingertips, the two small bumps of bone are much larger now. None of it is covered by skin. Or, at least, not the skin from my back. Maybe something else is covering the bone. A membrane, or something.

I should be thinking about how I'm turning into a literal monster, but the only thing running through my head is the question: How am I going to go out in public with *wings*?

I lie back in the earth, pondering this.

Maybe I don't go out in public? Maybe I stay right here in the dirt?

"Syrsee." I say her name out loud as last night comes back to me. Then I really do get up. I step up out of the hole, realize I'm fully naked—which I wasn't last night. Even while having sex—and then follow the tunnel back to the house.

When I get inside, I check the bedroom and find Syrsee fast asleep.

She drank me. Quite a bit, too.

But the mystery remains. My little trip to the tunnel, and subsequent imaginary conversation with Paul, has not solved any of my problems.

Which is: What is happening to us?

I want to think about this harder. Kinda... gather up clues and shit. Put them in some kind of order and then systematically come up with possibilities. But I can't think straight. I probably need to drink, but that craving that is usually there isn't.

Instead I have a craving for bacon. And dirt.

Which kinda feels OK. It's a weird combination. But also normal in a "pickles and ice cream" way. Except that's some cliché pregnancy thing.

I let out a breath, pausing here. Because I've gotten all my memories back. After Jane condemned me to an eternal Hell in my pre-third-birth delusion, I remembered everything. And now that I'm thinking about pregnancy cravings, I remember that Jane was always making me go get her Junior Mints.

The moment those two words form in my head I need Junior Mints. Do they even make them still?

I'm not sure, but my new mission in life is to hunt them down and find out.

I grab the truck key off the kitchen counter and walk towards the door, nearly pulling it open before I realize I'm naked, covered in dirt, wings are growing out of my back, and Syrsee should not be left alone.

This stops me.

I mean, the fuckery happening on my back should be what stops me. Or the fact that I haven't put on pants. But what stops me is the idea that I'm not thinking clearly.

Junior Mints, Ryet? What the hell?

I put the truck key back on the counter and take a breath. I feel like I'm stuck inside a manic episode where all the bright and shiny things need my attention. And by bright and shiny things, I mean food.

Yesterday, it was blood.

Today, it's food.

What changed?

But I already know what changed. Syrsee drank me and then I drank her back and this explains why she's craving blood.

Our cravings were passed in the blood exchange.

Weird.

And my response is also weird. Because this is kind of a big deal. If cravings can be passed through blood, what else?

Can we make each other sick by doing this?

Can we change things inside us? Like… genetically?

Paul is inside my head now. His voice, at least. "Don't you wish I was still here so you could ask?"

Reluctantly, I do. I wish he was here. Because I don't know what's happening, and what if we're doing something wrong?

"Why are you covered in dirt?"

I turn and find Syrsee standing in the doorway to the bedroom. She's wearing a flannel that's like five sizes too big for her and she's clutching it to her body like she's cold. I think it came from my closet.

"What?" I blink at her.

"Why are you covered in dirt?"

I look down at myself. Then at the floor. There's a trail of dirt in the shape of footprints leading to the door to the basement. My first instinct is to lie. Maybe lie is a strong word. My first instinct is to deny. Deny the fact that I went unconscious drinking her and woke up in a hole under the house that I dug myself.

"I… woke up in a hole under the house." There's really no other explanation for it, so why bother lying?

She tilts her head and kicks her hip to the side, grinning at me. Unfazed by what I just said. Which isn't exactly a normal reaction. "Are you hungry?"

"Uh. Yes. But." I hold up a finger. "Did you just hear me? I woke up in a hole under the house."

"I heard you. But I don't want you to go hungry."

"Right. About that. I'm actually not hungry for... *you*."

"What?" Her face shifts into confusion. "What's that mean? You're craving some other witch's blood?"

"No." I nearly laugh. As if there is any other witch. "I'm craving food, Syrsee. Real food. Like bacon." And dirt. But I don't say that last part out loud.

"Oh."

"And let me guess, you're craving blood?"

She hesitates. Which means yes, she's just not ready to admit it yet.

"It's OK." I think. Actually, it's probably not OK, but I don't wanna panic her. "I think it's the exchange we did." Now she's confused. "When I drank you, and then you drank me, we..." I shrug. "Passed something along in the blood."

"We passed along cravings?"

"It's the only explanation I have. But I'm not an expert. If Paul were here—" I stop, unable to believe that I just said that out loud.

"If Paul were here, *what?*" Her question comes with a *tone*, and I don't blame her.

"I could ask him, that's all."

"I thought that was why we were going to the Guild. To get answers."

"Yeah. But we're not there. We're here. And something weird is happening, so... sorry. It slipped out."

"I didn't have a choice, Ryet. If I didn't capture him—trap him, whatever it was that I did—then we'd both be prisoners in that compound."

I walk over to her, wanting to pull her close and give her a kiss. Touch her body. Maybe even fuck her. But I'm covered in dirt, so I keep a distance between us. "Do you wanna take a shower?"

She lets out a breath and drops her guard. "I do." Her fingertips touch her head. "Sorry. I just don't feel like myself. My head is—"

"Foggy?"

"Yeah."

"I think that's from the blood too."

"So I can't have anymore?" She's looking at me with sad eyes.

"Do you *want* more?"

I get a one-shoulder shrug and a tilt of her head. Meaning yes, but this is yet another thing that she doesn't want to admit.

"I think we should hold off. I won't drink you, either. Not until the craving comes back." I smile at her, reaching for her hand. "Sound fair?"

She nods, but I can tell she's still feeling confused.

"Come on." I tug her back into the bedroom. "You can wash my new wings." When I look over my shoulder I catch her sighing. And when her eyes meet mine, they are filled with doubts.

There is a crushing feeling in my chest. A feeling of loss. Because something has gone wrong here.

Something has gone terribly wrong.

All I can think about is the blood.

*H*e's not craving me anymore.
Well, that was fast. It was my number-one worry on the ride east. And then I just put it out of my mind because his cravings, just yesterday, were so strong I was getting pissed off about it.

But now, he's telling me that he's craving bacon.

We're in the bathroom now. Ryet steps around a stacked-stone wall to start the shower and then comes back out.

When my eyes slide up and meet his, all I see is doubt.

He places his hand on my shoulder and gives it a little squeeze. "It's fine. I promise."

But I'm already shrugging him off and shaking my head before he can get those last two words out. "It's not."

"We don't know that, Syrsee."

I scoff. "Don't start treating me like that."

"Like *what?*" His tone is defensive.

"Like I can be placated with lies."

"'Lie' is a strong word. We don't understand anything right now. It could all be fine—"

"And it could all be going to shit. Suddenly, you don't need to drink, Ryet? And I have a craving for blood?" A wave of dizziness washes over me, forcing me to reach out and place a flat palm against the log-sided wall. He reaches for me again, but I just stumble forward and sit down on a small bench just outside the shower.

"Are you OK?"

"No, Ryet. I'm not OK." I look up at him, and I'm suddenly angry and scared. "I'm not OK. We"—I point at him, then me—"*we* are not OK. You're turning into a vampire and I'm turning into... well, I have no idea, but the odds are good that it's something much, much worse. And now, in the middle of all this, you're threatening me?"

"How the hell am I threatening you?"

"You're not going to give me the blood?" Even *I* am surprised when these words come out of my mouth. But the look on Ryet's face is more than surprise. It's... shock.

He laughs. It's a small laugh that has nothing to do with anything being funny. "You're worried..." He stops, letting out a breath and sucking in a new one so he can start again. "This is what you're worried about? The blood? Because if all it takes to make you happy right now is to give you a drink of my blood"—he lifts his palm up to his mouth, bites, and a rivulet of scarlet drips down his wrist—"then by all means, Syrsee, have a *drink*."

My heart thumps inside my chest as my eyes follow the red line as it slides down his arm, and then I am transfixed by a single drop as it splats on the tile floor.

I almost kneel down and lick it. But instead I close my eyes, lean forward, and breathe through the compulsion.

Ryet says nothing. And the silence just hangs there between us like something real and heavy.

Finally, after almost a minute of this, he bends down in front of me. One hand on my knee, the other pushing my hanging hair out of my face so he can look me in the eyes. "If you need it, of course you can have it. I just didn't think it was..." He stops. Watches me. Probably noting how I'm not looking him in the eyes. I'm staring at the blood on his arm.

Then he's lifting it to my lips. I wish I could turn my head, or at least put up the pretense of an objection, but I can't. I reach for his hand and then the next thing I know, my mouth is pressed up against his skin and a sense of peace and calm washes through me as a purple and gold mist rises up in the steam of the shower.

This mist becomes thick, almost like a curtain. Separating me from the room, and Ryet, and the whole world. Then it thins again, splitting in half, almost making a hallway. This is when I realize I'm alone now. There is no shower, there is no cabin, and there is no Ryet.

There is just a way forward.

I take a step, then another, and another. And soon there is no purple, just darkness.

I should be afraid—I should be terrified, actually. Because the blood is doing something to me. It's acting like a very powerful drug and it's fucking with my head. Just as I think this I see, in my mind's eye, Ryet sitting on the couch all limp and satisfied, his head rolled back into the cushions.

Like an addict. He looked like an overdosing addict yesterday when we got here. The only thing missing from that memory of him is the cliché needle sticking out of his arm.

But inside this new reality I'm not afraid. I can smell blood up ahead and it's drawing me forward. Suddenly the space around me is bright and golden, all traces of purple gone now.

A part of me knows that this is a dreamwalk—not a kind I've ever experienced before, but the gold is like the purple. It takes me places.

The brightness slowly dims and as it does this, I start to make out shapes. A man with his back to me. He is tall and cut with muscles. His blond hair is shoulder-length and the ends curl up just a little. But while it is a very nice back, what really catches my attention is the wings.

Well, the buds of wings. Like Ryet's. But this is not Ryet.

The man looks over his shoulder at me, scowling. "What do you want?"

He can *see* me?

He turns all the way around, facing me, and I realize this is Paul. Not the Paul I know, but another version of him. Something much, much younger. And if the wing buds are any kind of indication, he is newly born. Second-born, I think Ryet calls it. Newly second-born. Paul's feet are bare and he's only wearing a pair of loose-fitting linen pants.

"Do you know who I am?" My voice is surprisingly calm.

Young Paul snarls at me. "A ghost. A demon. The Dark Slut. I don't give a *fuck* who you are. *Get out.*"

"I'm afraid it's not that easy." I sound very in control. And as soon as I think these words, I *am* in control.

"Why not?" He's still growling at me. Eyes narrowed down into thin slits. He's angry and control is something this version of him has yet to master.

"Because I didn't choose to come here, Paul."

He tries not to show his shock when I say his name, but I can tell this revelation unsettles him. "Who are you?"

"I'm Syrsee. We're... acquaintances. In the future."

His brow furrows, then he looks over his shoulder. I glance in that direction too. And this is when I realize we're in a room. Something old-looking. Walls made of stone, elaborate cornices made of plaster, and marble slabs for the floor. There is a large pool of water in the middle of the room. That's what he's standing in front of. But his glance right now is in the direction of a door. It's closed, and this seems to be what he was checking, because then he looks back at me. "What do you want?"

Torches placed at regular intervals along the stone walls make flickering shadows across my body as I step away from the darkness. I'm naked. He and I realize this at the same time and he takes a long, casual look down and back up my body before meeting my gaze again, giving me his full attention. Which I do not waste.

"How old are you?" Which seems like a stupid way to start this conversation, but I don't feel in control of this question. The words come out like they've already been spoken. Like I've been here before. Like I'm just playing out a memory.

"Two hours."

"*Hours?* But your wings—they are already sprouting."

He reaches up and over his shoulder, like he's trying to feel the little bumps pushing through the skin back there. "They itch."

"Would you like me to wash them for you?"

His eyebrows go up in surprise. And I have to admit, this young version of Paul—a version that displays confusion, and hesitation, and vulnerability—well, it's a good look for him. Once again, his eyes travel down my body, then back up to meet my gaze. He doesn't smile, but he does wave a hand at the large pool of water—which I realize now is a bath. Something Roman, probably. "Join me then."

His hesitation is gone. He might be a newborn vampire, but he's still Paul. And I get the feeling that Paul and sex are synonymous. Wings growing out of his back might still be a mystery to him, but a naked woman in his bathroom is not.

This is when I realize I'm about to bathe with the monster and the inner voice—the one that is supposed to caution me from doing stupid things—is snapping into action. *What the fuck are you doing, Syrsee? Go back!*

But I didn't come here just to go back. And anyway, this has already happened.

I walk towards him, then past him. His body turns with me and I can practically feel his gaze as he watches me slowly step down into the pool, descending until the warm water is up past my breasts.

That's when I turn to face him again. He has dropped the pants he was wearing and his cock is long and hard. His eyes lock with mine as he descends down the steps and into the water as well.

He bites his lip and a little stream of blood drips out.

Immediately, the cravings inside me come back to life. I want that blood much, much more than I want sex or answers.

But the weird thing is, I don't think he did this on purpose. This realization is the only thing holding me back. He's not the Paul I know. He's not in control at all right now. He's not tempting me, he's just... nervous, I think.

"What?" He snaps this word out and it's true. I'm making him nervous.

I suck in a deep breath, then slowly let it out. He watches me do this, his brow furrowing again. Then I look around, spy a shallow wooden dish filled with sponges, and walk through the water towards it. I pick up a large sponge that looks like it was harvested directly from the ocean floor this morning and didn't come from a mall store filled with skincare products.

There is a cake of soap too. And I take that with me as I walk back over to Paul. He doesn't say anything, just accepts the cake of soap in his palm when I offer it. Then I dip the sponge in the water, rub it against the soap, and look up into Paul's eyes. "Turn around. I'll wash them for you."

He clenches his jaw, but then relaxes it and does as I ask.

Now that I can see them up close, I realize the skin around his emerging wing bones is very red, so I am careful when I touch the sponge to the scabs. He flinches when this happens. Just his skin, though. The way a horse might flinch when bitten by a fly. But he doesn't protest or tell me to stop.

I dip the sponge in water, apply more soap, and gently rub the scabs until they melt away and begin to bleed. Not a lot, and it's mostly mixed with water, so I'm able to control my urges. But the desire to lick him is still fairly strong.

"Well?" Paul breaks our silence. "Are you going to tell me why you're here?"

I continue to gently clean his wounds—which is a good word for what these wing bones look like—as I answer him. "I don't know why I'm here. It just happened."

"Where do you come from?"

"The future."

He looks over his shoulder at me. "How far in the future?"

"Couple thousand years, maybe?"

"Am I there, in your future? Do you know me?"

"Unfortunately, I do."

My answer makes him chuckle. "Are we not friends?"

"We are not."

"Are we enemies?"

"We're…" I sigh. "I'm not sure."

"Why are you serving me then?"

"*Serving* you?"

"Cleaning my back like a slave."

"I don't think it was my idea."

This makes him go quiet and this quiet lasts for nearly a

minute. I simply continue to gently wash the wounds until finally, I have to stop when he turns to face me.

The cut where he bit his lip has already healed, but just the memory of the blood when I look at his mouth is enough to make the cravings start.

He reaches out, wrapping his fingers around my wrists—not tightly, but definitely with intention. My gaze slides up to meet his.

"What did I do to you? To make you hate me?"

I shrug. "I'm not really sure."

"What *are* you?"

I shrug again. Just one shoulder this time. "I don't know."

"A Black witch?"

"Definitely that. But not *just* that."

"Did I make you?"

"I… you… well… yeah." I let out a breath. "I guess you did. You made me when you made Ryet."

"Who is this Ryet?"

"Your scion. And I am his food."

Paul is staring at me with a stoic face, his eyes brightening and then dulling, a dark shade of red. And when they do this, all I can think about is his blood. And how much I want it. And how if he were to turn around again, I could simply lean forward and swipe my tongue against his wounds.

"You're hungry, Syrsee? For my blood?" His voice is different now. More congenial, less angry. More intentional, less confused. This is the Paul I know. The confident one. A monster who takes almost nothing seriously.

But still, all I'm really thinking about is his blood and how much I want to lick him. It takes every bit of self-control I have not to reach out and pull him towards me, begging for it.

I hate myself for this. I do. But I'm out of control. This is not a want. This is a need.

"Would you like some?"

I can only nod my head as I press my lips together. Because if I open my mouth right now—

"Drink, Syrsee. Can you hear me? Drink. Just drink."

The hallucination fades and I'm on the floor of Ryet's cabin bathroom. He's got one arm under me, his upper body leaning over me, and the purple and gold mist is still thick like a curtain. But then he's holding his palm to my mouth and all I can think about is the blood.

11 - Josep

A new nation. A new race. A new destiny.

They are making a noise upstairs. Lots of noises, actually. Loud thumping ones from the music, sharp cracking ones from the firearms, and other, smaller, more desperate noises that come from the hunger they are now feeling.

Of course, I know the world above my bunker is filled with halfbreeds. And I've been perfectly OK with this since Lucia started collecting them, but that's because I never thought I'd actually have to deal with them myself. Not like this.

But—I sigh, resigned to my fate—it is what it is.

I straighten up, then turn to face the side of my cavern that leads to the bunker. I am leaving. Something I have not done in a very long time. Years. Probably decades, at this point, but I haven't been keeping track.

Halfbreeds. What a nuisance.

However, they are part of the plan. One of them, at least. Otherwise Paul would not have tolerated them.

Paul is… missing. Kind of. I'm really not sure what happened during Ryet's ascension—he didn't come back with my promised blood, so something happened—but that blood was for storage and experiments. It wasn't anything necessary for my present objective.

Paul does not require a babysitter and I am not about to spend time worrying about him. He can figure it out himself.

Ryet and the little witch have gone east to his home. A home Paul provided him. A safe haven where Ryet can retreat and have space to think. All part of the plan and, like the whereabouts of Paul, none of my concern.

I have one goal now and I am focused.

I come out of the bunker and enter Paul's bedroom, stopping short in front of a full-length mirror. It's one thing to see your reflection in a rippling dark pool of water and quite another to get all the details presented to you in glass coated with silver.

I am dirty and naked. My hair is a darker blond, than I remember but the body is in good shape for my age. I'm still tall and muscular, but in a lean way. Attractive.

Of course, all vampires have this look once they master the monster stage. We all end up pretty much the same. Different versions of this. Paul is a special shade of beautiful, but that's another story for another time.

We are in the middle of the greatest ascension in history. If we pull it off, and there is no reason to think that we won't at this point, we will change the world. Every last inch of it.

Ryet was the bottleneck. Getting a scion to transform into a vampire with only two fathers was a feat. There were many mistakes and it took us hundreds of years, but here we are.

The birth of a new nation. A new race. A new destiny.

The American Vampires.

*I shower, **and when this is done**,* I walk over to the door, still naked and still wet, and open it up.

The thumping of music has been non-stop for weeks already. But once the door is open, it's much louder than I can stand. So I close my eyes, find the vibration, follow it backwards to the source, and then cut the power.

The lodge goes quiet for a moment, but then the protests from the halfbreeds fill in the silence. They are yelling and screaming for someone to turn the music back on.

I open my eyes and find a young woman with pink hair standing in front of me. Her eyes are wide and blue, her mouth open in shock. She blinks. "My... lord?"

"If you insist."

Her brow furrows. "What?"

"I will be your lord if you insist."

"Are you... Josep?"

"I am. Who told you about me?"

"Ryet. I called him. Paul is missing. Did you know? Do you know where he is?"

"We don't need to concern ourselves with Paul at the moment. He can take care of himself. What we need to do... what is your name?"

"Echo."

"What we need to do, Echo, is release these halfbreeds."

"Release? I don't understand."

Echo has a very appealing face and I am pleased that she is the halfbreed waiting outside Paul's door. It feels like a reward. "No, Echo. You were not meant to understand. You were made to obey. Will you obey me?"

She nods her head enthusiastically. Then bows it and falls to her knees, pressing her forehead onto my bare feet. "I'm at your service, my lord."

"Of course you are, Echo. You have no choice in the matter. Now get up. We have a lot to do before we can leave." I take her back in the bedroom and motion to the bed. "Have a seat."

She looks at the bed, then at me—eyes falling down my body to my cock, then back to the bed—only then meeting my eyes again.

"Don't be a fool. I am not interested in having sex with you, Echo. You are not my type. But you need to feed, do you not?"

Echo blinks at me. And I can see the greed in her eyes. Halfbreeds don't need the blood. Normally. But if they've been feeding on it—and she has, it was planned that way—then they do crave it something terrible. It's an addiction.

"Go on," I encourage her. "Lie down. This feeding, it's going to take a little while. So you might as well get comfortable." Then I turn, close the door, and by the time I turn back, she's on the bed. Flat on her back, eyes already begging for that blood.

She will do anything for it.

I walk over to the bed, lie down next to her, and turn onto my side so I can see her better. I consider making myself at home with her body. Stroking her a little. Making her moan. But there's no time. I bite the fleshy part of my palm and put it up to her lips. The moment she tastes my blood, she is gone.

Not dead. Just somewhere else. A place called Bliss, I suppose.

As she drinks, I let my thoughts wander back to Paul and our history together.

It was his idea to make Syrsee for Ryet to feed on specifically. It took decades to collect the right blood to breed her. We were hunting down the donors for more than a century. There were many clans of Black witches in America when we arrived, but they were well hidden in the native tribes. They did things differently than in the Old World and it took us a while to form our own little coven to use as breeding stock. We needed genetics from all over the continent. We went up as far as the Arctic and as far south as we could without impinging on the territory of the Amazonian vampires.

Every Black witch we had was used to make Syrsee's genetics. And once we had that, we made Ryet. This was a much more difficult task than making Syrsee. We used one of our most precious Black witches as a surrogate and it didn't exactly go as planned. She was not going to make it through her third trimester, so we tried something very unconventional to save the experiment—we turned her halfbreed and fed her our blood until Ryet could be born.

This had never been done before and so we were not sure if he was the one.

Not until now, that is.

It worked. And it worked beautifully.

But Ryet's ascension is just the first phase of the plan.

There is much, much more to come.

ECHO STOPS **drinking** and when I look down at her, she's completely unconscious. But I don't require her to be conscious for what comes next, so I lean over, place my mouth on her neck, wait until I can feel the pulsing of her blood through her jugular, and then I bite her and drink.

Her blood is bitter and I pull back, letting it drip out of my mouth and onto her neck. It's been so long since I had to kill a halfbreed, I guess I'd forgotten how bad they taste. Almost as bad as a pureblood human.

But it's the only way, so I press my mouth back onto her neck and take her blood, sucking it out of her as fast as I can, just to get it over with.

Minutes later, she is drained, and pale, and limp. But this process is just getting started. I don't bother trying to rouse her, she's gone. I just bite the palm of my hand and let my blood drip into her mouth.

After a minute or so, she stirs. Moaning.

My reply to this is a whisper, low and sweet. "You're fine. Just keep still for another moment now."

I doubt she can hear me, but she doesn't try to wriggle away when I lean into her neck and take another bite.

This time she tastes a little less sour. Not good, by any means, but it's better than it was on the first round. After I've drained her a second time, she is much more eager to drink me back. And after the fifth round of performing this little ritual she tastes almost as good as Lucia once did.

At this point, I know I'm done. I've always compared Lucia's blood to a weird appetizer served at an elite party, something meant to spur conversation, if only to discuss how gross it is. So Echo's blood—while better than it was when we started—is by no means tasty.

And I have halfbreeds to kill.

I pick her up and leave the bedroom. There are many people downstairs and they stare up at me as I descend, looking confused.

One of them—a tall man with many tattoos—opens his mouth like he is going to speak. "No," I say, looking right at him. "You will not talk to me. I am not interested." My gaze sweeps around the room, and as I do this, they all go silent.

I have pushed the mute button on the whole lot of them. That's what Paul once called my power of silence. That was decades ago now. But the name stuck in my mind for some reason. So 'mute button' will go down in vampire history.

A chuckle escapes as I picture future generations of American Vampires learning their history and how they will snicker at the name of this power I will pass on to them. Mute button. How fun.

I paid a pretty price for the mute button but in this particular moment, it still feels worth it.

"I have a present for you." I declare this loudly to all the halfbreeds around me, my voice echoing off the high wood-beamed ceilings. "Her name is Echo. Do you know her?"

Of course, they can't answer me. The mute button is still very much pressed. But it was a rhetorical question anyway. Of course they know her.

I walk to the center of the foyer and set Echo down on the wood-planked floors. Then I look up at the halfbreeds that Lucia has been collecting since we arrived in the New World. None of these specific halfbreeds were there at the time. Their lifespan is only a few decades. But Lucia made them constantly. It was the gift the Darkness gave her. The only gift she had, so I can't really blame her for using it.

"Are you hungry?" I ask them.

They nod, enthusiastically, and I can only imagine the noise they'd be making if I hadn't rendered them silent. But they are anxious and eager for blood, so when I don't

JA HUSS

immediately explain, they shuffle their feet, becoming restless as their gazes wander up to my neck.

"Oh, no. You have misunderstood. *I* will not be feeding you." I point to the girl on the floor at my feet. "She will. But don't worry and don't make faces at me. I have given her some of my blood, so you will all get the proper dilution to ease your cravings and slip into bliss. How does that sound?"

I smile at them. Radiating warmth and compassion. Giving off a paternal vibe.

It's all lies, of course.

Because this is how I'm going to kill them.

They begin to rush forward but I put up both my hands, palms out, and push them back as I turn in a circle. "Do not. Rush me. Do not touch me, do not look at me, do not do anything without permission. Do you understand?"

They do. Or probably not, actually. They are addicts seeking a fix. Since when do addicts understand anything but their own lust?

The power of compulsion is what I use to keep them away. Passed on to me through the blood, just as I will pass on the mute button. The important thing is, the halfbreeds do not rush in like a horde and rip little Echo to pieces.

I hold up a finger and point it at the zombie-like creatures in front of me. "One at a time. You." I point to the one right in front of me. A woman, early thirties, maybe. Which makes her old compared to the rest, who all appear to be just a bit older than teenagers.

The woman comes forward, her eyes not on me now, but locked on Echo's body. Her only thought in this moment is the blood.

I can relate. I was hungry like that at one time, as well. But never as a lowly halfbreed.

"Kneel," I tell her. She does, looking up at me, practically salivating. "One. Sip. Do you understand me? One. There are dozens of others who need blood as well. If you are greedy, I will cut your head off. Do you understand me?"

She nods, but she's not really agreeing. She's not really capable of that. Not when the hunger is this bad. But I like giving them warnings like this so they know what to expect. I look at the rest of the horde and repeat my caution. "Do you all understand? One. Sip."

They nod, or don't. Doesn't matter.

I return my attention to the woman kneeling at my feet in front of Echo and nod my head. "Proceed."

The woman, whose face is gaunt but not ugly or evil-looking, attacks Echo's neck with a ferocity that surprises even me. Three seconds pass and she's already taken far more than just one sip. I reach out, grab her by the hair, fling her backwards into the crowd—which disperses in a disturbing silence—and then I reach down, grip her fragile throat in my hands, rip it out of her neck, and then, with my other hand, I pull her head off and drop it on the floor at the feet of a rough-looking man.

He's still looking at the head when I speak. "You're next." He looks up at me, eyes wide. Blinking. "Do not take more than your share. Do you understand?"

This one nods yes as he looks me in the eyes. I have his full attention. The blood can wait. He's listening for the rules.

"Good." I pan my hand at Echo's body. Part of her neck is missing and we're just getting started. But one does what one must. "Proceed."

This halfbreed is smarter, or better behaved, or has a much more developed sense of self-preservation than the last. Because he takes a deep breath as he approaches Echo, then lets it out slowly as he kneels down in front of her body.

He gives me one more glance, nods, and then bends down with his mouth open, going for the other side of Echo's neck.

He bites, he sips, he stops. He remains absolutely still for a few moments, then looks up at me for approval. I nod, then point in a random direction. "You may wait in the..." I've never actually seen the finished house. My bunker was completed first, before the lodge renovation. So I take a guess. "The... dining room." Surely, there must be one of those. Or something like it.

Surely. Because the man gets up, licking his lips—already craving that next drop—and stumbles off, deeper into the house.

"Very good. Who's next?" If they could speak, they would be shouting and begging. This is why I silenced them in the first place. Well, one of the reasons, anyway. I'm not in the mood to hear their voices, but everything I do has multiple goals. So I point at another random man, snap my fingers in the direction of Echo's body, and instruct him to repeat what he just saw.

When he's done, I send him to the dining room as well.

I do this several more times before one finally comes back, waving their arms at the hungry, waiting horde. Trying to warn them.

Reason number two for the silencing. I don't want them to be warned. This do-gooder came back from the dining room —probably because when she arrived there, she found a bunch of dead bodies. Perhaps they were sitting at a table, all slumped over? Or maybe they just fell face-forward onto the floor? Doesn't matter. The point is, they are dead.

Because that is the whole purpose of this little ritual.

I'm not feeding them. I'm killing them.

However, despite the fact that this disruptor is unable to communicate through speaking, the horde—which still consists of several dozen halfbreeds—takes notice of her distress and begins to look at me with suspicion.

I don't even bother caring. In fact, I take myself over to a leather-covered bench made of logs—Ryet's handiwork, no doubt—and take a seat. I cross my legs and smile at them.

What will they do now? Come at me with vengeance?

No. They all understand that something is very wrong here. But Echo's body has been bitten many times now. She's bleeding onto the floor. The scent of it alone is enough to drive them mad. The only reason they're still in control is because they think I will tear off their heads if I do not constrain themselves.

But now, with me seated, comfortable, seemingly uninterested in keeping order—along with the silent rage and caution, not to mention visible weakness and stumbling, of the halfbreed disruptor—they begin to care less and less about my threats as the seconds tick off.

What is happening, they ask?

They don't know. They have no idea. All they know is that they need blood, there is blood in a body on the floor, there is a vampire with considerable power in charge, and there is a friend in some kind of distress.

It's the distress that actually breaks the hold I have on them. Well, that and the fact that I'm sending off a vibe that I no longer care what they do.

And then there is a collective... *pause.* Where they do nothing, and don't move or think. It lasts for about three seconds.

Then they all come to the same conclusion at once.

They need blood and everything that is happening in these moments is telling them that they might not get this blood.

This is why they attack Echo's body on the floor.

And 'attack' really is the right word here. In less than a second, she is covered in halfbreeds. All of them trying their best to get a piece of her.

They take much, much more than a sip. And of course they do.

But the important thing is, as they're doing this—as they're in this feeding frenzy—they fail to notice how quickly the other others around them are dying off.

One sip of my blood—even diluted with Echo's—is really all it takes to kill a halfbreed. That's why I had to behead that first little rebel. If I had let her live for just a few more seconds, she would've died right in front of us.

That would've caused suspicion amongst the horde. Things could've gotten messy.

Not that they aren't messy now. There are already at least thirty dead bodies strewn across the foyer floor and the blood, my God. It's a wonder they ingested any at all, it's just everywhere.

It takes another couple of minutes for the struggling and gasping to stop and the foyer to fall silent.

I get up and walk over to the center of the floor where I placed Echo less than ten minutes ago. I can't even see her body at the moment, there are so many dead halfbreeds piled on top of her.

But I kick them off, drag them off, and finally find the pink-haired girl underneath.

She is in tatters. Literally. Her body looks like someone tried to flay her. Her eyes are dead and black. Her clothes ripped off. Bites all over her body.

I bend down, slip my arms underneath her, and pick her up. Then I carry her back upstairs.

When we get to Paul's bedroom I don't place her on the bed. I take her into the hallway that leads to my bunker. Her body flops as I descend back into my sacred underworld and the scent of dirt swirls around us.

When we get to the bunker the purple mist appears, billowing up from my feet as I walk forward into my cave.

I stop here, just past the threshold, and let out a breath. Happy to be home.

Then I kick the door closed behind me and the outside world disappears once again. In the new, comforting darkness I carry the ragged remains of Echo's body over to the pool near the waterfall and descend into the water. I settle us on a flat rock ledge, keeping what's left of her head above the water. Then I bite the palm of my hand and set it on top of the remains of her lips, letting the blood drip onto what's left of her tongue.

It takes a while. I don't keep track of time down here, but a good amount of it passes before she starts to show signs of life again.

Life, though? Is it life? It isn't. She has not been a living thing since the day she was made. Still, it's all she has.

She can't die, not the way the halfbreeds did in the foyer. Because she had *an exchange* with me and they didn't. The exchange is what matters. It's how you create things, it's how you change things, it's how you do everything in the world of vampires.

All those halfbreeds did was drink poison. I am poison. Perhaps they could've drunk Ryet the way they probably drank Lucia on occasion, because Ryet is new and his blood is still developing. Lucia was never a vampire. She and Syrsee share some similarities, but Syrsee is a pure Black witch. Lucia is the equivalent of a witch-vampire halfbreed and her blood is not poison to her little minions.

She was also giving them blood from the feeder. A no-no in our world—our old world, the one across the ocean. But this was part of Paul's plan, or else he would've stopped it.

He didn't like the fact that she did it, especially when he was not directing it, but ultimately, he didn't push back much. It was, after all, necessary to create this moment with Echo right now.

She stirs in my arms. Her skin—all of her skin—is still tattered, but even as I watch the skin begins to mend. She will not remember what happened. Not directly. So she will have some peace. This is how I'm going to repay her for doing me the favor of killing Lucia's horde.

There is a chance that her memory of the ritual will come back, but I doubt she will live that long. I can't let her die, not yet. She has yet another job to do for us.

But once that is done she will be on her way to Hell.

As I've been thinking this her body has been repairing itself. And by the time I'm done, she is looking much, much better. Still more deathlike than lifelike, but she's making progress.

I resituate her in my lap so I can swipe the hair out of her eyes. I like to watch the life come back into them. Also, her eyes will turn color. They were blue, but they are not blue now, nor will they ever be blue again. They will be orange or yellow, or something in between.

She stirs again. A good sign. And then, abruptly, she's back. Eyes fly open—gold, very nice—and she gasps. Her lips are a luscious pink color, her pale cheeks become flushed and rosy right before my eyes, and her hair—which was pink and cut into a bob before the horde tore it from her scalp—grows back right before my eyes. Long, then longer. And not pink, since that was not her natural color. It's more gold than blonde, just like her eyes.

I smile down at her. "Welcome back, little baby."

ECHO IS SITTING NEXT *to me* in the pool of water now. She's mostly naked, but not entirely. What's left of her clothes hangs on her upper arms and around her waist. She's staring straight ahead at the waterfall, saying nothing. She has not quite come to terms with things just yet.

But she will. She has no choice, really. She will accept what happened, though she won't remember it. And she will move on and proceed to live out the rest of her life, which will be short.

"What—" This single word of hers comes out as a croak. She coughs and clears her throat. Tries again. "What happened?"

"They attacked you."

"What?" She turns her body to look at me. "Who?"

"The horde, of course. Lucia's minions."

"They—" She squints her eyes. "They *attacked* me?" She's making a face of severe confusion.

"They did."

"But... why? I don't understand." Now she's shaking her

head. "I was *very* popular. Everything was under control. We were—"

"Little baby." I turn towards her and place my hand against her cheek, gently stroking it with my fingertips. Her skin has healed nicely. Spectacularly, actually. She looks like a little porcelain doll. "They were addicts. Who can predict the behavior of addicts?"

She's still squinting her beautiful golden eyes. My blood really made nice improvements on this one. I'm actually impressed with myself. She's... well, 'spectacular' really is the only word for her. "But... we were going to..." She can't finish her sentence because she can't remember.

"We were going to release them, Echo? Do you recall when I said that to you?"

She shakes her head no. And of course she doesn't. Because I never said that to her, and even if I did, she would not be able to remember it.

"I, since I am old, and a vampire, and contain the power of the Darkness inside me—I could release them from this blood lust they had."

Which is not even a lie, when you think about it. I did release them. From... life. This thought delights me, causing me to internally chuckle.

"They are... dead?"

I nod at her. "They are, little baby. I'm very sorry if they were friends of yours. But they attacked you."

"Why?"

"Because I fed you, remember? You had my blood inside you and... well, they wanted it. They were eating you. When I killed them."

"That's..." Her face scrunches up as she finds my eyes. "That's *gross*."

"It certainly is. But it's over now."

She blows out a breath. Then looks up at me. "Well, what's next?"

"We need to find Paul."

This makes her happy. She even smiles. "Yes! We do! I really, really need to find Paul."

I furrow my brow. "Do you love him?"

"Uhhhhh…" She makes a face of uncertainty. "Well, I'm not sure about that, but I do like him. And he's nice to me. And… I miss him. He disappeared from the castle room." She makes a vague motion with her finger pointing up. "Do you know what happened to him?"

"Lucia, that's what happened to him. And Syrsee, I imagine."

"The woman? The one they were feeding on?"

"Yes. Her. She's rather important in the grand scheme of things. But don't worry. We'll catch up to her later. Paul comes first."

"Will we punish her?" I do believe that I detect some hope in Echo's question. She certainly is loyal to Paul.

"It's a nice thought, isn't it? But don't get your hopes up. As I said, she's important. Also powerful. So if you ever come up against her, don't challenge her to a fight. She's a little bit dumb, I imagine, as she was kept ignorant on purpose." I take a moment to stroke Echo's cheek here. Because she is rather ignorant as well. "But she's capable of hurting us, little baby. Even without the knowledge of how to do so."

"OK. But how do we find Paul?"

"We will have to look in the mist, of course." When I say this word Echo looks up at the mist that floats all around us. "Yes," I tell her. "That mist. But not this literal mist. Not here, in this cavern. We must go deeper into the dirt where the mist comes from. There are pathways under the earth."

"Like tunnels?"

"Y...yes. Sure. Like tunnels." I smile down at her. "Once we find these tunnels, they will take us places. Places where Paul might be."

"Will he be OK?"

"I'm sure he will. He's Paul, after all. Quite a powerful monster."

"If he's so powerful, then why can't he find his way back? Why is he lost? And how did he get down in those tunnels?"

I hold up fingers so I can tick off answers to each question. "It's complicated. The mist is deceptive. And I already told you—Lucia and the little witch did some magic on him."

"What happens then?"

"Then?"

"After we find Paul in the tunnels?"

"Then..." I pause to smile as I picture what actually comes next. "Then... a new nation. A new race. A new destiny."

She doesn't understand, but that's OK. I stand up in the water, extending my hand down to her. She hesitates, but only for a moment. Then she places her fingers across my palm and squeezes her hand, helping her rise.

Since she is mostly naked, and since she has taken my blood—quite a lot of it now—her breasts are a sight to behold. I let my gaze linger on them. Then down between her legs where there is a bit of blonde fuzz to entice me. "I would like to fuck you, but I'm afraid there's no time."

She scoffs. Like she wants to point out that she wasn't offering herself up. But she knows better and leaves it at that.

We walk towards the back of my cavern together. She's still fairly amicable, but when we arrive at the entrance to a tunnel that glows with a lavender mist, she hesitates. "Now where are we going?"

"Into the earth, little baby. I've explained this." I grab a hold of her arm—just in case—and tug her into a passageway where, at the end, there is a large tapestry covering the wall of rock.

When we get there, I keep a hold of her with one hand and use the other to pull the tapestry away, revealing a dark hole in the side of the earth.

"What's in there?" She's facing the hole, nearly under the threshold, when she says this. So her question bounces off the ceiling of the new cavern.

"Our destination, love."

I push her forward and she stumbles, then turns, trying to get past me. I grab her, hard, and push her up against the wall. "I just explained to you that you're coming with me. There is no way out, little baby. None at all. So stop. Because if you resist, *you will piss me off.*" This last part comes out mean, almost a growl. "You're not going to die. You're already dead. And I will be with you every step of the way." I reach down, making her flinch, and swipe a strand of hair away from her sweaty face. "Do you understand?"

Echo forces herself to take a deep breath, then nods her head as she presses her lips together. She's terrified. And she should be.

Because while I *will* be with her every step of the way, we will certainly be parting ways once we arrive at our destination.

She must read my mind because she makes one last attempt to get around me. But this time I am forceful and committed. I grab her wrists, spin her around, and then shove her forward.

She screams when she realizes there's no earth under her feet. And I have just enough time to grab her tight around the middle, and unfurl my wings, before we start falling.

With the wings comes the transformation. It creeps across my skin like a spider weaving a web of death. Turning it blue-black. Making my teeth grow into long, sharp fangs, and claws appear at the end of my hands and feet.

This is why I didn't bother putting on clothes.

When one goes into the dirt, one must become one's self.

12 - Ryet

We'll meet again one day.

*S*yrsee's fever has not yet broken and it's been nearly a week. I did have to leave her alone for about an hour several days back because I ran out of bacon. But other than that, I've been by her side this whole time, giving her small amounts of my blood to bring her fever down.

Meanwhile, as I've been doing this, I've also been eating real food non-stop and taking regular trips down to the basement tunnel to cover myself in dirt.

What the actual fuck is happening to us?

If I could leave Syrsee alone I'd be in town right now trying to find that fucking Guild Lounge. I'd turn myself in to them just to get answers.

I'm almost to the point of putting her in the truck and carrying her into that general store with me because I don't know how long I can go on like this. When will she wake up? What is happening to her? What's happening to me?

Paul, where the fuck are you when I need you?

Oh, I've been having regular conversations with him too. Not real him, of course. Some kind of hallucination, I think. There's no purple to indicate I'm in a dreamwalk, but I know it's not real because he looks blurry and smudgy. Like he's been in the dirt too.

He's also annoying in that smarmy way I hate. The ultimate smooth talker, always demanding that I come find him so he can illuminate me with the answers to all my questions.

And, actually, I probably would. More than likely, if Syrsee wasn't so sick and I wasn't afraid to leave her alone, I'd be back in the truck driving to Montana to go look for him. Because I don't understand what is happening and it's entirely possible that I'm fucking up really critical things that will affect our futures.

Also, I feel guilty about Syrsee. Because the last conversation we had was a fight over me having to feed her. And I just can't take the irony of it. She was *just* pissed at me because she was *my* food and less than a day later, our roles were reversed. And we were having the same fight, but in reverse.

What the fuck is happening?

And, oh, yeah, the wings? Leaving again to go shopping in town for more bacon is a fantasy because the fucking wings are growing like... well, like nothing I've ever seen in nature. A weed, I guess. My wings are like weeds. Getting bigger, and thicker, and heavier by the hour. There aren't any feathers yet —and it's *not* a good look. It's like wearing a skeleton on my back. At least fucking Paul had bat wings. My wings make me feel like I'm carrying around something that has died and rotted away.

And don't even get me started on the dirt. I crave bacon and dirt.

This is my life. Frying bacon and eating it by the pound. Bleeding myself out to keep Syrsee alive—or... something. And lying in the hole I dug under the house so I can cover myself with dirt.

It's been eight and a half days and I feel like I'm going crazy.

No. I feel like Syrsee when she stood out on the side of the highway in Arizona, looking up at that horse and rider sign, yelling at me because I had been sick for ten days and she had been taking care of me that whole time, all by herself, and she had reached her limit.

I pause my mental rant here and think about this.

Ten days.

Maybe she's on her own ten-day transformation? Maybe this will break in another day and a half?

A little bit of hope swells up inside me.

But what if it doesn't? What if she never wakes up again?

It could happen.

The phone in the kitchen rings, shocking me back into the present. It's probably Echo again. And even though I'm not in the mood to talk to her, or hear her complaints about how all the halfbreeds are starving, I get up and answer it anyway.

"Now what, Echo?" And all my irritation, and annoyance, and resentment comes out in these three words.

"Um." There's a pause. Then—"Is this... Ryet?"

"Who's this?" It's definitely not Echo and my aggravation is building.

"Zusi. I know Syrsee is there and I know she's mad at me, but please... *please* let me talk to her."

"Where are you?" Now I'm beyond annoyed, I'm pissed. Because she's got this phone number and she's bothering me when I have more pressing matters to concern myself with.

"I'm in town."

"At the lounge?"

"You know about the lounge?"

"Syrsee told me some guy named Tristin was waiting for her when she went into town to shop."

"Did she say anything about me?" Zusi sounds a little desperate for information.

I don't feel sorry for her. She hurt Syrsee. She betrayed her. And to me, how that betrayal happened, or whether or not she knew about the plan hatched between Paul and the Guild, doesn't matter. She hurt Syrsee and now I want to hurt her back. "No, Zusi. She didn't mention you at all."

All I get in response is a long breath of air.

"Is that it?"

"Wait—you're not going to let me talk to her? You're not even gonna tell her I'm on the phone?"

I hesitate here, which is a mistake. Because obviously Syrsee is unconscious and can't come to the phone, so there is no reason for me to tell her anything.

And apparently Zusi is wise to the way of hesitations because she picks up on it immediately. "What? What's wrong? Is she OK?"

"She's fine. She just doesn't want to talk to you."

"Syrsee!" Zusi is yelling into the phone so I have to hold it away from my ear. "Syrsee, just talk to me. Please! Let me tell my side of the story! It's not what you think! I would never betray you!"

I hang up the phone, then pick it back up, check for a dial tone, and leave it off the hook. The vintage way to block someone from calling you back.

Then it hits me that it wasn't Echo calling and I kinda want to talk to her. So I depress the switch, get a dial tone, and call the kitchen landline at the lodge.

It rings. And rings. And rings. After fifteen of them, I hang up, wishing I had my cell phone so I could call her directly, but I don't even remember the last time I saw that phone.

Also, what the fuck? Even if Echo is busy, there are dozens

of halfbreeds at the compound. Someone should've been within earshot of the kitchen and picked it up.

This has me wondering just how bad things are getting out west.

Paul appears sitting at my little table. He's leaning back in the chair wearing a vintage suit that reminds me of our time in San Francisco, back when I was newly second-born. "I have all the answers you're looking for, Ryet. All you have to do is come find me."

I know he's not there. I'm hungry, that's all. For blood, not bacon. And feeding from an unconscious Syrsee feels a little bit too coercive for my comfort level. I don't need a lot of blood right now—I'm seriously surviving on the bacon. But every couple of days I do need *some*. I'm going on day three since my last drink and I'm trying my best to put the next feeding off as long as possible, hoping she will wake up before I absolutely have to do it, so Paul's ghost isn't exactly a surprise.

Still, I'm tired of being alone. Illusion Paul is better than nothing, I guess. I take a seat at the table across from him, letting out a long breath. "I can't come find you, Paul."

"Why not?"

"Because Syrsee is sick and I can't leave her alone."

Paul chuckles in that disingenuous way he has. Like he's laughing at me. "You don't have to *leave*, Ryet."

"What do you mean?"

"You're a vampire with the gift of dreamwalking. Why do you think you're so attracted to that dirt under the house?"

I just stare at him. Almost unable to think, my head is so foggy. "*What?*"

"The dirt, Ryet. Why do you think I go into the earth? Do you think I sleep there?"

"Well…" I kinda did think that. And then I'm so tired of these fucking mysteries, and unanswered questions, and loss of control over my own life that I just give up. "Why don't you just tell me what the dirt is for, Paul? And why don't you just tell me what you want me to do with it? Let's make it all very simple for once."

"You would like me to tell you what to do so you can follow directions?" He laughs here. "Since when?"

"Since *now*. What is the dirt for?"

That smarmy smile of his is back as he relaxes into his chair. "It's a conduit. It runs between worlds, through this world, all over the place, actually. You can go anywhere you want in the dirt, Ryet. And you don't even have to move." He taps his head. "It's all up here." He pauses again, eyes practically twinkling. "Of course, there is… *a catch*."

I open my mouth to reply, but he's gone. Like he was never sitting in that chair in the first place. Or… maybe… like he *was* here and he just ran out of time.

Was he not an illusion? Was that really him? Is being stuck in the purple like being in the dirt? Only he's unable to come out of it?

I get up and start pacing the room, my boots thudding on the wide-plank hardwood floors.

If so, this whole purple thing doesn't sound like much of a punishment. He can come and go places as… what? A ghost? Not a ghost. Ghosts are dead people. He's not dead, he's just stuck. So he comes and goes as a… well, I don't have a word for that. A kind of energy, maybe.

Of course, being pure energy has its limitations. Maybe he can't hang around for long because he runs out of energy. Maybe it costs him a lot to come visit me like this, so being corporeal is a need. So he can affect the real world.

It makes sense, in a vampire way, I guess.

I blow out a long breath as I walk into the bedroom to check on Syrsee. She looks the same. Sweaty, pale, and unconscious. I sit down next to her on the bed, bite my palm, and then trickle the blood past her lips. After about a minute of this, she swallows. And I wait—like I do every single time—to see if this is the limit. To see if we've crossed some kind of threshold. To see if this is enough to wake her up.

It's not.

So my next decision isn't really a choice, it's a foregone conclusion.

I get up, take off my clothes, then go down to the tunnel that leads to the root cellar. The whole passage has been torn up at this point. It's nothing but dark, rich, loose earth. And not only does it feel soothing under my bare feet, it smells pretty fucking good too.

Not really sure how this whole dirt road thing works, I figure I must be on the right track if all my instincts are telling me to just lie down in the hole and cover myself up. So that's what I do. And as soon as I've got a good layer of it over me, I feel better. Like I've been carrying a weight and I just put it down.

I'm not completely covered and my face isn't covered at all, but I begin to wonder what would happen if I was truly immersed in the earth. And for long periods of time, the way Paul does it.

It's not something I'm going to try now. How would I breathe? Do I need to breathe? I have so many questions and the only way to get answers is to initiate this conduit through the purple that vision-Paul was talking about.

I don't know how one might do that, but I am pretty familiar with dreamwalking. And the moment I think this, I close my eyes and there it is. The lavender mist, floating all around me. Only I'm not lying down in a hole, I'm standing in the middle of that forest. The winter one where I saw Paul sitting on the fallen tree trunk while holding that baby.

And then there he is, minus the baby—naked and covered in dirt, just like me.

He just stares at me for a long moment. It's unsettling because normally this stare would be accompanied by the smarmy smile, and this time he's not smiling.

"What's wrong? Why are you looking at me like that?"

He lets out a breath, and with it comes a small smile. But the tone of his voice is different. It's not that fake congeniality, but low, and deep, and serious. "I just... I can't believe it worked. Do you have any idea how long I've been trying to make this happen?"

"Hundreds of years?"

"*Yes*. Hundreds of years. It was Syrsee who made it happen. Well"—he sighs—"it was all of us. Me, Josep, the Darkness. And reluctantly, I have to give Lucia credit as well. She was the origin witch for Syrsee's bloodline, after all. Of course, I've used the blood of every single Black witch I've ever tasted since landing in America for that purpose as well. But without Lucia, we wouldn't have been able to create a new strain."

"New strain of *what*?" He's calm and sounding very rational. But I'm not. And this question comes out with a lot of anger and pent-up frustration.

"Of..." He pauses, like he's struggling to find the right word. "Of... *sustenance*, Ryet."

"Sustenance? What a gross word, Paul. She's not food."

Paul doesn't even argue with me. Just kinda shrugs his shoulders. Then redirects the conversation away from Syrsee with another question. "What do you think of them?"

"Them? Could you be any less specific?"

"The wings, Ryet. What do you think of the wings?"

I look over my shoulder and find that they are complete and all the bones have been covered with a thin grayish-purple membrane. I raise one shoulder and the corresponding wing flutters a little. I can suddenly feel all the new muscles along my back that control this movement. Then I redirect my attention back to Paul. "What are they for?"

He tilts his head at me, like he doesn't understand the question. "What?"

"Why do we have wings, Paul? It feels... cliché."

Paul almost laughs. "Cliché? That's funny."

"Why?"

"Because I've found that the human lore tends to leave the wings out in most of their fictions."

He's right, I guess. "Who cares about that. Why do we need wings?"

"For flying, of course."

He says this like I'm an idiot. Which isn't even fair. "I can count on one hand the number of times I've even seen your wings, so don't act like I should know this."

"Well, that's because the flying isn't for *out there*, Ryet. It's for in here."

I have exhausted my patience for Paul's explanation of vampire wings. But at least he's provided me with a logical segue between that subject and the more important one, which is where I'm currently at. "What is this place? Some kind of advanced dreamwalk or something?"

"No, Ryet. It's not a dreamwalk. It's reality. The reality that exists to feed the Darkness. The only reality that really matters, when you boil it all down to nothing."

I close my eyes, shake my head, and force myself to be

patient. I open them back up. Breathe. "Can you maybe explain that in a little more detail?"

"How about this?" As he talks the space around me changes from a snowy forest to a luxury hotel suite located someplace very sunny. It's the hotel room where I woke up from being second-born.

We're both on the bed now, side by side and leaning back against the headboard. Clothed—thank God—but close enough to each other that I have a compulsion to move over and put some distance between us. Which I do.

Paul chuckles. "You've always been so resistant, Ryet."

"What are you talking about? There were times that I was begging you for blood."

He turns his head, that fucking smarmy smile back. "You know damn well I'm not talking about the blood." The smiles fades. "I'm talking about us, Ryet."

"There is no 'us,' Paul."

"See? This is what I mean. You say that and you know it's not true. It's always been us, Ryet. Us against... *everything*." He pans a hand through the air, trying to give the meaning of 'everything' some actuality. "I understand that you hate me. I do. I don't even mind that you hate me because you don't understand anything about what's happening to you, and Syrsee, and me, and Josep."

I scoff. "How the hell did Josep get included in that list? I've never even met the guy."

"See, this is what I mean. You don't understand. But I do. I understand your hatred for me. I can't blame you—not really. I was, after all, the monster that killed your family."

"Oh. My God. Did you really just go there?"

"I did. For a good reason. You see, if I hadn't killed them in that fire, Ryet, you would've taken them to Hell with you."

I blink. "What?"

He puts up a hand. "Not Jane, of course. She was safe. But your children?" Paul shakes his head. "They had the Darkness in them because they were part of you. They were damned from the moment they were conceived. Burning them in that church while they were still young and innocent was the only way I could set their souls free. It was the best possible outcome."

Something happens here because everything in front of me—on all sides of me—narrows down into a dark tunnel of empty blackness with just a little bit of light in the center allowing me to see. Like I'm looking at life through a telescope.

Maybe like I'm seeing it for the first time.

Is this true? Were my children damned?

I can't speak, so I don't ask. But I don't need to ask. I *know* he's telling the truth. I was *made*. Produced. Bred. I was never a man, ever. I have always been the monster.

And maybe I didn't always know this, but I felt it. That's probably why I was such a fucking church boy. That's probably why I was compelled to be *good*.

I was born evil. I am evil. I am one of *them* now.

No, Ryet. I huff out a little air. *You have always been one of them. And if you were one of them, then all your children were too.*

It's true. Burning them *was* the best possible outcome.

Wow. I huff out a little laugh, shaking my head. I am a gullible fool if I believe this. I am making excuses for my... abuser? Not quite the right word. Captor? Doesn't really fit either. Master?

There we go. Master. As in, I am a slave. And this master just told me that he killed my entire family—burned them alive in a fire—to save their souls.

The problem is, it kinda makes sense. Now that I have a few more details about who and what I am. About where I come from. And even in the human world, genetics is passed through blood. It's a little more complicated than that—germ cells, and chromosomes, and heritable traits and all that science bullshit. But it's not a far-fetched theory to conclude that because my children had my blood that they were also part of the dark world just below the surface.

I take in a breath. I let out a breath. And with that breath I let my family go again. It's done. Jane made that very clear. She is saved and I am damned and if this fire did burn the evil out of my children and save their souls, well... Paul's right. It truly was the best possible outcome.

"Would you like to know where Josep fits in?"

The tunnel vision fades when I turn my head to look at Paul. "What?"

"Would you like to know what's happening? Or do you need a little more time?"

I don't answer that question. Instead, I ask one of my own. "Where are you?"

"I'm right here, as you can see."

"Where is this place? Where *are* you?"

"Do you have an urge to come save me?"

"Do you *need* saving?"

He hesitates for a moment. "Perhaps." He hesitates again. "But don't bother coming to find me. It needs to be Syrsee, Ryet. It's her spell. She's the one who needs to break it. If you come..."

Another hesitation. So he's either lying or unsure of himself. I don't like either of these possibilities. If he's lying, well, that would be very Paul of him. Which is bad, because untangling his lies would confuse me further, waste time, and put Syrsee in more danger. But if he's hesitating because he's unsure... I dunno. I think that's probably worse. Because I've always counted on Paul to be my... leader. To be in charge of making sure things turned out—well, not OK. Nothing is OK —but making sure things turned out the way they *should*.

"If I come... what? What were you gonna say?" I'm looking at him now. Straight in the eyes.

"If you come any further into the Darkness, it'll get you, Ryet."

"What the fuck does that mean?"

"You belong to the Darkness. You understand that, don't you? You're made of it. Just like me, just like Josep, just like Syrsee. And once you meet it, you can't go back from that. Of course, there's no way to stop this meeting. It is going to happen, but it needs to happen a specific way. I was selfish, earlier. When I was provoking you to come find me. I just wanted to know that you needed me. Now that I know you do"—his smile is big now. He's very satisfied with himself— "well, I can let it go. I will see you soon enough. We will be together again and I don't want to jeopardize our chance."

"Our chance at what?"

He smiles here, and it's not a smarmy one. It's... diabolical. "At revenge, of course. What else is there?" These words come out low, and mean, and absolutely evil. Sending a chill down my spine that reverberates all the way out to the tips of my wings.

I just stare at him for a few moments, unable to speak.

He breaks the building silence. "I'm going to send you back now. You found the medicine I left for you?"

I have to shake my head a little to focus. "What?"

"The jars and vials in the root cellar?"

"Those were from you?"

"Who else?"

"I don't know. I don't know anything right now."

"Of course you don't. I've kept you ignorant, Ryet. It's all very need-to-know. And up until now, you didn't need to know. But things are progressing nicely at the present. Your transformation has reached critical mass and Syrsee is just about there as well. Once she comes out of it, it will all go fast. She will need things, Ryet. Things only *we* can give her. And that is when you will need to meet your Maker."

"She will need things? What does that even mean?"

"One step at a time. First, go into the root cellar and use those jars and vials. They are for the both of you to share."

"Which ones? There are a lot of them."

"I can't tell you that because I'm not there. I cannot see her symptoms. You'll have to figure that out yourself. But don't worry. She's safe, for now. Because she's not in the purple, she's in the gold."

I make a face of what-the-fuck-does-that-mean.

"It's a witch thing. Not a place for vampires. But if you can bring her out of it, just long enough for me to find her, then I will be able to prepare her for what's coming."

I should ask. I know I should ask. *Prepare her for what?* But I'm almost certain he's not gonna tell me, and to be honest, I'm really not sure I want to know. Not yet. One thing at a time.

This feels a little bit like giving up, but what else can I do? I am one hundred percent certain that we are moving forward with whatever plan he's cooked up, so maybe letting him lead is the best course of action.

"Go now, Ryet. Get the jars and vials and take them inside."

Suddenly everything around me is starting to fade.

Including Paul. "Wait! Don't leave yet! How do I use the stuff in the jars and vials to make her better?"

And just as everything goes black, I hear his voice, low and distant. "You'll know what to do. Trust yourself."

The next thing I know I'm waking up in the dirt, sitting up and letting it all fall off of me. It's dark, but I can see just fine. And when I look over my shoulder, my wings are exactly as they were in the dream—complete and the bones are covered in a membrane. Except I don't think it was a dream. I think Paul and I really did just have that conversation.

Then I remember the last thing he said and get up. I pick my way over the various dirt mounds I've accumulated in the tunnel over the past week and finally stumble into the root cellar. There's an old produce basket on the ground, so I just start filling it up with the jars and vials.

Once that's done, I make my way back through the tunnel and up into the house. I check Syrsee first—still sleeping. Her fever is back. Well, it never really went all the way down to normal, but she's very hot again. So I take the basket of vials into the kitchen and use a dishcloth to clean the dirt and grime off the bottles, being careful not to get the labels too wet so I don't smudge what's left of the old ink.

Then I line them all up on the counter and take stock of what I have.

For jars I have 'Thirst.' 'Hunger.' 'Gasping.' 'Purging.' 'Chills.' 'Sweats.' 'Fatigue.'

For vials I have 'Despair.' 'Loneliness.' 'Regret.' 'Contempt.' 'Estrangement.' 'Fear.' 'Shame.' 'Guilt.'

The jars are for physical symptoms and the vials are for emotions.

Well, I can't read Syrsee's mind, so the vials will have to wait. I choose 'Sweats,' since she has a fever, and open the lid of the jar. I expect it to smell rancid—everything in the root cellar looks like it was made decades ago—but it actually smells sweet. A cross between ginger ale and honey. It looks like a pudding or custard and when I dip a finger into it and give it a taste, it *is* sweet.

There are no directions on any of the jars or vials, but at this point, I might as well trust Paul. It's not like I have many choices. I'm not sure how I'm going to get her to eat the pudding since she's unconscious, but then I get an idea—maybe I could mix the pudding with some of my blood and feed it to her that way? But then I get another idea—maybe *I* should eat the pudding and then just feed her my blood?

I've done dumber things in my life, that's for sure. And for some reason, this feels right. The exchange of blood feels important. At least it's familiar.

I go into the kitchen, grab a spoon, and then, without thinking too hard about what I'm actually putting in my mouth, I eat the whole thing.

Then I go back into the bedroom, sit down in the bed next to Syrsee, bite my palm, and put it up to her lips. Like every other time I've fed her since she fell sick, the blood stimulates some kind of involuntary instinct to suck. I give her a little more than I normally would—wanting to make sure she gets enough for the medicine to take hold—and then pull back and start thinking about my own hunger.

There's another jar, one specifically called 'Hunger,' and my first idea is to eat it myself. But would it be better if I feed it to Syrsee and then take her blood the way she just took mine?

Unless she wakes up, that's not possible.

But I could just bleed her out a little and mix it in, then eat it.

I decide to do this because while it would be much simpler to just bite her neck and take what I need, leaving the potions or whatever out of it, that is a temporary fix. What if this jar can make my hunger go away? Maybe not forever—it's not likely that it's a cure. But even if it's just long enough for her to wake up and make informed decisions about being my food, wouldn't it be worth it?

It would. Time. All I can do is buy myself time. Because whatever is happening to us, it's coming no matter how many jars of pudding we eat. And I just want a little more time before I truly turn into something evil and take my girlfriend along for the ride.

I position Syrsee's wrist over my mouth and then nick her vein with my teeth. Then I hold it over the open jar of 'Hunger' and fill it up to the top. When that's done, I lick the wound on Syrsee's wrist until it heals. Then I get a spoon, mix the blood into the pudding, and eat it. Again, like the first one, it doesn't taste bad at all. Not like honey and ginger ale, more like… meat. Which is kinda gross. Should be gross enough to stop me, actually. But by the time I'm actually having this thought, the jar is empty.

I just stand there in the kitchen, waiting. For what? I'm not sure. *Something* has to happen.

A moan from the bedroom draws my attention and when I enter the bedroom, I find Syrsee covered in sweat.

"No." I say this out loud, trying to give the word power. But I already know that I've made a big mistake. I go over to her, place my hand on her wet forehead, and find her cold.

My heart thumps inside my chest, ready to panic. But I force myself to stay calm. Cold is better than hot, isn't it? Plus, she's not dying. She's not human, so she's not dying. She's going to live to be very old. This is not the end. Paul did not just tell me how to kill her—he *needs* her.

It's this last thought that finally snaps me out of the urge to panic. Paul needs her. He would not have gone to all this trouble if all he wanted to do was kill her.

I go back out in the kitchen and read the labels in the jars again. Then pick up the one that says 'Chills.'

I eat it as I'm walking back into the bedroom. Then I sit next to her, bite the palm of my hand, and put it over her lips.

She reaches up and grabs my arm, pulling it down to her mouth. And this reaction is so sudden and unexpected, and I am so on edge, that I nearly pull away. Especially when I realize that she's not awake. Her eyes are still closed. But I calm down, get a hold of myself, and watch as she feeds on me like I'm food.

It's kind of erotic. I can feel her pulling the blood out of my hand and it sends a weird sensation through my entire body. My mind swims and floats and I have a sudden urge to drink her dry. Not a sip, but all of her.

Then I nearly laugh out loud. Because of course I do! 'Thirst' is a label on a jar in my kitchen.

I grab it, milk the blood from Syrsee, mix it in, eat it.

Relief.

But then I hear gasping from the bedroom and at the same time, I'm looking at the jar on the counter that says 'Gasping.' I don't even hesitate this time. I bite, I milk myself, I mix. I eat. I go back into the bedroom, teeth already puncturing the skin on my palm, and I hold my hand over Syrsee's mouth. She's too busy grabbing at her throat, trying to breathe—eyes still closed—to grab at me this time. But when I place my hand over her mouth the instincts kick in and she feeds.

A few moments later, she's breathing normally again.

But this time, her feeding doesn't elicit an unwanted erotic response. This time she sucks all the energy out of me. I barely have enough strength to pull my hand away and stand up. And it takes a real, concentrated effort to make my way back out to the kitchen and open the lid on the jar labeled 'Fatigue.'

Only the understanding that this Black magic is going to help me makes it possible for me to bleed myself out yet another time and mix my blood into the pudding.

I eat it. And from the very first spoonful, I feel stronger. By the time I'm done, I feel like a brand-new man. Or, rather, a brand-new monster.

There is only one jar left. 'Purging.' And if the pattern holds, this one is for Syrsee. I prepare the pudding with my blood and then grab a bucket from the little kitchen closet, put some water in it, and take it into the bedroom.

Syrsee is sleeping, but it's coming, so I'm ready.

And by the time she's done with her purging, her fever is gone, her face is flushed pink with blood, and she is the most beautiful creature that ever lived.

But really, the point is that by the time she's done I have eaten all the jars and she has eaten me.

I want to be pissed off about this. I want to hate Paul for what he just did to us—even though I don't even understand what he just did to us. But I can't be angry with him. Not anymore. I don't feel it. I want to see him. I want to save him. I want...

"Ryet?"

I startle at the voice, because I'm looking down at Syrsee as this word appears. And it's not coming from her.

"That's what he calls you, right?"

I look up and find Jane standing at the end of the bed.

She leans forward a little. "Can you see me?"

I nod.

"Can you... talk?"

I nod again.

"So... are you going to?"

"Talk to you?" My words come out as a breath. "Am I going to talk to *you*?"

"Yes. That's why I'm here. So we can talk."

I'm suddenly angry. No. Anger is not a strong enough word to describe my feelings towards Jane. I'm enraged. I feel a lot of hate for this woman.

It's unreasonable and probably related to the guilt about the blood magic I just did on myself and my girlfriend, but I don't care. I don't even try to subdue the fury inside me. I send all that rage out towards the woman who used to be my wife.

"So we can *talk*?" I am spitting words at her.

She smiles at me. That same angelic smile I remember from when she was my wife. "I know you're angry."

I stand up, walk to the end of the bed, loom over her, and growl right down into her face. "You have no idea what anger even is."

She stares up at me with those innocent eyes of hers. So wide. So calm. "I'm not afraid of you."

"Well, you should be." I sound evil. And if I wasn't shaking with hostility, I would think a little harder about this new me. But I don't have room for self-reflection right now. "Why are you here?"

Something has changed in the way I speak. My mouth has changed. And this is when I realize that I have *fangs*. Not the sharp and dainty points that were there when I woke up in

Syrsee's truck. But fucking fangs. Like I now possess the mouth of a lion, or a bear, or a... a fucking *vampire*.

That's not the only change, either. I can feel the new heaviness of the wings. I want to look—I want this bitch to go away so I can figure out what the fuck just happened to me—but I don't look. I stare straight down into her stupid, innocent eyes.

"I want to tell you," she says, "that I loved you."

"*Loved?*" I scoff. Not because I think she's lying. I know she loved me. And I loved her too. I scoff because it's past tense. She gave up on me. And all that time, when I didn't remember—when Paul was hiding the memories from me—I *never* gave up on her. I always knew she was there, in my past, and I never stopped trying to find her in my head and I certainly never stopped loving her.

"You didn't know, so I can't blame you—"

"Blame me?" Is this bitch for real? "*Blame*. Me?"

The world around me changes and suddenly I'm in our kitchen. And my kids—Charlie, Nancy, and Susan—are all sitting at the dinner table. I'm holding Jane in my arms and she's leaning back, her face pointed at the ceiling, happy and laughing.

I close my eyes and shake my head, forcing the memory to go away. I don't want to see it. I don't want to see what I lost.

"I don't blame you, Ryet."

"That's not even my name. You know that's not my name! Stop fucking calling me that!"

"We're OK. That's all I came to say. The children, they *were* saved."

I shake my head and laugh. Looking up at the ceiling. Looking all around me. Looking at anything but this ghost in front of me. "Paul. This is you, isn't you? You sick freak! You sick fuck! Come out—show yourself!"

"Goodbye, Ryet."

I look back at Jane. "Go, then. Get the fuck away from me."

"We'll meet again one day."

"I doubt that very much. Unless you're planning a vacation to Hell."

She smiles at me. But it's a sad smile, something that conveys pity. "You're not going to Hell, Ryet. You'll be forgiven in the end because this isn't about evil. But I guess you'll have to figure that out for yourself."

And then she's gone.

And I'm not standing at the end of the bed. I'm not in the cabin.

I'm not anywhere.

But everything around me is gold.

13 - Syrsee

This is what it means to be a vampire.

I **sit up straight in bed**, gasping, simultaneously feverish and chilled, and with an urge to vomit. But then I realize I'm not in bed. I'm not anywhere. I'm sitting on the ground—except there is no ground. I'm just in a golden mist.

"Well, at least it's not purple."

I turn and find Paul standing a little bit away, wearing a very nice black suit and with his feet hidden in the swirls of gold. I get out of the bed. "What is this? Why am I here? What do you want?"

Paul smiles. And for some reason, this smile of his—while gross, it's always been gross—is also comforting. Not really the smile. Just... him. The fact that he's here. I let out a breath in the same moment when he speaks again. "You came to me, dear Syrsee. I should be the one asking you that question."

I get to my feet, disagreeing with him by shaking my head. "I don't even know where I am, so stop with the lies."

Paul pans a hand through the space in front of him, parting a path through the gold mist. The space around me changes to a room. A very nice room, actually. Like a penthouse sort of place with high ceilings and massive windows that show a cityscape blurred through a haze of sheer white curtains. "Relax, Syrsee. We're going to be here for a little while. You might as well get comfortable."

I walk over to the window and pull the curtain aside. I

don't recognize the city, but it's not America, that's for certain. The scene is nothing but old, weathered, gray buildings outlined by an even gloomier sky. "Where is this?" I turn to face him. "Where did you bring me?"

"It's anywhere you want it to be. Because it's nowhere at all. We're in the gold now. You saw it."

"I don't know what that is."

"Don't be silly. Of course you know what it is. You just don't *remember* what it is."

"Same difference. What is it?"

"It's your magic, of course. Your *new* magic. Black witch magic. You had the purple because I gave that to you. It's mine to give, you see. I gave that purple magic to Ryet. And Josep, as well. You're all under my spell at the moment."

This makes me recoil. "What does that mean?"

Paul walks forward to a seating arrangement in the center of the large room. Two golden wingback chairs face each other. There is a small table between them with a tea service for two. He pans his hand to the chair nearest me. "Have a seat. Let's tea."

I scoff. "Let's tea?"

"We have things to discuss, why not get comfortable?"

There is a three-tiered tray of cookies and finger sandwiches on the table with the tea service and I'm suddenly very hungry for food, so I walk over to the chair and sit.

Paul waits for me to settle before taking his own seat across from me. Then he reaches for the teapot and pours us both a cup. "Go ahead. Help yourself to sugar and milk." His smile is big and feels genuine.

If anything coming from a monster like him is ever genuine.

I add some milk to my tea, then sigh and take a sip as I lean back in my chair. It's surprisingly good. And sweet, even though I didn't add sugar.

Paul takes a sip of his as well, but while I hold the hot tea cup in my hands—loving the warmth—he puts his down. "Take a cake, if you'd like. They're delicious."

"This is a dream. Why are we eating and drinking in a dream?"

"It's not a dream. It's like a dream, but you know as well as anyone that the dreamwalk isn't really a dream. The purple isn't exactly real, but it's definitely not imaginary, either. The gold acts in a similar way, but it's far more powerful than the purple."

"Why?"

"Why is it more powerful? Well, it's Black magic, Syrsee. That's the most powerful magic in the whole realm. I literally live off it. All vampires do and we do nothing but suck up energy. That's why we need your blood."

I sigh. Because I hate that he knows so much and I know so little. I hate that I need him to feed me this information. Someone should've taught me this shit. The Guild should've taught me this shit.

"You'll understand it more once you start using it regularly."

I feign disinterest with a shrug. "Whatever. I don't even care."

"Good. We're not here to discuss the power, we're here to discuss your future."

"Ya know, you're pretty confident that you're allowed to have an opinion about my future. I mean, this is nice and all" —I wave my hand at the room—"but you're stuck. I can leave and do whatever I want. You can't."

I'm not actually sure this is true, but I'm running with it

anyway. Because there's something to it, that's for sure. Otherwise, why meet up with me here? He has to know we're at Ryet's home. And even if he doesn't actually have that information, it's a logical first guess.

But he didn't come to the cabin. He's controlling this experience, I do understand that. But he's not really in control.

I am.

"You're very astute, Syrsee. Do you know that?"

I'm so used to him being smarmy and assholishly charming that I find his new serious, calm, deliberate, and almost cold nature off-putting.

Frightening, actually. That's a better word. Because only people who know they've won act like this. And I didn't even know we were playing a game, so there's no way I'm the winner here.

"Why are we here, Paul?"

"I just told you. To discuss your future. And you took us off track to try to convince yourself that I'm not really in control of your future, but as your maker, I disagree. You are mine. I've already told you this. Ryet is mine. I've told you that as well. We're doing this together whether you want to or not."

"Doing what, though?"

"That's all very need-to-know. And you don't need to know. Yet."

"Then why should I help you?"

"I don't need your help. Well"—he pauses to smile. It's a very confident smile—"I don't need your permission to take your help."

'Take my help.' It feels like a weird way to phrase things.

"Then, again, why am I here?"

As soon as I say this, Ryet appears. Not standing in front of me, or sitting next to us having tea—but in the bed. He's naked and lying on top of the covers. All stretched out on his stomach and showing off that glorious body of his.

I look over at Paul with an eyebrow raised. "What's going on?"

"Do you love him?"

"You don't have the right to ask me that question. We're not *friends*."

"I'll take that as a yes."

"Well, you would be wrong. I like him, but love him? No, Paul. I do not love him. I'm his food."

Paul laughs. "My darling, he is *your* food."

"What? How the hell do you figure? He feeds on me!"

"He feeds on you so he can feed you back. It's a symbiotic relationship. That means—"

"I know what it means, you asshole. I'm not stupid."

Paul flicks a finger in the air. "Of course you're not. I know that better than anyone. I am, after all, the one who educated you."

"You didn't—" But I don't even bother finishing. Because of course, he was the one who sent me to college. He was probably the one who chose all my classes.

The moment this thought runs through my head, he smiles. "Did you enjoy the piano?"

"What?"

"You took two semesters of it. I like the piano, myself. I had fantasies of you playing for me one day, but I suppose that's all they were. Fantasies. You did like it, though, didn't you?"

"Is that why Ryet plays instruments? So he can play for you one day?"

169

"Why does Ryet do anything? Why does he make things with his hands? Why does he build houses, and fix cars, and all those other things he does?"

"So he's got no free will?"

"I never expected you to be such an either-or person, Syrsee. I have to admit, it's throwing me. There is no black and white, my sweet."

I curl up my lip at the term of endearment. Sweet. That's probably how he literally sees me. A piece of candy to suck on.

"It's all very gray."

"Well"—I sigh—"I just don't see it that way."

"Then you're going to have a very hard time adjusting to what's coming next."

My stomach sinks and I suddenly feel sick. "What's that mean?"

"It means, if you want to survive with your mind intact, you will learn to love the gray." He gets up and walks over to the bed, stopping next to Ryet.

Paul begins to loosen his tie. His head turns so he can meet my gaze as he does this, undoing the knot and pulling on the tie so the silk slides through his collar. He drops it to the floor and tugs his dress shirt out of his pants.

I should look away. Should get up and try to leave, because I know where this is going. But I can't. I'm watching his fingers as he unbuttons his white shirt. It opens, revealing his muscular chest.

It's an illusion. I know this. I've seen the real him. He's gross. Blue-black skin and horns. He literally looks like a demon. But that's not how he looks right now. Right now—as he slips his suit coat off and lets the dress shirt slide down his arms—he looks like a god.

My eyes slide down his chest and once again find his fingertips, watching as they unbutton his trousers, then pull the zipper down. I might even be holding my breath at this point, that's how captivated I am.

Ryet groans and rolls over and my gaze immediately goes to him. He's hard. Like he knows what Paul is doing. But he can't possibly—his eyes are still closed.

I get up and walk over to the bed. "Ryet? Ryet, wake up."

"He can't wake up."

I look over at Paul. We are on opposite sides of the bed with Ryet between us. "Why not?"

"Because he's busy taking care of you. Out there. Where your physical body lives. You're sick. He's fixing you. So his spirit is otherwise occupied."

"Why bring him into this at all, then? Just... *stop*."

"I brought him here for you, Syrsee."

"If that's true, then you would leave. And let us be alone. But instead, you're taking off your clothes. So if you brought him here for me, then why are you doing that?"

"You really do think the worst of me, don't you?"

"You've given me no reason to think the best of you, that's for sure."

"Haven't I? I seem to recall that I was the one who saved you. Just like I saved Ryet's children by burning them alive all those years ago. Your soul is filthy and so is Ryet's. And although those children of his were innocent, they were tainted. I've already explained it to Ryet. He's accepted it as truth. And now, dear Syrsee, it's time for you to accept your truth."

Once again, I feel sick. Like I might throw up. "What is my truth?"

Paul's smile is warm now. "Don't worry, it's not as bad as his truth. You're going to have Ryet's baby, Syrsee."

I let out a breath and a little bit of relief washes over me. I knew this. I mean, not exactly knew this. But that is my destiny as a Black witch, right? That's our purpose in life. To make new Black witches. So I've known for a while now that this was coming. "OK. Is that it? Just... make a baby with Ryet?" I point to his naked body displayed before me on the bed.

But as soon as the words are out of my mouth, I know this is not it. Why would Paul be here, undressing himself in front of me, if all I had to do was make a baby with Ryet?

"You're part of this baby as well?" I have to force these words out past the lump forming in my throat.

Paul nods. "I am. I play a different role than Ryet. I won't be inside you. Well"—he stops to chuckle—"I've already been inside you. Many times."

I'm shaking my head. I did have that dream, but—

"It wasn't a dream, Syrsee. It was a dream*walk*. There is a very big difference. But that's not what I'm talking about. You see, I *am* Ryet."

I replay these words in my head. "What... what does that mean?"

"We're connected. I made him. I'm inside him. Which means every time he's been inside you, I've been inside you." He whispers these last few words, making them intimate. "Sometimes I take over. Like that first time, when he was very sick. It was me between your legs, Syrsee. It was my mouth. It was my tongue. I was the one who made you come."

I'm shaking my head again.

"Do you want me to describe it? Do you want me to tell

you what your pussy tasted like? Shall I tell you how you moaned and screamed?"

"Why are you doing this?"

"I already told you. I'm preparing you"—he nods his head to Ryet—"for your future." He slips his trousers down his hips and grabs his cock, fisting it as he looks me in the eyes. He smiles, then kneels down on the bed next to Ryet. Positioning his hips right up next to Ryet's.

Then he lies down on his side, tilting his head to look at me. "Join us?"

"Syrsee?" I look down and find Ryet awake. "What are you doing? Get back in bed."

I blink at him, then look at Paul. "He can't see me. This is your space, Syrsee. Not his."

"Why are you dressed? Are you going somewhere?" Ryet sits up and when I look back over at him, he looks a little bit scared. Like I was trying to leave him.

"No." I say this quickly before that wrong idea of his has time to take hold.

Which makes his smile and reach for me as his eyes find mine. "Then take off your clothes and get in bed with me."

This is when I realize he doesn't have wings. He looks like he did that day in that shitty cottage in White River. He looks like a really hot man.

"You want him. Why deny it, Syrsee? You tell yourself that you don't love him, but you do. I made you that way."

My mouth opens, ready to protest.

But Paul puts up a hand, silencing me. "But even if I didn't bake it into the cake, so to speak, you would still love him. I mean…" He chuckles. "*Look* at him, Syrsee. Have you ever seen a more beautiful man in your life? He's fucking hot. I made him this way for you. To make it easier. It's always easier to love the darkness when it's beautiful."

"Syrsee?"

I look back over at Ryet. "Hm?"

"Come back to bed." He lies back, getting comfortable and smirking at me as his hand slides down his stomach and fists his cock. He begins to jerk off, looking me straight in the eyes. "Well, if you're not coming to bed, take off your clothes, Syrsee. Let me watch."

Let me watch? "I don't think that's something Ryet would say."

"You don't think so?"

I look over at Paul and find him looking at me. "No. You've got it wrong. You're ruining the illusion."

"No, dear Syrsee. You've got *him* all wrong. He didn't fuck a lot of women. In that time after Jane and before you, I mean. But when he did…" Paul winks. "I was there, remember. In his head? He's dirty, Syrsee. You just haven't seen that side of him yet."

My thoughts drift back to that first night we met and how filthy hot the sex was. If that was Ryet, and not Paul, then yeah. He is dirty. "You said that was you, though. The first time Ryet and I had sex?"

"It was me. But I take my cues from him. He would've eaten your pussy with the same enthusiasm, trust me. Or don't, actually. Just… take off your clothes, get into bed, and see for yourself."

"With you watching? I'm sure you'd love that."

"Watching? Hardly. I'm going to participate."

"No, you're not."

"Yes. I am. Because I want to drink you, Syrsee. And you

like to be fed on, don't you? You're addicted to the pull already, aren't you?"

I don't know what to say to this. I mean, I'm definitely not addicted. Not yet. But I do like it. And this… offer of his. To drink me. I've got to admit, it's compelling.

Not only that, I'm fantasizing now. Ryet on one side of my neck, Paul on the other. Both of them pulling the blood out of me at the same time. Just picturing it turns me on.

But it doesn't have to be just a fantasy. I have them both, naked, right here in front of me.

I pull my shirt up over my head, forcing myself not to look at Paul. Then I slip my pants down my legs. Ryet opens his arms to me and I slide into bed next to him.

I'm acutely aware that Paul—naked Paul—is just inches away. But Ryet is kissing me now. His hands exploring my body, sliding up and down my thigh as his tongue twists inside my mouth.

Time skips, or something, because the next thing I know I'm lying on my back and Ryet is positioned over top of me. Paul is leaning in to my neck. I expect him to bite. Expect him to drink. But he whispers instead. "It's him, see? It's just him. And I'm here to remind you of that."

Then his hand slides down to my thigh, gripping my leg as he pulls it open.

Ryet is between my legs now, looking down at me like he's hungry. But I don't mind. Because Paul is finally at my neck, his teeth grazing over my skin, and I'm waiting for the bite. Wanting it. And when it happens, I close my eyes just as Ryet slips inside me.

My back arches. The pull of blood and the fucking—it feels good. Both at once feels more than good. It's glorious. I have them both and I suddenly realize, I *want* them both.

Ryet and Paul.

This is when Paul pulls back and whispers in my ear. "We serve very different purposes. Learn to love us that way, Syrsee. And everything will be fine."

I don't know what that means. I don't even care what that means because Ryet is thrusting inside of me, his movements hard now, more urgent. And I'm gripping him, my fingernails digging into the skin of his shoulders.

Ryet leans down, his mouth on mine, moaning things about babies, and all I can do is agree. "Yes," that's what I'm saying back. "Babies. Anything. Just keep going."

Paul is sucking the blood out of me, but then I'm sucking the blood out of him.

This is what it means to be a vampire.

Sharing.

The blood, the sex, each other.

"You're right." Paul's voice is right up in my ear. "That's what it means. That's what we're getting ready for. The share, Syrsee. It must happen in your physical body, not just the spiritual one. But don't worry. By the time that happens, you'll be more than ready."

A phone rings and I sit up in bed, blinking.

I'm not in some luxury hotel room having sex with Paul and Ryet. I'm in the cabin. Ryet is lying next to me, but he's not a man. His black wings are long and leathery. His body is... well, bruised is the first word that comes to mind. But I've never seen a human with skin the color of a bruise.

This is when I remember the phone is ringing. But I only remember because it stops.

That's when I see all the jars lined up on the nightstand nearest the door.

I let out a breath, feeling sick and both feverish and cold at the same time. I shudder, then lean over and press my hand against Ryet's back. He feels the same. The black-blue skin feels like regular skin. But it's very hot. Like that time in his cottage up in White River.

He needs blood. I don't know what he's been doing with those jars, but whatever it was, it's not enough. He needs blood. And that's my job here in this arrangement. So I don't even hesitate. I scoot up next to him—as close to him as I can get. "Ryet."

"Hmmm." It's not a word, just a low rumble.

"You need to drink."

He moves a little, aiming his mouth in my direction. And then he latches on to the side of my neck, making me wince from the force of his fangs. They feel different. Not little needle pricks, but more like the bite of an animal.

But the pain doesn't last. The moment he starts taking blood from me, all those feelings rush in. The ones that make me like what we're doing. The ones that make me crave it.

I close my eyes and enjoy it. Because why not? There's no way to change what's happening.

But before I can even do that, it's over. Too soon. Ryet pulls away and falls back asleep.

The phone rings again, so I open my eyes and get up. I grab a flannel shirt off the floor and put it on as I walk out of the bedroom. The ringing is coming from a landline phone in the kitchen. I pick up the handle and put it to my ear. "Hello?"

"Oh. My God! Syrsee! What the fuck! I've been calling there for hours!"

"Zusi?"

"Are you OK? I'm coming to see you."

"*No.*" Normally Zusi is the not the kind of girl you can deter with a simple objection. She is a bulldozer. She plows

JA HUSS

right through simple objections. But this one is not simple, nor is it an objection.

It's a command.

"You will not come see me. Do you understand me, Zusannah?"

This stops her too. She hates when people call her Zusannah. Only Tristin calls her Zusannah and that's only when he's trying to make her listen to him by pissing her off.

She blows out a breath on the other end of the phone. "Why? Because you're mad? I didn't betray you. You have to know that. If you're my best friend, then you *do* know that."

She's right. I do know that. After the dreamwalk I just came out of, it's very, *very* clear that everything is need-to-know and Paul is the one who decides who needs to know.

He would never think of telling Zusi his plans. Or the Guild, for that matter. I don't care what kind of deal they have going, there is no way the Guild knows more about what is happening to Ryet and me than we do. Or I do. My part, at least.

"I have to go. Do not call back. I mean it." Then I slam the phone down and start trying to make sense of the kitchen.

The phone rings again and I answer it through clenched teeth. "*What?*"

"Syrsee?"

I sigh, closing my eyes. Because it's not Zusi, it's Tristin. "What do you want?"

"Listen, you know how Zusi is. When she wants something, she does not give up."

"I don't want to see her, or talk to her, Tristin. I don't have time for this shit."

"Which is why I'm calling."

"Explain."

"There are things you need to know. And if you're not going to listen to us, will you at least take a look at some of the research?"

"What research?"

"It's a project that Zusi has been working on in secret since —I dunno. Grade eleven, I think."

"A *project?*"

"Will you at least write down the URL? It's all on a website."

"Hold on." I'm so annoyed right now. "I need to find a pen and paper." I start opening drawers, finally finding one with what I'm looking for. Then I pick up the receiver again. "Go ahead." He gives me the URL, then the log-in credentials, and I write it down. "Is that it?"

"Will you promise to look at it?"

"Fine, Tristin. I'll look at it. Please don't call back. And pass this message along to Zusi as well. Tell her..." I sigh, frustrated. "Tell her we'll talk soon. But only if she gives me my space."

Then I just hang up the phone without waiting for an answer.

I leave the kitchen and go back into the bedroom to check on Ryet. He's still a vampire. A very scary-looking vampire. But when I place my hand flat on his back, right between those wings, he feels much cooler than he was before he fed.

How much longer? How much longer will it go on like this?

And what is the deal with all the sickness? First him, then me, now him again. It's like a cycle of... something. I got a little information out of Paul, but not nearly enough.

My eyes involuntarily track a path through the open bedroom door and to the counter where I left the notepad. I doubt it's going to be much help, but at this point, any new information is better than none.

I leave Ryet to sleep it off—feeling a little sick myself, but trying not to think about it—and go back out to get the notepad. Then I find the cellphone I bought while Ryet was feeding off me those first ten days, and navigate to the website.

I'm immediately presented with a log-in page. I enter the credentials that Zusi gave me—they are not words or anything. Both the username and the password are just long strings of numbers, letters, and characters. The kind of super-strong combination that is automatically generated by a browser AI.

The webpage reloads and I lean in, squinting my eyes at the small screen as it populates.

Then I gasp. Because the first thing I see is some kind of digital art depicting the Ice Maiden I saw in my dreamwalk with Lucia that night I banished Paul.

The whole scene is there, actually. The horse and rider. Coyrah, the Ice Maiden, taming the aquis equī out on the ice and turning into the night mare.

"What is this?" I whisper these words out loud as I navigate the menu. There are a couple dozen folders and all of them have something to do with me. 'Syrsee's Ancestors.' 'Syrsee's Dreams.' 'Syrsee's Nightmares.' 'Syrsee's Diet.' 'Syrsee's Education.' 'Syrsee's Habits.' On and on like that.

Research? This isn't research. This is… a *dossier*.

Zusi *was* spying on me.

The whole fucking time.

14 - Josep

A little baby taste.

*L*ittle **Baby screams** the whole fall down as I hold her against my chest. Then the landing is so hard, I lose my grip and she goes flying forward, falling face-first into the ragged rock floor.

She makes noises of pain, then she starts sobbing.

I let out a breath. Then take in another one, filling my lungs with the pungent, humid air that one only finds at the entrance to Hell. The mist is thin, but it's very purple down here. Purple that is almost black. Purple the color of a feeder's blood.

It's the past, it's the future—the mist down here is all possibilities at once.

It's only been about six weeks since I last visited the gates, but it feels like forever since I was deep in the earth like this.

This is where vampires come from. Not the physical location at the bottom of a cave drop found off a hallway. 'Here' isn't a definitive term. You can find Hell just about anywhere underground if you're a vampire blessed by the Darkness, as I am.

We not only like it here, we want to be here. That's why we love the Darkness. That's why we try to please it so badly. This is where we belong.

Little Baby—the creature formerly known as Echo—does not belong here.

She gets to her feet, sobbing through her screams. "What's going on? *Where the hell are we?*"

I chuckle at her little accidental pun. "Well, you got it in one, dear girl. We are at Hell's Gates."

Her eyes go wide, then they wildly dart around, looking past me. Like she might be able to go back. To escape. To evade her future.

"Oh, good luck with that." I chuckle these words out. "There is nothing behind me but rock. To leave now, Little Baby, you must go up." I watch, fascinated by this girl, as her eyes track above my head, squinting because she can't see in the dark.

But I can. And there is fear all over her face. This fear manifests as a screech. "Take me back! I want to go back! Right now!"

"I'm sorry, Little Baby. That's just not possible."

"Stop calling me that! And you're gonna be in so much trouble! Paul will come back. He'll come back and he'll be looking for me! I'm the loyal one! I'm the one he loves now! And he will look for me! And when he finds out that you kidnapped me—"

I put up a hand and her mouth goes silent. She's still moving her lips, but the mute button has been pressed. Once she realizes this, she starts grabbing at her throat, freaking out.

I reach out, snatch both her hands in mine, and then look her in the eyes. "Well, you're right about one thing. You are Paul's favorite. But let me be clear. Paul is the one who chose you, Little Baby. You endeared yourself to him. To get noticed. To get fed. To be the special one in the house. Isn't that right?"

She can't answer me and doesn't even try to mouth words of agreement. She just stares at me in shock.

"Well, you did such an excellent job—you were such a good little slave, such a good little halfbreed slave—that he decided to *give you* to the Darkness. You're a present, you see. A gift. An offering. Oh, let's be real, shall we? You're a sacrifice, Little Baby."

She opens her mouth in a silent scream.

"And now it's time for your reward, dear girl. You're about to witness something rare, and powerful, and life-changing."

She has given up on the screaming. Now she's motionless. Eyes open, mouth open, still shocked, but under a spell.

I lean into her neck, nipping the skin right over her jugular. Teasing it open, little by little. Exposing the vein without tearing it. Little Baby squirms, trying to unbalance me as I continue to pin her to the ground. "Shhhhhhhh." I say this right into her ear. "You'll be OK again, eventually. It won't last long. And no matter what happens next, you won't remember it."

She chokes on air, trying to inhale. And when I pull back so I can see her face, her eyes are going wide in a panic. This is what it looks like. This is what the end looks like. This girl right here. So young, and sweet, and filled with plans for the future that will never be realized.

I stroke her cheek and gaze lovingly into her eyes, willing her to calm down.

Little Baby has no power here. She was never given a choice. Lucia presented her with an opportunity, as she did all her halfbreeds. 'Live bigger, better, unconventionally.' That was her favorite phrase back when I was still paying attention to what she was doing. That's how she convinced the humans to shorten their natural lifespans by decades and join her.

Lucia was never a loner. It was always the main thing that set her apart from Paul and I. And while I am a much lesser vampire than Paul because I was made so long ago—long before the definition of vampire started to change—compared to Lucia, I'm a textbook example.

She has always needed humans. But witches come in family groups. Covens, or clans, or whatever they call themselves these days. Black witches included. They all come from somewhere. Though the Black witches are cast out at birth, of course. In one way or another. Killed for their magic or given as a blood gift to the vampire who made them.

Lucia was not a Black witch, but she was not an ordinary witch, either. She was something in between. A pet to one of the Obscurati masters in Rome back in the ancient days. She was older than Paul by a couple hundred years, even though she looked like a child when she joined our small group and took the trip across the ocean with us.

A pet to be experimented on. Much magic was done to her in the name of progress back in the Old World. She was not a witch but she was not a vampire, either. She was a mongrel? Or, if one is poetic and sees the glass as half full, a hybrid. The first and last of her kind.

A mistake, actually.

But I prefer to call her a fortunate turn of events.

And she served her purpose with us. We used her blood, after all, to make Syrsee. Well, we did that experiment hundreds of times before Syrsee came along. All of them failures until that glorious day when she was born and her grandmother killed her mother, took her power, and gave it to the little girl.

That was the part we were missing in the other attempts

to make the perfect symbiotic feeder for our perfect new line of American Vampires.

You need evil to make new evil. And what that grandmother did—sacrificed her own daughter, more than once, just so she could do it all over again with her granddaughter—that is one of the ultimate evils. Of course, all black magic acts done against children are evil. But what the Black witches do to their offspring is a whole other level of evil.

Little Baby moans in my arms, but she is calm now. My gaze has overpowered her instincts to be afraid.

It is time.

I stand up, holding Little Baby in my arms, and walk forward into the blackness. I can see a good way down the tunnel with my night vision, but even I have limits. And this is why it's called the Darkness, isn't it?

Because at the limit of my vision is a hole. Blank and empty, but full at the same time. This hole leads everywhere and nowhere all at once. I have gone in there on more than one occasion. It is a container for all that was and all that will be.

It is the Darkness.

I take my time as I approach, waiting for signs of recognition. It won't kill me. Can't kill me—at least I don't think. It's not that kind of entity. The Darkness sucks things up. It takes. That's all it wants, just to take. But it's not looking for souls, or thoughts, or bodies. That's not what it eats. It feeds on blood, just like us.

But we are part of it. It doesn't want *our* blood. Paul and I. It will take our blood, then give it back. That's how we make new vampires, after all. And new Black witches, in a roundabout way.

No, what the Darkness really wants is a nice sample of what it lacks. A mixture of the outside world.

And this is where Little Baby comes in. A little baby sample of what the Darkness lacks. Something... other. That was bitten, and torn to shreds, and fouled up with the saliva of the other halfbreeds as they fed.

Little Baby's blood is a gift to the Darkness. She is a toy. Something to keep it occupied. A puzzle to put back together. Busy hands are happy hands, isn't that what they say?

In giving the Darkness a little baby taste of the outside world, I give it something unique. Something it has not seen before. Something intriguing.

And in return, it gives me power.

I came up with this idea hundreds of years ago. Of course, I told Paul about it. We could've used a sullied, shredded halfbreed at any time in the past two hundred years to distract the Darkness, but only just the once.

Every time you ask the Darkness for a favor, you must give it something unique. It never works twice. So we saved this opportunity for just the right time.

Right now, as it is.

The Darkness hovers before me, an opaque circular disc that undulates like ink flowing through water, one moment oily and wet, the next like powder or smoke. It is everything, but it is nothing like anything anyone has ever seen before. It is an ending, not a beginning.

The end of everything, actually.

It hovers and waits. It needs an invitation, you see. *It* is what needs permission to enter, not the vampire. And while Little Baby cannot give this permission—she is not the one in control here—as her representative, I can.

So I do.

15 - Ryet

This is how it's done.
This is how it's always been done.

*T*he gold mist is thick. Very thick. But it's narrow too. And on either side of it there is a very dark purple. A purple so dark, it almost looks black.

Which means... what? That's the past, or the future, or something unreal? But the gold is... I'm not sure. The gold is new. It's not the present. At least, that's not my first choice as far definitions go. Because in my extensive experience with dreamwalking, the light purple is the present.

But looking at the mist all around me, what it really looks like is... the Yellow Brick Road. From *The Wizard of Oz*. Except not a road, of course. Just a thick, misty path. But it's definitely giving off the impression that it leads somewhere.

I look around. But I don't feel like I'm anywhere. The two different-colored mists are giving off a tunnel vibe.

So. I dunno. There is really only one choice. I guess I'll just follow the Yellow Brick Road. It's probably gonna take me to a witch. But what the hell, witches aren't so bad. I think I might be in bed with one right now, since this is a dreamwalk and, last I recall, I was nursing Syrsee back to health.

Time feels relative here, so I'm not sure how much passes when I notice that the purple on either side of the tunnel disappears, leaving nothing but gold. The worst thing about this is that now there is no road. There's no path. So I stop and throw up my hands. "Now what?" I say this out loud to the mist.

Which doesn't answer back. Not exactly, anyway. But there is a voice in my head—my own voice, actually—telling me that the gold is just like the purple. *If you can imagine it, you can make it.*

So where do I want it to take me?

My first instinct is Syrsee, but it's not the right one. I know where Syrsee is. I have physical access to her. I can talk to her any time I want if I take myself out of this.

But the person I don't have access to in the physical world is Paul.

And the moment I think his name in my head, we're back in that hotel room. The one where I woke up from being second-born.

Paul and I are on the bed again. Backs up against the headboard. So close, our shoulders are touching.

"Aren't you going to move away from me, Ryet?"

I shrug, looking straight ahead. "What's the point. I'm stuck with you forever."

"You're the one who came to me."

"I know." I'm kind of snarling at him. I feel like a much angrier man since turning into a vampire. "Because I have questions."

"So? Ask them."

I feel like he's a much angrier guy since I became a vampire too. "Why are you angry?"

"I'm not angry."

"You sound angry."

"It's just the tendency."

"Of? Because that doesn't explain anything."

"Master and slave. You and me. Father and son. But"—Paul looks at me—"please don't think of me as your father. That would make our future... difficult. And... out of my comfort zone."

I scoff. "Don't worry. I do *not* think of you as a father."

"Good. Because it wasn't actually me who created you, it was the Darkness."

"Doesn't really answer why you're angry."

"I'm not angry. I'm... you're... challenging me."

I turn my head to look at him, chuckling. "I'm seriously not."

"It's not a conscious thing, Ryet. It's just your monstrous nature. Like two stallions meeting out on the plains. Only one is needed, after all. One stud per herd."

I'm making a face of disgust. "Herd?"

"If we had a herd, it would be easier. Right now, all we have is Syrsee. So we must share."

"You're kidding, right? Tell me this is a joke."

"It's temporary. Black witches are hard to farm."

"*Farm?*"

"We need many more, Ryet. But don't worry. We have all the time in the world. And now that Syrsee is on board—"

"Oh"—I laugh—"you have grossly misunderstood what's happening here. Syrsee is not on board with anything you've got planned. That's for certain."

"Well, it's like this, Ryet. She doesn't have much of a choice. You fed her the jars?"

My stomach clenches up. "What did you do?"

"I did what I had to. I gave her a push. And you a push as well."

"What are you talking about?"

"The *babies*, Ryet. We need more Black witches. It's critical for my plan."

"What plan?"

"Need-to-know."

"Fuck that. I've got wings, Paul. It's time for me to know."

He turns in bed, lowering himself into a more horizontal position. His smile is wide and genuine. Which surprises me, because he's typically a less-than-sincere guy. "We. Are. The American Vampires. It's a brand-new dynasty. By now, several things have happened. One, Josep is with the Darkness, making an offering. We're bartering with it to get power. And two, the Obscurati know you've been born. You, Ryet, are the very first American Vampire. I'm in charge, of course, since I am your maker. But you..." He's nodding his head at me. "You are the one we've been waiting for. And together, you and Syrsee are the parents of our bloodline. A brand-new bloodline. Or, well, you will be. As soon as she begins having babies."

I concentrate on this last part of his little speech first. "Why are you acting like Syrsee can just create a whole coven of witches in no time at all? Because human reproduction doesn't work that way."

"Are we human, Ryet?"

I get that sick feeling in my stomach again. "Don't play with me." These words come out angry and low.

"We're not human, you know this. She will have your baby. Your *specific* baby. That is a given. But there are other ways to make more of us. And that is what we need. A population *explosion*, Ryet. We need minions."

"What are you talking about? Like... halfbreeds?"

"No!" He laughs. "And you know what I'm talking about.

You *were* one, Ryet. A scion, of course. We can make dozens of them at once."

"How? You said you planned me from birth and that's the only reason it worked."

"Does one put all one's eggs in the same basket, Ryet?"

"Stop talking about yourself in the third person. You sound ridiculous."

"The sentiment remains. I have dozens of scions, Ryet. All we need now is the blood to take them across the finish line."

"*What?*"

"I did not pin all my hopes and dreams on you. I have more. But, to be clear, you will always be my first."

I look away, staring out the sunny window. "So you... and me..."

"Oh, we are. It's a special bond, Ryet."

I turn to look at him again. "That's not what I'm talking about. I'm not jealous of your stupid fucking scions. I'm asking if I'm tied to you forever or if I'm allowed to just... fuck off."

Paul throws his head back and laughs.

"What's so funny?"

"You're so serious."

"Of course I'm serious. I didn't ask for any of this. And I've spent the last sixty-five fucking years being your bitch. I want freedom. I want Syrsee. I want to take her places, and fuck her senseless, and drink her blood, and feed her mine, and whatever. I want to enjoy myself now. I'm done with you and your plan."

"Not quite yet, Ryet. Don't get ahead of yourself." I open my mouth to protest, but he puts up a hand. "If you want to take Syrsee and explore the world, be my guest. Go." He goes serious again now. "But we must complete what we started. We must."

"Which is what?"

"The baby, Ryet. Her blood is good, but with another infusion of Darkness we can make... a kind of... Type O."

I squint my eyes. "You're talking about blood typing."

"That's the secret. The scion's immune system must be able to handle the Black blood. And with this baby—"

"Hold on." I put up a hand. "You're telling me that you want Syrsee and I to make a baby and give it to you to use as food to turn more scions into vampires."

"Correct."

"This is not happening."

"Of course it is."

"No." I'm shaking my head. "This is a very firm no, Paul. No. I will not breed a child for you to feed your new dynasty of vampires."

"OK." This OK comes out way too confident. "How do you propose to stop it?"

"Stop what? The baby? Well, protocol dictates that you would need my cooperation in getting her pregnant?"

"Of course."

"Well, I'm not going to agree to this. It's as simple as that."

"I'm offering you a good deal here, Ryet. You and Syrsee can raise it—up to a point. And then I will take over."

"No. You're insane if you think Syrsee and I will be having a baby and then handing it over to you."

"Did you miss the part where I said the two of you could raise it? The part where I take it away from you is over a decade away. You'll have another by then. Probably four or five."

"She's not a fucking broodmare."

"*She is*, Ryet. She absolutely is a broodmare. *My* broodmare. And you are my stud. It's a match made in heaven, don't you think?" It's a rhetorical question. "You love her, she loves you. Making babies has always been fun. You remember that, right?"

All the muscles in my neck go tight when he alludes to my human children.

"Well, making Black witch babies is *more* than fun, Ryet." He's practically chuckling these words out. "It's... well, you're going to find out soon enough. Just as soon as you talk Syrsee into freeing me from this prison."

"Wait." I smile. "You're stuck here, aren't you? So none of this happens unless Syrsee and I agree to it. Otherwise, you stay right where you are."

"Let me guess. Now you're thinking... *Maybe we should leave him here?* Well, let me caution you, Ryet. You do not want me to be *here* when she goes into heat."

"Heat?"

"When she cycles. It will happen very soon. That's why she's sick."

My mind is spinning. Trying to parse all these words into something coherent. She's coming into *heat?*

"And it's not as simple," Paul continues, "as just sticking your cock in her and coming. That's not enough, Ryet. It needs to be done properly. And only I know how to do that."

"So? Maybe we don't need a baby."

"Need as in want, or need as in require? Because whether you want one or not isn't the issue here. She must be pregnant in her first cycle or she will die, Ryet."

"Bullshit."

"In fact, she must be pregnant for *every* cycle or she will die, Ryet."

"You're lying."

"Am I? Ask yourself this, if a Black witch could choose to not have a baby—a girl child that she must either hand over to me as a feeder or kill and steal her power—don't you think that at a least a portion of them would refuse to have a baby and not put themselves into this hopeless position?"

I just... stare at him.

"She doesn't have a choice any more than her mother or grandmother did. She must be pregnant by the time her first cycle ends or she will fade quickly. Within hours, Ryet. But don't worry. I've changed things. It's going to be much better for her—and you—in this new way going forward."

"Explain this, Paul. And do not tell me it's need-to-know. I need to fucking know."

He smiles. Like me begging him for information was part of his plan all along. And it is. It must be. Because he is Paul, the vampire. And he knows way more than me. "You're ready then? To hear the plan I have for you and her. And... me."

"You?"

"In order to make a Black witch you need two vampires. That's how Josep and I have done it all this time. *But* you can make something else—something more than just a Black witch—if you have *three* vampires."

"Me."

"You. And me. And Josep."

"With Syrsee? At the same time?"

Paul nods, smiling. Maybe even picturing this in his head. Which infuriates me.

"No. I'm saying no."

"Then you just want me, do you? Or Josep? Because regardless of your feelings on the matter, there will be two vampires involved in the conception of your child with Syrsee. You and I? You and him? Or… all three of us?"

"Fucking her?" I'm growling now.

"No, Ryet. You can be the fucker." He pauses to laugh. Diabolically, I might add. "She's yours. Black witches aren't made with sperm. Not *just* sperm, anyway. It's a blood transfer. Between you, the Darkness, me, Josep, and Syrsee. Josep and I will be there, drinking and sharing with her. And you and the Darkness will be there fucking. And sharing."

"Wait. The Darkness is gonna—"

"*You* are the Darkness, Ryet. Or, at least, you will be. It will be inside you when you take her. It will be the actual one fucking her."

I just stare at him.

"When we're all reunited in the physical world Josep will come to us filled with the Dark gift. You will drink him and you will not give the blood back. You will keep it. The Darkness will live inside you for a time, and then, at the proper moment, when Syrsee is in full heat, we'll all get in bed, snuggle up to one another, and the Darkness will spill its seed inside her, using your cock to do it."

He reaches for me, placing his hand on my face. I don't even pull away. I'm not even thinking about him. I'm thinking about all those horrible words that just came out of his mouth.

He kisses me. Then bites his lip, letting his blood spill into my mouth.

I want to resist and pull away, but the craving is suddenly there. That overpowering lust for his blood that I had all these decades since he made me.

He pulls back, licking his lips as he looks me in the eyes. "It will be fun, you'll see. You'll love it. And we'll do it over and over again, in that same way, every single time Syrsee comes into heat. She will love it too. You'll see. She will be moaning. She will come so hard when you plant the seed of darkness inside her. And all the while, Josep and I will be drinking her. And then you will drink us and she will drink us. And we will come too. All of us. You will love it, Ryet. You will dream about it when it's over. It will be the only thing you ever think about again."

I picture this in my head and I believe him. I know how he made me crave his kiss of blood all these years. It was powerful and every time I fed, those little drops were enough to drive me mad with lust.

His hand slips down to my cock and I realize I'm naked. It's a dreamwalk, so reality is relative, I guess. But the weird thing is, I don't mind.

He grips me tight, sliding his hand up and down my shaft. And all I want to do is close my eyes and enjoy it. Just give in for once. Stop fighting him every step of the way. I'm so tired of fighting him.

And he's right. I don't think I will mind.

It's a terrible thought and I hate myself for thinking it, but when I picture the three of us—and Josep, I guess, but I don't even know what he looks like—when I picture us all drinking each other, it's the only thing I ever want to think about.

So I let him touch me.

And I let myself enjoy it too.

I will do this thing. He will be there, and Josep will be there, and Syrsee will be there and we are going to make Dark babies.

"That's it." Paul is whispering this in my ear. And then he's biting me. Pulling my blood out of me as I breathe through it, grabbing his hand on my cock so I can force him to go faster.

His lips are on mine and the blood is flowing into me too.

This is how it's done. This is how it's always been done.

Paul pulls back. "Listen to me, Ryet. Listen now. Because we can't do this if I'm locked away in the purple. Save me, save her, save yourself, Ryet. This is how it's done. This is how it's always been done. *You need to set me free.*"

16 - Syrsee

It was the worst feeling ever.

I read the names of the files off in my head. 'Syrsee's Ancestors.' 'Syrsee's Dreams.' 'Syrsee's Nightmares.' 'Syrsee's Diet.' 'Syrsee's Education.' 'Syrsee's Habits.'

But it's the last folder that makes me stop and hold my breath.

'Syrsee and Paul.'

All the rest of it is interesting. Especially the ancestors. I *really* need the complete Ice Maiden-sea dragon story.

But it's the folder with Paul's name that I click first.

I expect there to be documents. Maybe some photos. But it's… a presentation. A PowerPoint presentation.

"Are you fucking kidding me?" I just stare at the little icon sitting all by itself in the folder for a few moments before I even have the ability to close my shocked-open mouth and click back out. I move the cursor over to the folder that says 'Syrsee's Dreams,' click, and find the same thing. One PowerPoint file.

I check them all, but the results are all the same.

She gave presentations on me.

The anger, the hate, the… the… the *loathing* I feel for my former best friend right now is nauseating. My whole body goes hot. I break out in a sweat. Suddenly, I can smell everything. The wood in this cabin, the lingering scent of food from the kitchen, even the garbage can. All of it makes me want to vomit.

I put the phone down, sure this is going to happen, and then rush to the front door, go outside onto the porch, and bend over, holding on to the railing.

It's nighttime. I didn't even realize that. But it's a good thing because the air is still cold from a lingering winter and after a few moments I feel better and lower myself to the top step, head in my hands.

That website, it's a gut punch.

"It's reality, Syrsee." I say this out loud, but in my head it comes out in Paul's voice. And it's his voice, in my head, that continues, not mine. "Zusi cannot change who she is any more than you can. You don't have to take it all so personally."

"So personally?" I turn my head and look at lavender Paul. Is he here? Is he there? I don't know. But I feel like I'm at the end of some kind of line here. I've reached a limit and I can't take it anymore. I can't cope. "She betrayed me, Paul."

"Everyone betrays everyone eventually." He sighs, leaning back against the porch railing. He looks normal right now. I mean, he's hazy and covered in a purple mist. But he's wearing regular clothes. Things Ryet might wear. Jeans, and a t-shirt, and a leather jacket that looks like it was born five or six decades ago. His hair is a little messy too. And he's got stubble on his face.

He looks kinda hot, actually.

Not hot, like how he usually looks. He usually looks put-together hot. In-control hot. Alpha-male hot. This is... everyday-man hot. Just some guy trying to make his way in this world.

In other words, hot like Ryet.

"That can't be true."

Paul slowly turns his head to look at me. His eyes are

purple. Like violet purple. And they are glowing. "Given enough time all alliances turn."

"It wasn't an alliance, Paul. It was a friendship." But then I shake my head and put up a hand. "No. It wasn't a friendship. I thought it was a friendship, but this whole time—the entire time I was there at the Guild—she was a spy."

Paul looks at me thoughtfully. "She didn't know you when she accepted the job."

"Why are you sticking up for her?"

"I'm not. I'm just playing devil's advocate. Thinking clearly is a skill you need to learn. You can't just go off emotions, Syrsee. It won't help in the end."

"What the hell does that mean?"

"Your future is filled with…" He pauses here so he can choose his words carefully.

And this makes me sigh. "Filled with *what?*"

He looks me in the eyes. His are still glowing. "Filled with opportunities. For power, for vengeance, for money, for happiness." He smiles when he says happiness. "But you need to learn how to navigate the negotiations without letting the feelings get in the way."

"What negotiations? With the Guild? I'm not negotiating shit with those people."

He looks away and shrugs one shoulder, like he's no longer interested in my problems.

Which annoys me. "Why are you here?"

"Because your emotions got in the way and I'm stuck in the purple." He slowly turns his head to look back at me. "We're wasting time here. You need to let me out."

"I don't even know how to do that. And if we're all betrayed eventually, what's the point? What's the point of any of it? Nothing's permanent in this world. Even winning is nothing more than a temporary reprieve from being the loser."

He smiles at me. "Now you're catching on."

I wait for him to say more, but he goes quiet. And then he starts to fade.

"Wait!" I reach over, trying to grab his shoulder, but he's gone. Like he was never here.

And he wasn't. I'm going insane. I'm fucking psycho.

And I'm not going to let him out. He wants to turn me into a breeder. I won't. I was falling for it in the last encounter. But he was... seducing me.

Really, Syrsee? That's your lame excuse? He was seducing you?

Fine. I will admit this, to myself, at least, that I was... turned on.

But I've been betrayed a lot of times over the past few months. I'm learning. I might not be the quickest woman when it comes to untwisting the twisted plans of the Guild and Paul, but I'm learning.

I'm not going to set him free. It's still possible that I can just... walk away from all of it.

Even... Ryet. Potentially. I mean, he's pretty sick. He could still die. And if he did—

"Oh, Syrsee." I shake my head. "That's not the answer and you know it."

Maybe I *could* get away. Leave Paul in the purple, let Ryet waste away, pretend that I never knew Zusi. Maybe... do some magic to cloak myself the way my grandma did. Somehow figure it out. Find a... a *bookstore witch* who knows more than most to help me. If I put my mind to it, I think I could make it work.

But I would be alone again. And while I wasn't alone all growing up—I was literally in the middle of a magical school filled with other magical kids—I *felt* alone. And it was the worst feeling ever. Zusi made it better, but that was a lie. And I don't even think I could take a lie right now, let alone a truly singular existence.

A bookstore witch who knows more than most isn't going to fill the emptiness inside me.

Ryet could, though.

And, I have to reluctantly admit, Paul could too.

He's not lying. Not about this. He's telling me the truth. He's trying to, at least. I'm sure there's more. A lot more. And I don't think I'm ready for more right now. I'm still trying to deal with what's in front of me.

So I understand that Paul is tricking me. I know it. I feel it. And even if Ryet isn't, Paul is tricking him too. Tricking him into tricking me.

I get up and go back inside. The smells are still there and my stomach is still upset, but I can't run from this. I need to figure it out right now.

This is when I remember the vials on the kitchen counter. I walk over to them, picking them up one at a time so I can study their labels. 'Despair.' 'Loneliness.' 'Regret.' 'Contempt.' 'Estrangement.' 'Fear.' 'Shame.' 'Guilt.'

All things I feel in this very moment.

Then I glance at the jars. They are empty, but they still have their labels on them. 'Thirst.' 'Hunger.' 'Gasping.' 'Purging.' 'Chills.' 'Sweats.' 'Fatigue.'

They are all physical symptoms. And Ryet ate them all.

I look towards the bedroom and see his sweaty bruise-colored body lying face down on the bed. Those wings of his draped over his shoulders. The one on the side facing me is drooping over the side of the bed, spread out along the hardwood floor.

I don't know what these jars are about, but before he ate them, he looked like a man. Mostly. And after he ate them, he looked like this.

A demon. A vampire. Because that's what he is.

No, Syrsee. That's what he's always been.

It's Paul's voice in my head now. Real or imaginary, doesn't matter. Because it's true. Ryet was never a man. He was always a potential vampire.

And now, after a long sequence of events that culminated with the eating of whatever was in these jars, he's reached some kind of... stasis. A state of... completion?

Doubtful. But he's much further along than the last time I was awake.

I look down at the vials again. Maybe if I drink these potions it will change me into whatever I've always been too? Isn't it better to just embrace the inevitable? So I can get past it and move on?

Before I can talk myself out of it, I uncork the tops and line them up on the counter. Then, one by one, I drink them like I'm doing shots of tequila.

They are very small amounts. Maybe a teaspoon each. So it's all over in a matter of seconds.

I wipe my mouth, trying to decipher the lingering aftertaste.

It's not bitter. It's actually kind of sweet.

This is when I hear the crunching of gravel outside. I go to the window, pull the curtain back, and see a matte-gray Jeep, almost glowing in the moonlight. It looks more like one of those tricked-out off-road things than anything one might drive on the daily.

The driver's door opens and Tristin steps out.

"Holy shit." These words come out on a breath as I'm

rushing to the door. He cannot come in here. I know he understands that Ryet is here, and he probably knows a lot more than me about what Ryet actually is—but he is *not* coming in here.

I pull the door open, step outside, and close it behind me.

Tristin is already walking up the stairs. So we're looking each other in the eyes as this all happens.

"What are you doing here, Tristin? I told you guys I need some space."

"I came to bring you this." This is when I notice he's holding a wooden box. Maybe six inches long by six inches wide, but thin and shallow too. One or two inches in depth.

"What is it?"

He thrusts it towards me. "A present. From the Guild."

I don't know what to say. I chew on my lip for a moment, trying to add this puzzle piece to the big picture trying to take shape before me.

"Take it, Syrsee. It's yours. It's always been yours."

I don't take it. I don't think I want it. But I don't think I have a choice, either, because Tristin sets it down on the top step and then turns and walks back towards that Jeep.

"Hey," I call out.

He lets out a long sigh. Slowly turning his head towards me. Looking very... weary.

Maybe he's faking it, but I can't tell, so it comes off real.

"What?"

"Why, Tristin? Why is all this happening?"

He gives a very small shrug. "I know more than you about some things." Then he nods his head towards the box. "But I have no idea what that is. I'm just a fuckin' messenger, Syrsee. I'm just a fuckin' errand boy."

Then he gets back in his Jeep, backs up, making the gravel

fly out from under his tires, and drives back down the way he came.

I stare at the empty driveway for a moment, then resign myself to this new twist of fate, pick up the box, and take it inside.

Here is a body, here is a soul.
Take it, do as you will.

I *walk towards the oily*, black disc hovering the air before me. I have Little Baby by the wrist so she comes too. She's writhing, and resisting, and screaming as she attempts to plant her feet into the rough, rocky ground, trying to pull free from my grip. But when I am this close to the Darkness, I lose any sense of everything around me. So my world has gone mute.

I have a good hold of her though. She's not getting away. Even if she did, there's nowhere to go. We are in the Dark House now. We are in the Dark World. The only way out is up and the only way up is with wings.

My fingertip comes up and makes a mark on the slick surface of the Dark disc. I scratch out my name—not in a human language, but in the symbols of my maker. To it, I am not Josep. I am a circle—all vampires are represented by circles—with a line right down the center that oversteps its bounds on either end. Then, along the line encompassed inside the circle, I scratch many more circles. Nine, to be exact. Attached to the circles are other designs, ancient letters that no one remembers. But when we are born, when the transformation is truly complete, there is a name carved on our black hearts.

And if someone were to open me up, they would see it. A vein of gold in this exact design.

This is the name the Darkness gave me.

I make the sign for me, pushing the tip of my now-clawed finger into the oil slick, parting it as I draw. When I'm done I make the sign for Paul too, because I'm not even here for me. None of this is about me. It was always Paul's idea and the Darkness needs to know that. It has forsaken him. That happened hundreds of years ago now. But whenever I come down here, I remind it that Paul exists and this gift is really from him. I make the Darkness remember Paul.

Once that is done, I turn back to Little Baby, unmuting her.

"Please! Please!" She's screaming and begging. "No! No!" Saying very little, but her message is being conveyed just fine. She does not want to be here. And while I haven't told her anything about what comes next, obviously, she knows. I mean, at this point, there are only two ways this ends.

With her staying here and with her leaving.

She absolutely knows she's not leaving here.

At least not yet.

I yank her arm, pulling it hard enough to slip her shoulder out of the joint. Which wasn't my intention, obviously, since I'm trying to quiet her and this just makes her scream louder. "I'm sorry." I say this as I pop her shoulder back in. "I don't often live in this form, so I forget how strong I am. I just need you to be quiet, Little Baby. This is a solemn experience you're about to go through. A once-in-a-lifetime opportunity. Take it all in, girl. Don't miss a moment. Because it will never happen again."

She went quiet the moment I started talking. And now she's just staring at me. She blinks. "What?"

"Lie down on the ground."

"Why? What are you gonna do?" She's calmer now, but it's not a true calm. Just a state of shock.

"You're going to the Darkness, Little Baby." I nod my head at the undulating oil slick hovering in the air behind me. "You're a gift. An offering. A sacrifice." I've got her locked now, her eyes on mine. Entranced. I take a step forward, pressing my monstrous body right up against hers as I continue to look down, bewitching her with my eyes. Then I kiss her and with that kiss I make a promise, whispering, "You have not been forsaken," before pulling back.

She falls limp now and I catch her in my arms so I can carefully lay her down on the ground. I position her body. Legs spread, arms wide, back straight. Then I take off the remains of the tattered threads that used to be her clothes.

I pause here—it's been a long time since Paul and I made an offering like this. So I take a moment to reflect on what I have set out to accomplish here.

Then I suck in a breath and start carving. I trace my claw through Little Baby's skin, marking my name on her first—a big symbol, right over her chest. Then I mark Paul's name just below that, on her belly. All the other carvings are nothing more than artistic embellishments. To add power, or direct it, or whatever. Paul didn't care. Didn't have any opinions on this part. He's never been much of an artist when it comes to the Dark Death. But he's only done it once and that was the source of all his problems back in the Old World.

Let's just say his artistic vision doesn't match up with mine.

I like to take my time with the symbols I carve into the skin. The Darkness, after all, doesn't care about time. If you take ten seconds to mark your offering or ten years, it wouldn't notice. It's not alive, you see. Not really. Not the way humans are. Not the way I am. It's just... an interdimensional medium. A metaphor for God, or the opposite, if that's your preference.

But it does have desires. If one can call them that. It desires creativity and ideas. Because it has none of its own. It's merely existing without us. The vampire gives the Darkness meaning, and in return the Darkness makes the vampire a creator. A god. It gives us the power to bring our imaginations to life.

Again, Paul and I differ here. He is inclined to make monsters. Hideous, ugly, evil things.

While I am inclined to make beauty. I like refined symmetry and graceful elegance. Though my creations, in the eyes of everyone *but* me, are horrible as well.

I lie down on my side next to Little Baby, propping myself up on my left elbow so I can use the razor-sharp claw on my right fingertip to make symbols. I make some ritualistic ones that have magical meanings. Sigils I have come up with over the years to focus and convey energy, and strength, and courage. Then I just draw pictures. A sun, a moon, stick people. Me, and Paul, and Lucia—even though she's gone. I never disliked her. She wasn't a friend, but she was useful and always there. Part of the plan, but separate as well. Still, I use Little Baby's body to say my goodbyes. Then I carve two more figures—Ryet and Syrsee. We lost one, but we gained two.

One step back, two steps forward. It worked out.

I draw a house. A house that will be our house. A place, finally, to settle and start the dynasty of the American Vampire. I can't make it very grand—there is only so much skin I can carve up on this girl's body. I could turn her over, carve up the back too, but it would be unnecessary. So I make a simple house because our dreams are rather simple.

We want a family and a place of our own.

Isn't that what everyone wants?

Once I'm done with the major ideas, I fill the remaining skin with stars. Simple crisscross stars. And then, finally, Little Baby's body is nothing but lashes. Blood seeps out, mostly obscuring my drawings. But it doesn't matter. The Darkness doesn't see. Not the way we do. It senses the blood and the way it seeps through her skin. And anyway, it can read my intentions.

I look up at the oil slick, still hovering in the air where it was when I started the ritual.

Then all that's left to do is invite it in.

There are many ways to do this. With my mind, with a beckoning finger, with words.

This might be the last time I ever see the Darkness—one can't ever predict the future, after all—so I make it a formal request using careful words in the ancient language of the Obscurati. It roughly translates to:

Here is a body, here is a soul.

Take it, do as you will.

The Darkness begins to move forward towards us and I stay right where I am, ready to receive my gift. The room glows purple now—a color so lavender and soft, not even a princess in a fairy tale could imagine such beauty. And this beauty is reflected off the slick surface of the entity that hovers over top of me.

It knows what we're doing and it approves.

It wants Syrsee's baby even more than we do.

This is true, but it doesn't think like that. There is no biological brain inside the oil slick. But at the same time, it is nothing *but* brain. Finally, the outside world has caught up with what is happening deep under the earth. Paul told me once, a couple years back, that he knew what the Darkness is.

Nanotech.

Billions, maybe even trillions, of nanoparticles. Where it came from, I have no idea. What it wants, I do not know.

But it likes me. I know this because when it descends down onto Little Baby's body—seeping into the blood weeping out of her—it covers me too. Caresses me too. Touches me too.

It has always favored me. Why?

Because I'm beautiful?

Paul is beautiful too, but he makes hideous things with the power of the Darkness.

So it's something more than beauty. It's the gentleness of a spirit, maybe? Or, more likely—since I am not particularly gentle—the spirit's artistic vision?

Creativity is what it longs for, after all.

Suddenly, Little Baby screams and every muscle in her body locks tight. Her back comes up in an arch and I watch as the last of the Darkness disappears inside her.

I was holding my breath, so I let it out. Smiling.

Now the glow starts. The purple. It begins very light— even lighter than the pretty lavender mist all around us. So light, it's nearly white.

But as the moments tick off, and as Little Baby's blood mixes with the lavender, it turns dark. This is how to make Black blood, after all. Which was never black in the first place. It was always just purple.

And now, the magic begins.

Little Baby goes limp again. But as I watch, the Darkness is crawling under her skin. Like she is filled with wriggling worms. The first time I saw this—thousands of years ago—I was terrified. I really thought it was worms. Or something worse. Botflies, fruit flies, eye worms, mites.

I shudder just thinking about the horror.

Finally, the Darkness settles inside her. Of course, there are no textbooks to explain the process to me. That's why I had to write my own. So what I think is happening now is just a guess. An educated one. The Darkness doesn't just get inside the blood, it gets inside the cells. And once in the cells, it gets inside the nucleus. And once inside the nucleus, it gets inside the DNA.

Deoxyribonucleic acid. Base pairs, and hydrogen bonds, and helixes. A very specific structure with very specific instructions on what this body looks like, and sounds like, and how it behaves.

From here, it's a simple act of rearranging.

Well, it's not really simple. It's very complicated and I doubt there is much of anything in the human tech world that can rewrite the DNA of a living organism and then keep it alive as it morphs.

Only the Darkness can do that.

That's how vampires are made.

And that's why it's so difficult to make new ones. You must have the blessing of this dark god. You must have a vessel with the Black blood, and you must have a partner to help you. Not a human. Not a witch—she is the vessel, not the partner.

So you need two vampires and a witch.

That is how we make the babies.

But... if you have three vampires—oh, that's when things get very, very special.

Little Baby is a gift. Something I'm using to entice the Darkness to take part in what comes next.

She is pale now—nearly silver in this light. Dead. Very, *very* dead. But we're just getting started with this little ritual.

It's my turn now.

I lean back on the ground, spreading my legs and arms. Little Baby is kind of in my way, but I just flop a leg and an arm over her, pretending she's not there. Her body begins to shake—another seizure as the Darkness works magic inside her cells. And then there is a long gasp from her. A breath of life.

I have seen this done many times. So even though my eyes are closed and my mouth open in anticipation of what comes next, I know the Darkness—in all its purple glory—is leaving her body with that breath. And just as I have this thought, it enters me. Filling my mouth with oily, slick nanoparticles. Choking me, forcing itself down my throat.

I make myself lie as still as I can.

In the early times I would fight this, the instinct to cough and pull it out so overwhelming, I'd usually pass out from the fear. Which was a good thing, since choking is no fun.

But I have learned to control the instinct to expel the alien invader. My mouth is open wide and so is my mind.

Give it to me, I tell the Darkness.

Give me everything you have.

Give me all the magic, give me all the darkness, give me all the power.

Make me the creator.

Give me the blood.

My body swells with it. All of Little Baby's blood is put inside me. And when I can take no more, I turn over, positioning myself on top of her lifeless body, and then I kiss her, expelling the darkness out of me and back into her. A moment later, she gasps too, expelling the Darkness again. My mouth is right over hers, so it comes back into me.

We do this—a special version of the long drink—many more times. Hundreds of times. Enough times so that the

Darkness can enter my cells too, change my DNA too, and give me its power.

It's not for me, though. I am but a vessel. A delivery mechanism.

This blood of mine will be shared when Paul, Ryet, and I help Syrsee make a baby.

She will get some, they will get some—and they will give it back to me. And then we'll do that again, and again, and again until a new Darkness is growing inside her.

WHEN I WAKE up the Darkness is gone.

There is no trace of purple mist, just the dampness that exists everywhere under the earth.

Little Baby's body is beside me. She is not dead. It won't let her die, not yet. It will play with her for a while. Use her to make things, I suppose. Experiment a little. She's a lab rat now.

And I am ever so thankful. So I turn on my side and caress her sliced-up cheek as I gaze into her traumatized eyes. I think they were originally green? Or blue? I can't remember. Then they turned gold but they are pink now. It looks good on her.

I lean down and press my lips to hers. Then I bite my tongue and give her a little parting gift. Just a few drops to get her through the pain. After that I whisper, "Be a good little baby. I've got to run."

I don't want to leave. I rather like it down here. Love the smell. Love it so much. And the mist, even though it's just a regular mist of humidity now that the Darkness has retreated.

But big things are happening topside and I must participate.

So I get to my feet, lift my arms up above my head as I arch my back, stretching. And then I let out a sigh.

"Until next time, my Darkness."

Then I take my leave.

Unfurling my wings and gliding back up to the outside world.

This is how I got here.

I **open the box up and find**... I have no idea. Something old and, from the look of the patina, made of copper.

It's a disc with an elaborate design that might've been pulled straight out of the dreamwalk I took with Lucia after Paul beheaded her.

The exact moment when Coyrah, the Ice Maiden, tamed the aquis equī and turned into the night mare.

The Horse and Rider. Which, now that I think about it, feels like a very important symbol for the Guild and not so much any kind of representation of me.

It's off-putting. Why does the Guild identify with this horse and rider symbol? I mean, they've put it up everywhere. And I get it, it's a logo for the Guild Lounge, or whatever. But why this symbol if it's all about *me*?

This is when I notice that there is an aged yellow envelope attached to the underside of the lid. The flap has been sealed with purple wax that is turning black along the edges and embossed with the same horse and rider symbol.

It appears to my untrained eye that this envelope has never been opened. There is clearly something inside the envelope because it's bulging a bit.

I pause here. Am I supposed to unseal this thing? What if it's a trap? What if there's a curse inside? What if there's some kind of poisonous powder that pops out at me?

I roll my eyes and sigh, then grip the edge of the paper and rip the seal open. The wax lifts up, taking a layer of the paper with it. I pull out a small book that has a stitched binding. When I open it up, I find seven small watercolor paintings, again depicting the scene that Lucia showed me in that dreamwalk. Coyrah, the Ice Maiden, taming the aquis equī.

But the last picture is different. It's an illustration of a woman—who may or may not be me—holding the disc up. Looking into it and seeing her reflection. There is writing, which I don't understand, along with a few symbols, also indecipherable, but I think it's showing me a mirror.

I look back down at the disc. The design of the horse and rider is in copper relief. But when I pick it up, I find a shiny surface on the other side and my own face staring back at me.

It *is* a mirror. A very old, very intricate mirror.

And even though I can't read that writing I know it's a magical item. One made for me.

I smile and hold it to my chest. Something mine. All mine.

"What's that?"

I look over, surprised, and find Ryet—in all his vampire glory—bracing himself against the doorjamb to the bedroom. He's pale, and weak, and breathing heavy. Like it's a labor to even be alive.

"You're awake!" I put the mirror down and rush over to him, placing a hand on his cheek. He's cool now. Maybe too cool. "How are you feeling?"

Ryet attempts a smile, doesn't quite manage it, and hoarsely croaks out his words. "Better, I think. But not great. How long was I out?"

"A day or so? I kinda lost track of time, so I don't really know."

"How are *you* feeling? My last memory is of taking care of

you. I ate some…" His gaze goes over to the complement of jars on the kitchen counter. "Some of those. And fed you my blood. Did it work?"

"I think so? I'm not sure. I don't feel all the way better. My stomach is really upset. But I don't have a craving for blood and I'm not unconscious, so… jars for the win?"

He manages a bigger smile and nods his head over at the box. "What's that?"

"Tristin just dropped it off." I take Ryet's hand and lead him over to the table. "Come on, sit down. Let's look at it because I don't really know what it is."

He sits, his wings drooping to the floor like he hasn't got the energy to hold them up. He lets out a long sigh, then reluctantly slides his eyes up to meet mine. "I look like a monster."

I shrug one shoulder and take the seat across from him.

"Don't I repulse you, Syrsee?"

I sigh as well. "It's… just… who you are, Ryet. And I've already seen the hot version, so that's how you are in my mind." I pause, think about what I just said, then add, "Wow. That was really shallow and inconsiderate of me."

He attempts a chuckle. "At least it's the truth."

"I don't think you'll always look like this. Paul doesn't look like that most of the time."

"He hides it."

"Well." I swallow. Because this is… hard. "I can't deny that you're scary, Ryet. You look like a demon."

"I am a demon."

"Right. But… you're *my* demon." My smile is real when it comes out. "And this"—I reach for the copper disc and hold it up—"this is mine too. Two things. I have two things in this world that are mine. Just mine and no one else's. You, and this

JA HUSS

thing right here. So... whatever you look like, it doesn't matter. That's what I meant when I said I see you as hot-Ryet. I wasn't trying to say I prefer you as a man, I'm saying that all I care about is the man inside."

He stretches his arms across the table and takes my hand in both of his, giving it a squeeze and letting out a breath at the same time. "Thank you. I needed to hear that."

"It's gonna be OK, Ryet. I really think it is."

He doesn't look convinced. In fact, he winces. Like he knows something. Something bad.

Which makes me want to change the subject, so that's what I do. "I never explained what happened to me when I was in that room up in the Montana mansion. But *this* is what happened to me." I hand him the little book of watercolor illustrations and he takes it from me, shuffling through the pages slowly, studying each one.

When he's done, he starts over and looks through them again. Then, finally, he looks at me. "What is this?"

"A myth? The truth? I'm not really sure. But that girl—she tamed this monster and..."

I begin to tell the story, trying to recall all the little details, like how Lucia took me underwater and I thought I was gonna drown. And the ice, and the little girl who tames the sea monster that looked like a cross between a seahorse and an octopus.

"But what does it mean?"

I shrug. "I don't know, Ryet. It's just the beginning of my bloodline. I think."

He sighs and looks past me. "Your bloodline." Then he looks me in the eyes. "Everything's about blood these days. You drank me. Do you remember?"

I nod. "I do."

228

"It's… well… I have something to tell you."

A weird feeling passes through my body. Like my muscles release every bit of stored energy inside them and it floods my bloodstream all at once. It's a sudden burst of adrenaline, and then, a moment later, it's a feeling of being spent. Done. Drained.

As this is happening Ryet is talking. I'm watching his mouth, his words echoing in my head. I'm hearing them: "There is a cycle happening inside you, Syrsee. And this cycle requires you to be—" I'm hearing it. But it's not really sinking in. Because he can't be saying what I think he's saying.

"Syrsee?"

I blink. "Huh?"

"Did you hear what I said?"

I'm hot now. But not just now. I've been hot this whole time. Feverish. My stomach hurts. My head is spinning. Everything aches. And aside from that, I'm having feelings. A rush of feelings. Despair. Loneliness. Regret. Contempt. Estrangement. Fear. Shame. Guilt.

My eyes track over to the kitchen counter where all eight empty vials are lined up.

Ryet's gaze must follow mine because he gets up, chair scraping across the floor, and walks over to them. He just looks down, stares at them. Then points at one and looks at me. "Did you drink these?"

I nod. It's a slow, small act of acknowledgement.

"*Why?*"

I shrug. "I don't know. I was… compelled to. I worked out that you ate whatever was in the jars and…" A small breath comes out of me. And with this breath comes understanding. A realization hits me just like that adrenaline in my bloodstream a few minutes ago. And once again, I feel spent. Drained.

Also stupid.

Because I walked right into it. All of it, from that moment when I stood outside my grandma's cabin door up in the Colorado mountains, thinking about how wrong I was to abandon her for ten years and how I was compelled to risk my life to see her again before she died, up to this very moment right here—or, actually, however long ago it's been now since I drank the contents of those vials.

"The magic will be gone with me," Grandma says.

I'm in her disgusting death cabin again, right in this moment. It's enveloped in a purple and gold mist. Particles are dancing in the drafts coming from the shitty windows and under the front door. My grandma is dying and I am stupid.

"You must learn to do it on your own," she croaks. "You must make your own choices now, Syrsee. I did what I could, but I can't live your life for you." And then she nods to the beautiful man I now know as Paul. He's drinking blood from a child just a few feet away from us. "He will come for you too. He will get you. And he will make you offers, dear heart." She frowns and smiles at the same time. "These offers will tear at you."

"What kind of offers?" It doesn't even sound like me. Back then I was sweet. A Guild librarian. Maybe I wasn't innocent, but I was... ignorant, I guess. It's the only word that fits. And while it's not quite a synonym for 'innocent,' it implies a certain amount of blamelessness. If only due to lack of information.

"*What?*" When Ryet speaks the illusion all around me shimmers. But just for a moment.

"They will tear at you," Grandma continues. "At your heart,

and your soul, and your desires. He will make promises, darling." She's cupping my face with her hands. "You need to be ready to hear them. Because they will be magnificent promises."

"I'm not going to—"

"Oh, but you will."

"Grandma, I have the entire Guild of Guardians on my side. They're not gonna let him—"

"They don't get a say, Syrsee. Only you get a say. And you. Will. Say. Yes."

"But I won't."

"You're not listening."

And she was right about that. More than any of it. Because I wasn't listening. At that time, which was only a couple of months ago, I could not imagine giving in to the demon vampire's whims and desires.

Yet here I am.

"This is done," Grandma says. "It is known. He is going to promise you something you want very badly."

"Syrsee." Again, the gold and purple illusion shimmers when Ryet interrupts.

But once again, I push on. I need to hear this last part. I need to face the truth. "What, though? I don't need anything."

"*Syrsee.*" Ryet's tone is more insistent.

"No. You don't," Grandma says. "But someone you love will. So be very sure about the man you give your heart to, my love. Because he will be your downfall. He will *steal your soul.*"

But she was wrong about that part.

Ryet didn't steal my soul. He didn't have to. I just… gave it away.

"*Syrsee!*" He's raising his voice now. "You need to listen to me. I need you to pay attention. This is important. You need to face the truth."

Well, he's not wrong about that.

If Paul were here, I would give him one of those slow, dramatic claps. *Well played, vampire. Well played.* Because I have done everything according to plan. *His* plan.

My grandmother warned me. And wow, was my inclination to hate her right on point, or what? It's the only thing I got right, actually. She didn't save me, she sold me. Well, fine. *Sold* is a very strong and specific word. It implies a transaction.

There was no transaction. Not only did I never put up a fight, I didn't even get anything in return. For any of this.

I guess maybe I could put a monetary value on my Guild education. I am not a literal idiot. But they didn't teach me anything important. They didn't teach me to suss out liars, or how to protect my eternal soul, or how to come to terms with my pre-planned future.

They just... kept me occupied. Like a... fuckin'... hamster on a wheel.

I'm a hen, I'm a hamster... I'm a *fool*.

I look up at Ryet and find him staring at me. His eyes are glowing *gold*. His body is black and purple, the color of a bruise. His wings like a bat. His hunger a vibration, a low one right now, but I can still feel it. "Did you hear me?"

Oh, I heard him. But hearing something and processing something are two very different things.

"I think you need to drink."

These words should be coming out of my mouth. These words should be directed at the fucking vampire standing in front of me. He's the one who drinks blood. Not me.

But I'm the one who needs it.

I'm sweating now. Profusely. My head is spinning and the dreamwalk is gone. Or whatever that was. It's gone. Grandma is dead, Ryet is a vampire, and I am... a hen.

I'm making eggs inside me right now.

Eggs that will be used to make babies.

Babies that will be handed over to Paul so he can complete whatever it is he's doing.

That's what Ryet just told me. I am in the middle of a cycle. That's why I'm sick.

And just as I realize this, I also realize that I'm in bed now. Ryet is placing a cold washcloth on my forehead. Then another around my throat.

I blink. Meet his gaze with clear vision. "What's happening?"

He's holding my mirror. The present Tristin gave me. The one thing that is mine. "I think this is how we get Paul out."

I laugh. It's borderline hysterical. Because of course it's how we get Paul out. Of course it's how we save his demon ass. This whole thing is about *him*. My life has nothing to do with me.

"You need blood, Syrsee." Ryet is kneeling down on the bed next me. "Take a drink."

I think I lost time. I think this because his words come out in a certain tone. Like he's told me this before—which he has —and I've rejected the offer. Which I don't remember doing. So I lost some time.

He's lying down next to me now, pulling me towards him so we are face to face. Just inches apart. "It's not my fault. You can't blame me, Syrsee."

He's right about that. I can't. He didn't do this to me. I did this to myself. Every step of the way I made choices. This is how I got here. I made choices.

Still, I *will* blame Ryet for this until the end of my days. I will spend my life feeding him like a hen and when I am taking the long drink, I will still be blaming him. And when I stare into those now-gold eyes of his, I say this, but leave it unspoken.

And he hears me. Because he sighs. A long, tired breath of inevitability. "We're both sick."

I laugh right out loud.

"We're both sick, Syrsee. We need each other. I'm not using you. You're not using me. We're just..."

"Using each other?" I'm surprised at how weak I sound.

"That's one way to put it. But it's more like... a symbiosis. It's an alliance, Syrsee. We're a team. We exist, not as singular people, but a pair."

I might believe that if I hadn't heard what else he was saying during my... episode of truth-facing. "You said we need to save Paul because he's..." I shake my head, unable to come up with a word for what Ryet said. "He's... part father? To this demon baby I must have?"

"Not exactly."

I sit up. Straight up. Staring at those devil eyes of his. "Not. *Exactly?*"

"He drinks. Josep drinks. I'm the only one who needs to—"

"*Fuck me?*" I blink. And we stare at each other for what seems like forever. "That's what you said, right? The four of us. Them drinking me—"

"And you drinking them."

"You say that like it matters, Ryet. Like I'm getting something out of this!"

He exhales. It's a long one. "I didn't create this game, OK? It wasn't me. I'm just stuck in it like you are. I'm trying to—"

"You're trying to get me to accept the fact that you're going to implant a demon baby inside me while your blood brothers drink my soul. That's what you're trying to do, Ryet."

He shrugs. "Fine. If you want to see it that way, then fine. But I would like to see it another way."

I laugh. "Oh, I'm sure you would."

"I would like to see it as us saving each other."

"I'm going to be impregnated with a *demon*, Ryet."

"It's not a demon, Syrsee. It's a vampire. Like me. It's like us. It's ours. It will be *ours*."

I'm repulsed. Just thinking about a vampire growing inside me makes me want to vomit.

"Paul is not going to take it to feed on. And let's face it, if this wasn't happening to you, then that would be the other outcome. You're a Black witch. I didn't make you a Black witch. Someone else did."

"Paul?"

"I don't know, Syrsee. I don't have all the facts. I don't have all the answers. All I can tell you is that we don't have a choice. It's either... you get pregnant. Like... *now*"—he points at the ground when he says that last word—"or we're both gonna die. Because if you don't get pregnant, you die. And if I don't have your blood, I die. This is the sick, sad reality of our lives."

"Maybe we *should* die?" I shrug. "Maybe we're supposed to die? Did you ever consider that maybe this is just a test and if we refuse to give up the last crumbs of our souls, perhaps there is a better future waiting for us?"

Ryet guffaws. "A better future where? *Heaven*, Syrsee? Are you really trying to convince me that if we kill ourselves tonight, we'll save our souls and go to *Heaven*?" He laughs again. "You're not that stupid. I know you're not."

I want to fight with him. I want to scream at him. But I'm

sick. And my head is not spinning now, it's pounding. And even if I had the strength and fortitude to give up my life for my eternal soul, they're not gonna let me.

He's not gonna let me. I know this because he's holding up the mirror. Right in front of our faces. I recoil at my reflection. I'm pale with black circles under my eyes. I look old, and worn down, and ugly.

That can't be me. It can't be.

"Just stare into it." We lock eyes in the mirror.

And the moment we do this, reality shifts.

The bedroom is gone and in its place is the snowy clearing in the woods. Paul is right where he always is.

Sitting on the fallen tree trunk holding that baby.

.

19 - Ryet

With permission.

Syrsee and I enter the dreamwalk together. It's different now. Not purple, but purple and gold. I don't know what the gold means. Eventually, once I've got a better grip on things, I'll ask Paul about it. But right now, all I want is to get this over with.

There is no way to change what Syrsee is. I told her the truth, I didn't lie. But I can't tell her the whole truth right now. Not yet. Not until we get through this first stage and I've got her in a better place.

She hates me. And I don't even blame her. In fact, I kinda feel the same way about her.

I mean, if we'd never met, I'd have died a scion. If she hadn't fed me, I'd be dead now. And she'd be… the other half, left behind. Better off.

And this is pretty much where we're at. I'd rather be dead and Syrsee would be better off without me. Just like Jane. But Jane is both dead *and* better off without me, so… kinda different.

We're in that winter clearing again. The one Paul's been showing up in since my whole metamorphosis started happening. He's holding that baby and he's wearing those furs. Like he's some kind of Viking.

It was weird at first, but now… I dunno. It kinda suits him. He looks like a Viking. Well, he's too pretty to be a Viking, so… whatever. Doesn't matter.

JA HUSS

I'm holding Syrsee's hand and when I look over at her she's wearing a long, flowing white gown. Not like a ball gown. More like a nightgown. But very pretty and over-the-top for something you'd just be sleeping in.

In fact, she looks like some kind of princess. And she doesn't look sick at all. Her complexion is glowing. Nice, tanned skin and rosy cheeks. Like she just fed.

Which she did. But in real life, it didn't help her much. Not in the looks department. In real life she looks like a witch on her deathbed.

When I look down at myself, I'm still me. Black-blue body that comes across as a bruise. Like someone beat the shit out of me from head to toe. And my wings are here, heavy and drooping because I don't think my back muscles are strong enough to actually hold them up. Flying anywhere with these things feels very out of the question.

"Hello, Syrsee. Don't you look lovely tonight." Paul, who normally comes across as a charming asshole, is somber and his tone is a little bit angry. It's been that way since he got stuck here, I realize. I just hadn't noticed because he was talking to me. But now that he's talking to Syrsee in this same tone, it makes me bristle and I take offense.

Syrsee doesn't say anything. She hates him, I'm certain of that. But she's not blaming him for this. She's blaming me. I'm the new bad guy in her mind. So she can afford to disregard Paul and his moods right now.

Paul directs his gaze to me. He smiles, kinda holding the baby up. "You were such a beautiful boy."

I make a face. "That baby is *me?*"

"Who else, Ryet? You're..." He shakes his head a little like he's searching for words. "You're my everything."

Syrsee scoffs.

I roll my eyes.

Paul stands up. "Should we get things started?" Neither of us answer him. He directs his gaze to Syrsee. "Has everything been explained to your satisfaction?"

I expect a pretty big protest from her. I mean, it took almost two hours of nursing her, feeding her, explaining things to her before she finally gave in and listened. But she doesn't protest. She asks a question.

"I don't understand why we're in the dreamwalk. I'm supposed to set you free?" She waves a hand through the purple-gold mist. "This isn't real."

Paul snaps his fingers. "How about this? Better?" We're not in the forest any more, the baby is gone, and we're all naked and standing in a luxury hotel room. "Real enough for you?"

Syrsee isn't satisfied. "It's just another illusion." Then she looks at me. Looks me up and down, actually.

Which makes me look down at myself. I'm a man again. No bruised body, no wings. Just a male human in his prime looking very much the same way I did when Paul killed my family to try to save their souls.

"It's not an illusion." Paul is speaking again, so I look up at him. "It's reality, Syrsee. You know this. The dreamwalk was never an illusion." He comes towards us and I grip her hand tighter.

But she doesn't recoil or shrink back from him as he approaches. In fact, she straightens when he's so close to us that she has to tilt her head and look up to keep meeting his gaze.

He places a hand on her face, his palm flat against her cheek. She doesn't even flinch. "It was real when we were together. This is the same. Josep will be here, so it's a little different. But he's very pretty, Syrsee. You'll like him, you'll see. It's going to be OK." Then Paul looks at me. "Ryet loves you. Don't you, Ryet?"

I have an urge to disagree with him just because that's what I do. But it's a pointless urge because I don't disagree with him. "I do." I look at Syrsee, though she's not looking at me. She's still fixated on Paul. "You probably don't believe me, but I'm doing this for you."

Syrsee swallows and nods her head. "To save me." Now she meets my gaze. "You left something out."

"What?"

"When you explained this to me." She nods her head at Paul. "He's going to drink. Josep is going to drink. I'm going to drink. At some point you'll drink. You'll be…" I wait for her to say 'fucking me,' ready to recoil at the vulgarity. But she catches herself. "You'll be inside me. And when it's over, I'll be pregnant."

"Right." I nod.

"But what you didn't say, Ryet, is what comes after that."

"You'll be—"

She puts up a hand to shut Paul up. Doesn't even look at him. She's staring straight at me. "I don't want to hear it from you, Paul. I want to hear it from Ryet. After I'm pregnant, what comes next?"

I take in a breath and let it out in a long exhale. "You'll have the baby."

"And then?"

"Then…" I look at Paul. He's sympathetic, I can tell. But he can't help me. "Then we do it again. The cycle starts again."

"Mm-hm." Syrsee nods. "I'm a broodmare." Her eyes are locked with mine. She is glaring at me. "I'm a breeder. I'm the blood mother. Is this what you're telling me?"

I nod now too. "Yes. That's what you are." I want to

elaborate. To tell her that's not all she'll be. She will have a life and... yeah. Not even I believe that shit.

She's going to make demons and once they are made, she's going to make more.

Now she looks at Paul. That same stoic expression on her face. "How many? How many times will I be in this cycle?"

"Well—"

"*Guess.*" She snaps this word out. "If you don't know, then guess. I want a fucking number."

Paul shrugs. "Ten or twelve."

Syrsee exhales loudly. Like it's a much higher number than she expected. It takes a moment for her to gather herself again, but once she does, she walks over to the massive bed, kneels on the mattress, crawls over to the middle, and then lies back. "Let's do this then. Let's get on with it."

"Where's Josep?" I'm looking at Paul. Because I agree, let's just get this over with.

Paul is smiling. Not even looking at me. He's only got eyes for Syrsee's naked body on the bed. And when I glance down, I find him already hard for her.

Has he always lusted after Syrsee? Was this his goal all along? I understand that he said he would not be inside her. It would be me and only me. It's the only way to make this tolerable.

But now I'm wondering if there's more to it.

He's crossing the room now too, and when he gets to the end of the bed he kneels down and crawls up alongside her. Fitting his body right up against hers. His hands wandering. Going anywhere he chooses.

She doesn't stop him. In fact, she closes her eyes and seems to enjoy his touch.

This is when I feel a body slide up behind me and a hand slip around my waist as a face presses into my neck.

It's Josep, of course. Materializing from nowhere.

I've never met him. I don't even know what he looks like. And oddly enough, I don't care. Just like Syrsee, I don't mind what he's doing. Even when he reaches between my legs and finds me hard for him already, just like Paul was hard for Syrsee.

His teeth graze over my skin, ripping it open just a little bit, right under my ear. "Nice to finally meet you, Ryet. Are you ready for your gift?"

He's pressing himself into me. He's hard as well. I manage to open my eyes when Syrsee moans and I see that Paul is already taking her. His fingers are between her legs and his face is hovering over hers like he's going to kiss her. I want to watch them. I want to see what he does next. But Josep is nibbling on me and I want that too. I want that bite. I want him to pull the blood out of me and take it in his mouth. So I force myself to pay attention. "What gift?"

"The gift of the Darkness."

I'm like a hundred percent sure I'm not ready for this, but there's no turning back now. It has to be done. I don't even understand what 'it' is. All I know is that Syrsee needs to be pregnant at the end of this encounter, because if she's not, she will die. And if she dies, I die.

And it's not even me I'm worried about. I don't care about the feeding. I don't care about her blood. I just want what was stolen from me when I was born. I want my chance at happiness and Syrsee is that chance. Even if it comes with being *this*.

"Well?" Josep asks. "You can't be a passive participant, Ryet.

It's always been a choice. This is no different. You have to give me permission."

He's right. I have made all the choices. Fine. It's all my fault.

But it doesn't change anything. I still want my chance.

"I'm ready. Do it."

His teeth are in me before the last two words are out of my mouth. And the moment he starts pulling blood out of me, I don't care about the consequences.

This is temptation. Straight out of the Bible.

Sexual immorality, sensuality, sorcery, orgies.

I understand this. It's a test. It's evil.

I warn you, as I warned you before—

And I'm in the middle of failing.

—that those who do such things will not inherit the kingdom of God.

I am sinning.

This is when I bite Josep. This is my sin. Not giving him my blood, but taking his blood back.

That is how the Darkness gets inside me.

With permission.

And the moment I think this, I'm gone.

I am not in that bedroom with Syrsee, and Paul, and Josep.

I'm in the gold. I'm in the purple.

And I'm alone.

We are all we have left.

I'm writing on the bed, my back arching as Paul strokes me between my legs. I want to stop him— at least, I tell myself that. Because I want to believe it. But I'm justifying what's happening in so many ways right now, there isn't a chance in hell that I'm going to stop him.

I'm rationalizing. I'm in full-on justification mode. Telling myself that it's been Paul all along. He's been in Ryet's head every time we've had sex. Every time we've done anything.

I'm his. I belong to Paul, not Ryet.

And I'm so disgusted with myself that I let him get to me like this. That I'm believing his lies.

Except they're not lies. It's true.

I am Paul's. Ryet is Paul's. This game we're playing isn't ours and this moment right here is destiny. It's what we were made for. I'm going to die if this ritual between me and the blood brothers doesn't happen. And that death might actually be worse than death.

But the real reason this is happening is because... I like it.

I want to be with Paul. And I want to be with Ryet. Josep, I'm not sure about, but even if I didn't want him, it's not enough to stop me now.

This is the only thing that matters, really. I can blame Paul all I want, I can justify and find all kinds of completely true reasons that explain my behavior.

But in the end, this is my choice.

"Are you ready?" I open my eyes and find Paul's face hovering over mine. Then I am drawn to movement at the end of the bed. Ryet and another man—Josep—are clinging to each other in a tight embrace. Ryet's mouth on Josep's neck. Josep's mouth on Ryet's neck. Drinking each other at the same time. But it's more than that. They are naked, and hard, and grinding into each other. Moaning, blood dripping out of their mouths. Snarling and growling like animals. Josep has Ryet's cock in his hand, fisting it tight. And Ryet's hand is pumping up and down Josep's shaft.

It's unrestrained lust.

It's evil desires.

And I can't. Stop. Watching.

Josep pulls back from Ryet's neck, blood dripping down his face. He is the most beautiful man I've ever laid eyes on. He is Ryet times a hundred. He is Paul times a thousand. And it takes every bit of self-control I have not to beckon him into my bed with a finger.

Paul wipes my sweaty hair away from my face. He has stopped drinking me and the craving I have for blood—all the blood—suddenly takes over.

Josep and I lock eyes. His are black. Nothing but pits. And this should terrify me, but it doesn't. It makes me crave him more. He sticks his tongue out, wiggling it at me. "Do you want me to eat your pussy, Syrsee?" He fists Ryet's hair, yanking him off his neck. Ryet is growling and hissing, trying to latch back on. "We have a little bit of time, if that's how you want to spend it."

I'm lost. I don't know what's happening. I don't really understand what he's talking about. *Time?*

But I don't care, either. I say, "Yes. Come here." And then he's dragging Ryet to the bed with him. Crawling up between my legs. Paul spreads them open for Josep, Ryet is back to drinking, making animal noises as he sucks the blood from Josep.

I'm focused on Josep too. Because he's smiling like an evil demon as he flicks his tongue back and forth, teasing me for a few seconds. Making me agonize with the anticipation.

And then, when the tip of his tongue glides over my pussy, Paul's neck is pressing against my lips. I bite into the skin and Paul starts to moan as the blood rushes out of the ragged wound I just made.

It's hot, and sweet, and I can't get enough. I swallow it down in gulps as Josep slides his mouth over to the inside of my leg. I know it's coming and when his teeth sink into the tender skin of my inner thigh, I am so overwhelmed with hunger, I nearly attack Paul. My teeth snapping at his shoulder, his neck, any part of his body that gets close enough.

Then his mouth is covering mine. Biting me as I bite him, our bloody lips connected now.

Josep slides out from between my legs, lying on the opposite side of me.

It's like it was that night Paul was draining me. Him on one side, Ryet on the other.

But this time I'm between Paul and Josep and that's when I realize that they are opening my legs and Ryet is scooting up between them.

I open my eyes to watch him.

And then, finally, *I scream.*

Because this isn't Ryet.

This is the Darkness.

But something happens here. I'm screaming, but I'm not. It's in my head, or some place else, or maybe not even happening at all. I can't tell. Because I'm not in the bed anymore. I'm in a library. Not the Guild library filled with untouchable tomes, but something bright and public.

Ryet is standing next to me. Real Ryet. I know this because he's grinning at me and his eyes are twinkling and filled with good-natured mischief. This smile and these eyes are familiar in a long-lost way because this is the man, Ryet. Not the monster.

For some reason I'm deliriously happy. The kind of happy that comes after a long day of nothing but good things. So many good moments, you don't even have time to count them all up and sort them all out.

We're reaching for the same book on the shelf in front of us, our fingertips touching as we smile at the good fortune of being in the right place at the right time.

We are strangers. I know this, even though it doesn't make sense.

Neither of us lets go of the book. Neither of us surrenders to the other.

And then something washes over me. Like a memory of forgetting. And I'm not sure where I am, or why I'm here, or who this man is—I just know I must meet him. I have to say something to get his attention and lying about my claim on the book feels like the perfect opening.

"I was here first." I say this with confidence, even though I did actually see him reaching for it when my hand flew up to the spine. We were both browsing the same aisle of books for several minutes. Stealing glances at each other. Trying to be coy.

"Really?" The handsome stranger laughs this word out as he grins at me. He's amazingly beautiful. Like supernaturally beautiful. "That's your opening? 'I was here first?'"

"What? It's true. I had my hand on the book and you reached for it."

He chuckles, shaking his head. "You're just... gonna lean in to it, aren't you?"

I blink my eyes at him, feigning innocence. "I have no idea what you're talking about."

We're both still holding on the book. He nods his head at it. "Do you even know what this book is about?"

I have no idea what the title is, let alone what it's about. I glance at the spine—*Lovers Under a Bridge*—then look back at him with confidence. "Of course I know what it's about."

He smirks back at me, calling me out as a liar with his eyes, but it's not a serious call-out. It's more like a challenge-accepted call-out. "You think it's about lovers under a bridge, don't you?"

I shrug one shoulder up. "That's... part of it. But... it's got... deep, dark undertones."

"So you've read it?" His eyebrows have shot up to the top of his forehead. Like he's surprised. But it's not a real surprise, just a flirty one. We're playing a little game here. A little game called meet-cute banter.

We're probably gonna have sex. Maybe he'll take me back to his place, or maybe I'll take him back to my place, or maybe we'll just do it right here in the stacks like sex-addicted exhibitionists. But this is no ordinary chance meeting. It's… a beginning.

"Dozens of times."

He scoffs. But it's still in good-natured territory. "OK." He has to stop and chuckle here. "What are the main characters' names?"

I don't even hesitate. "Esmerelda and Tony."

He laughs so loud, it echoes off the library ceiling. Then takes a moment to look properly embarrassed while simultaneously peeking down and through the stacks to see if anyone will come chastise him. When he's sure the coast is clear, he directs those mischievous and twinkling eyes back at me. "Nailed it." I press my lips together, stifling my own outburst. "But you're not out of the woods yet. I'm gonna need a plot."

I tsk my tongue and stare at him in mock open-mouthed shock. "Are you really challenging me to a pop-quiz duel?"

"Is that a thing?"

I shrug. "I'm making it up as I go here."

"You're really good at it."

I curtsey, lifting up the hem of my little summer dress. "Thank you."

He holds up a finger. "But I've got my heart set on this book."

"So do I." We're both still holding the spine. I grip it a little tighter.

"Well, then I think a pop-quiz duel is the proper way to handle it."

"Challenge accepted."

His eyes are twinkling even brighter now. Like this is the best conversation he's had in years. "You seem pretty confident."

"Why wouldn't I be? I've practically memorized Emily and Toby's character arcs."

"Esmerelda and Tony." He chuckles the words out.

"That's what I said."

"Question number one."

"I'm ready. Let's do this."

"Where do the lovers meet?"

"Duh. Under the frickin' bridge."

"You're really gonna do this?" He's got that one eyebrow lifted up again.

"The quiz? Fuck, yeah, I am."

"It's not about a bridge. It's a metaphor."

"Oh. My God. That's what I just said."

"They're not even lovers. They're frenemies."

"I hate that word."

"Why?"

"It's so overused."

"*Frenemies?*" He laughs loudly again. And this time someone is close enough—though hidden in some other stack —to chastise him with a shush. He lowers his voice and leans in to me, whispering. "Where do you hail from where the word 'frenemies' is overused?"

"Where do I *hail* from?" Now it's my turn to laugh out loud. "What are you, some kind of out-of-time, old-fashioned bibliophile?"

He points at me with the hand not holding on to the spine of *Lovers Under a Bridge.* "Yes."

I put up my free hand in a full-motion stop. "No."

"No? You're just gonna say no? Like... I'm lying?"

"Well, here's the thing..."

He fills in the blank I just dropped. "Ryet."

"Here's the thing, Ryet. It's fine if you're an old-fashioned bibliophile. But you can't be an out-of-time one."

"Why not?"

I shrug up my shoulders. "Because time travel is fake."

He nods his head to the book. "Tell that to Esme and Tyler."

"You mean Elsa and Todd?"

"That's what I *said*."

Now we both laugh. And then we both let go of the stupid book. He backs up, leaning against the stack across the aisle, crossing his arms as he smirks at me with those amazing twinkling eyes.

I do the same, but on my side of the aisle. "Are we gonna have sex, Ryet?"

He nods his head. It's a slow nod. Giving him enough time to say paragraphs of words with just a look. "It's happening..."

Then I fill in the blank he just dropped. "Syrsee."

"It's happening, Syrsee. I'm pretty sure that not only are we going to have sex, we're gonna be best friends forever after it's over." He's completely serious too. The banter is gone and so is the twinkle in his eyes.

This is when I notice that there is a gold mist swirling up from the floor. Dancing around the hem of my flirty skirt and filling the space between us.

I suddenly want to cry because it's not real. And I want this to be real. "Something really bad is happening right now, Ryet."

He looks like he wants to cry too. "I know, Syrsee. That's why we're here. I don't want you to remember it. I don't want you to feel it. I don't want it to define you, or me, or us. So I brought you here. And you're never gonna know what happened."

"Won't it... haunt me? This missing piece of my history?"

He nods again. And again, it's slow. But now it's also sad. "It will. But... I'll do my best. I'll do anything to fill that ugly emptiness with something good. Something good like this." He waves a hand at what's left of the library. Which isn't much. It's really just the hint of a library. "What's happening in my cabin is not us, Syrsee. We are not a witch and a vampire. We're just Syrsee and Ryet. That's all there is to it. We're not them."

I nod. Swallow hard, still nodding. But I'm not sure I believe him. I want to believe him. It's just... too big of an ask, I think.

Ryet reaches across the aisle, plucks *Lovers Under a Bridge* off the shelf next to me, then gives it to me. "I'm gonna get you all the books, Syrsee. That's where we'll start. You're gonna get all the fucking books you want."

I look down at the book in my hands, then back up at him. "But how? They're locked up."

"I'll make a deal with them. With those Guild people. They can have me, do whatever they want with me, but in return, you get all the books."

"If you do that..." I pause to take a deep breath. Then try again. "If you do that, Ryet. I will... I will want to kill them. If they hurt you—"

"It's OK." He places his hand on my cheek, staring into my soul with eyes that no longer twinkle. "I'll be OK. They can't hurt me."

"How do you know?"

"Because if they could, they'd have done it by now."

"What if they're... I dunno, working on some secret project? Something that will hurt you. And the last piece of the puzzle is you giving in. Wouldn't you be trading yourself for something that will only make me temporarily happy?

Because the books are a good idea." I place a hand on his cheek, looking straight into his soul now too. "It's a really nice way to fill the ugly emptiness that's developing inside me right now. But I don't want knowledge, Ryet. Not if I have to trade it for you."

"We can... fix it. If anything goes wrong, Syrsee? We'll fix it. We're powerful. What's happening in the cabin bedroom is disgusting and tragic. But it's making us more powerful. We'll... bide our time, the way Paul did. But we'll never lose sight of the endgame."

"Revenge?"

"No. That's destructive. I don't want to live for revenge, do you?"

I shake my head. "No. I don't either. It's just the first option that came to mind."

"Our endgame is us. On our own terms. Everything we do from now on is about that. Freedom. That's our endgame. One day we will be free from these curses and we will never have to submit again."

I like the idea. But I don't want to live in a fantasy. So even if I don't say this out loud to him, I need to say it to myself.

What he just described—being free from these curses— well, that sounds a whole lot like death to me.

I think Ryet is probably having the same internal conversation with himself because he wraps his arms around me, pulling me tight into his chest, and all the stupid little things that were coming between us when we arrived at the cabin cease to matter. Whatever I am to him—food or otherwise—and whatever he is to me—I'm not sure—none of that is important.

Because we are not each other's enemy.

We are all we have left.

21 - Josep

There is only one way this ends.

Syrsee is **writhing** against me, mouth searching for more.

Paul is trying to comfort Ryet with words and soft touches.

I am… in shock, I think. That it actually worked.

We are in the dirt under Ryet's cabin, all of us squished together in a shallow grave about six feet wide and two feet deep, covered in loose, rich earth.

I know I have to leave—there is much to be done now. But I allow myself a few more moments of peace.

We did it.

We tricked it.

We controlled it.

And soon, we will be master and it will be slave.

Paul interrupts my thoughts, talking in hushed tones as he has a private moment with Ryet. But his whispers are hard to tune out and the level of anguish in his voice makes me turn my head. Syrsee is still writhing, nearly on top of me now, and Paul is lying on his side, hovering over Ryet's chest as he pushes sweaty hair away from his eyes.

"You're OK." This is what Paul is saying on repeat. "You're OK, Ryet. It's going to be OK."

Syrsee is panting heavily, unable to calm down because the blood lust in the beginning of every transformation is insatiable. Her mouth is still seeking my blood. She's licking me, and sucking on me, and writhing against me like she wants more sex.

But this isn't really her.

I could feel the moment when Ryet took her away into some kind of dreamwalk.

It doesn't matter. She didn't need to be mentally present in her body when the consummation took place. Ryet wasn't there, so it makes sense that he would take her with him.

But neither of them are back yet, while Paul and I are both awake.

That's why Paul is worried. He won't be able to stay long. He's here, but not. Because he's still under whatever spell Syrsee put on him.

I don't have much time either. I am really here, thanks to the Darkness. It's more than evil. It's always been more than that. It's made up of carbon and code too.

And it's everywhere under the earth.

Everywhere. Little veins of black, oily Darkness run under the surface of the entire planet like tree roots. That's how I got here and that's how I'll get home too.

It only has one objective: Replicate.

That's all it does, all day long. That's all it's been doing since it came into being long, long, long before I did.

It's very good at replication. What it is not good at is making more than itself. It's been here millions of years, it's been replicating this whole time, and all it can do is make more of *itself*.

It cannot make a new, independent copy.

In other words, it cannot make babies. It can only grow bigger, and longer, and more spread out.

That's why it needs the vampires.

It made the vampire to make a baby and it made the Black

witch to feed us their blood. The Black blood of Black witches comes from the Darkness because the Black blood *is* the Darkness. Its mission is to get inside us, and take over our cells, and rewrite what's in there, and make something new *from us*.

Something it cannot make itself.

A baby made of cold, coded carbon.

A new breed of vampire.

A vessel filled with nothing but Black blood.

Black blood that will one day, if the Darkness gets its way, leave the vessel behind and be a second.

And it's kind of ironic. Because we all want the same thing. Babies.

The problem is, each vision of what a baby is—human, vampire, witch, Darkness—is distinct.

A human baby is not a witch baby. A witch baby is not a vampire baby. And a vampire baby will never be the Darkness.

We cannot allow it.

We cannot allow the Darkness to extinguish our species. And that's what it's doing. Because in order for the Darkness to have the Dark baby—an exact replica of itself, existing on its own, outside the vessel that contains it—it must *kill* the vampire.

All these scions we've made... for what?

To die. We make them to die. It's murdering *us* to save *itself*.

That is why there are so few. It's not that we have a completely illogical life cycle—we are not the doomed panda. We are so few because this thing—this alien thing that doesn't belong here—kills us in its attempt to save itself.

I take a breath. Hold it. Let it out.

I took part in this genocide. I was favored and I took part. Just like everyone else in the Obscurati.

Paul was the one who stood up to it.

Paul was the one who made monsters instead of vampires.

Paul was the only one who ever tried to *save us*.

The only reason we're still here is because the protocol for making the third-born was detailed, and difficult, and required thousands of years of trial and error.

But that's over now.

We've done it. With Ryet, we have made a new vampire.

The American Vampire.

Will the Darkness inside Ryet be able to leave the vessel and be itself, alone, without the container?

It must.

It must.

Because we need that Dark baby if we want to win. We need a copy—a perfect copy of the Darkness—before Syrsee, the Blood Mother, gives birth.

It's the only way to fight it.

Ryet is the first sacrifice.

Paul will not be able to save him.

Just like Ryet will not be able to save Syrsee.

There is only one way this ends.

With another Darkness.

One that *we* control.

So *we* can be the masters instead of the puppets.

*I push **Syrsee off me*** and get to my feet. Paul looks up, unable to hide the panic in his eyes. This was all his idea, but that idea to make a new race of vampire in order to save the vampire came long before the man he's holding in his arms right now.

And he's having doubts.

I knew this was coming. And I have prepared for it.

If he turns on me—if he betrays me—he will regret it. And I want him to know this.

I refuse to be a slave. I refuse.

This moment, the very one he promised me all those hundreds of years ago when all I wanted was death, is here.

But we haven't won yet.

Ryet must die and Paul needs to accept it.

The moment I finish this thought he speaks it out loud. "He's going to die." Paul's words come out matter-of-factly. And I give him a lot of credit for the even tone of his voice as he speaks his worst fear out loud.

"He *is* going to die, Paul." I say it too, my voice even as well. Because he needs to hear it. He *must* accept it.

It's Ryet. Or us.

Is anyone surprised?

"*I've got to go.*"

I'm still staring at Josep when he says this. It's not unexpected. We have more work to do while the Darkness is still vulnerable.

But *he's* hesitating because he knows *I'm* hesitating.

"Yes. You go." I say this with confidence, abruptly letting go of Ryet. His head hits the hard ground with a thump. "I'll stay and take care of this one." I nod my head towards Syrsee, who is writhing against Josep's leg now. Trying to get off, I think.

It's a really bad look for her. But it's not *her* doing it. Both she and Ryet left their bodies back in the purple room. This is just the Darkness inside her now, craving blood and sex.

"I'll handle Ryet first. Then I'll get Syrsee to release me and I'll be back in the tower room, right where she left me, before you know it." I get to my feet and let out a breath as I meet Josep's questioning gaze with my own stoic one.

Josep puts a hand on my shoulder. "I can stay with you. If you need me to."

He doesn't trust me. But it's understandable. I wouldn't trust me either. I smile. "I would appreciate that, brother. The offer means a lot." I mimic his hand on my shoulder with my own on his. And this time, when I speak, I let a little emotion through. "He was my favorite."

Josep nods. "I know." His suspicion is reined in, his expression more solemn now.

Giving up Ryet was a sacrifice I made that Josep didn't have to. The biggest sacrifice Josep has made towards this monumental moment is the actual act of showing up here in this tunnel.

I give his shoulder a squeeze. "So your offer to stay is generous and appreciated. I know how much you hate being away from your space."

Josep hesitates, looking down the tunnel towards the door to Ryet's house. He doesn't *want* to stay. And he's not in some vague am-I-here-am-I-not existence, the way I am. He's *really, physically* here. He traveled through the Dark dirt. He left his bunker.

It's killing him. Maybe even literally. His anxiety about the outside world has always been pathological, but he's been locked in that bunker for decades now. It might even have slipped his mind how much anxiety the outside world causes. It's easy to forget one's shortcomings when one never has to face them.

And the only reason he agreed to come here, to this tunnel under the earth, was because I had Ryet build it specifically for this encounter and Josep has known about it since the nineteen seventies. We could've done this exchange upstairs, or outside, or anywhere, actually—if one of the major participants wasn't an agoraphobe. Josep prepared for the journey. Prepped himself mentally. And he did great.

But it's over now. It's done.

He *needs* to go home.

Not only that, he's got work to do there. Pressing, important work that will direct our path forward.

He looks back at me now. "The scions will be arriving shortly. Some of them might already be there."

"Well"—I smirk at him—"they won't be able to cause much trouble while we're away. There's no blood. There's no Lucia. And no halfbreeds to worry about either."

He hesitates again. His offer to stay with me was a bluff. His anxiety over being away from home far exceeds his mistrust of me. I mean, we came this far, didn't we? If I was going to pussy out over what comes next for Ryet, the time for that was *before* the transfer. Not now. What has been done to him cannot be undone. I don't have that kind of power. Not even Josep could pull off that miracle.

It *will* happen, regardless of how I feel about it.

And Josep knows this.

I hold up a finger and bend down to Syrsee. "Maybe I can make it go quick?" I take her face in my hands as she snaps her teeth at me, trying to bite. "Syrsee?"

She snarls, trying to wriggle free.

"Syrsee! I need you to release me from the purple. *Syrsee!*"

She's not in there. Josep knows this as well as I do. It's going to take a fair bit of coaxing to get Syrsee and Ryet to come back from the gold dream they are in right now.

Josep sighs. "You handle it. I'll go get everything ready at home."

I stand back up and look him in the eyes. "I won't be long. I'll draw her out, and the moment she releases me I'll be back in the tower bedroom, right where she left me. We'll probably arrive at the same time."

The Darkness is more than an oily blob of undulating shadow hiding in the dirt. It's a network in the earth. A highway, of sorts. A medium of transport for those with access to the purple. I'm the one who discovered this highway and how to travel on it. The purple is mine and everyone who has access to it is under my control. Including Josep.

This is another part of his anxiety. He won't go outside. The world could be ending—we could be in the middle of Armageddon itself—and Josep would just watch it happen from a window. Or pretend it wasn't happening at all and stay down in his bunker.

So he must travel in the Dark dirt if he wants to go anywhere.

He's got a system of tunnels connected to his bunker. They are like subway stations, linking different places. A direct route to the Darkness, of course. Here. Other places too, I'm sure. But in order to use Paul's Purple Line, he must walk my purple dream.

He must be under my control.

He doesn't like that.

He wants to go home far, *far* more than he wants to stay and make sure I follow the plan.

Which was *my* plan to begin with. Why wouldn't I follow it?

Josep gives me one last nod and then walks over to the earthen wall of the tunnel. It's been a long time since I've watched him travel through the dirt and for a moment, when his body takes on the appearance of a gossamer curtain and the Darkness that exists in all things underground looks more like the curling, serpentine tendrils of an evil demon than an oily vein of blackness, I am captivated by the process.

The way he flickers, like he's not there. The way the tentacles encircle his body from foot to head. And that one, last look over his shoulder as the purple mist begins at his feet and travels up, while at the same time the Darkness begins to pull him back into the earth where he belongs.

It's over in a matter of seconds. I was holding my breath as I watched, so I let it out. Forcing myself to be calm.

I'm going to betray him now and it's a big decision. One I've been mulling over since the very day Ryet was born. Trying—*desperately* trying—to figure out a way to have my cake and eat it too.

Is anyone surprised? I am the vampire Paul. If there's a way to get everything I want and not settle for less, then why wouldn't I?

First things first, though.

I need to talk to Syrsee and Ryet. And isn't it convenient that I'm already in the world between worlds and so are they?

One purple, one gold.

One vampire, one witch.

There are many things that set the two realms apart, but there are an equal number of ways to make them cross.

It's almost like it was planned this way.

I take a deep breath, hold it, let it out, and then focus myself into one of the three worlds I mentally reside in.

The purple is the first and the one closest to reality because it is mine. The gold world is the second, which isn't mine, but belongs to Syrsee. She has no idea how to control it —barely even knows it exists at this point—so the gold world is porous and can leak over into the other realms on either side of it.

The third is one I do not have access to. Yet. But it's close now. So, so, *so* close.

It doesn't take much to hop into the gold and as soon as I'm there, a reality begins to form. A library—of course. I should've known. With Ryet and Syrsee standing in the middle of a stack, hugging fiercely. As if they are about to say goodbye.

They *would* be saying goodbye, if it wasn't for my plan. "Am I interrupting?"

They break apart. Syrsee lets out a surprised gasp, but says nothing.

Ryet directs those constantly-angry eyes in my direction, then pushes Syrsee behind him. "What the hell are you doing here?"

It's an honorable gesture. Of course he wants to protect her. He loves her.

Not as much as I love him, but he'll get there with time.

Unfortunately, time isn't a luxury.

But it could be.

I put up a hand. "We don't have a lot of time. I need to explain some things—"

"You bet your ass you do." Syrsee spits these words at me. "You didn't tell me that I was literally going to be fucked by a demon! You said it was Ryet!"

I shrug with my hands. I mean, what was I going to say? *Syrsee, you're going to be fucked by a demon and have its baby?* That would've gone over well. And anyway, it *was* Ryet. The vessel that contains Ryet, at least. It is my professional opinion that this was not a lie because Syrsee didn't understand that the mind and the vessel are two separate things.

She does now.

All of this is beside the point. "We have more important things to discuss." Syrsee opens her mouth to protest, but I put up another hand, warning her off. "I'm sorry. OK? I apologize for leaving out the details. But the situation is very sensitive."

Ryet takes a breath, then looks me straight in the eyes. "What, exactly, is the situation?"

"Third-born's choice." I hold up a finger. "Long version?" I hold up another finger. "Or condensed?"

They both say, "Condensed," in unison.

"Good choice. Here's the deal, kids." I point at Ryet. "You're going in the ground. I'm going to bury you in the tunnel between the root cellar and the house. You're going to stay there for the foreseeable future." I point to Syrsee. "You're going to the Guild."

The both blink at me. Like they can't believe they're about to agree that this is a better outcome than they expected.

"But," I say—they both sigh—"there's a catch."

"Of course there is." Ryet is looking like the beautiful man he is in this moment. Not the blue-black thing back in the tunnel. "*Paul!*"

So he's a bit distracting and I missed most of what he just said. "What?"

"Stop looking at my dick and focus. I *said*"—he's really angry—"what is going on back in the tunnel?"

I wave a hand in the air. "Oh. It's all over." Then I point at Syrsee. "You, however? We have a little bit of a problem."

Syrsee goes pale. "What kind of problem?"

"You're addicted to the blood. You will need to continue feeding on a regular basis."

Ryet interjects. "Let me guess. I'll be in the ground so you'll be the one who needs to feed her."

"An intriguing possibility that I admit sounds a lot more fun than the path I'm on. But no, Ryet. *You* are going to feed her."

"But you just said he's going in the dirt."

"He is. But only *part* of him, Syrsee." I suck in a breath, steeling myself for the next revelation. Because this is the part they're going to hate. "Just like only part of you will be going to the Guild."

"Explain." Ryet is growling mad now.

"You can…" There is no good way to say this, so fuck it. I just spit it out. "You can split yourselves. In fact, this is not a 'could' situation. It's a done deal. Every time you enter the purple 'dreamwalk,' as we've been calling it, you split away from your true self to be there. But you *are* there." I look them both in the eye for this part. "It's not a dream. The two of you know this, right?"

They look at each other for a moment, then shrug. Ryet answers for both of them. "Yes. It's real."

"This is real too." I pan my hand at the library. "It just exists in another place. It's connected to the reality we experience through our magic." I wave a hand through the haze of gold and purple. "Which manifests as a mist. You're perfectly safe as long as the mist is around you because it's a connection to your physical body."

"Oh!" Syrsee puts up a finger. "It's like astral projection."

"Sort of. But it's really not. I, myself, am not an astral projection expert, so I can't say how related this might be to our particular circumstances. But I don't think the point of astral projection is to split away from your soul so you can be in two places at once." They blink at me. "Physically, I mean. You can be in two places at once physically."

"How?" This one word of Ryet's is filled with so much doubt, it comes out seething.

"You walk away from the soul."

The silence that comes after this revelation is thick, and heavy, and charged with unanswered questions.

"OK." Syrsee comes back first. "But… I don't understand.

One… clone, copy, whatever—this one has the soul, but the other one doesn't?"

"So what is the other one?" Ryet finishes that question for her. "A zombie, or something?"

"No." I laugh. It's absurd. "It's you." I point at both of them individually, but mean the word in a collective way. "Just… minus a soul."

"OK." Syrsee is back again. "The soul part of me is the one who gets to go to the Guild?"

She's so hopeful, it's sad. But she already knows this is not how it will happen.

I shake my head.

"So you expect us to live as soulless creatures?" Ryet is snarling now. "Something evil. That's what you're saying, right? Something forsaken."

"Ryet. I'm trying to be gentle here. But here's the reality for you, my love. You are *already* a soulless creature. Your soul was sold to me."

"That's a lie. You lied about all of it. You made me think that I chose this back in that alley when I was second-born, but it's a lie. You *made me*, Paul. From beginning to end." He's pointing at himself, eyes flashing red. "I didn't choose to be *born*."

"It's a complicated argument, Ryet. One we don't have time for now. So. For the sake of moving things along, I will just agree with you. It wasn't your choice and you bear no responsibility for any of this. How's that? Feel better now?"

Syrsee scoffs. "You don't have to be a dick, Paul. We just need to understand what's happening."

"Here's what's happening. Both of you have already split. And"—I look Ryet in the eyes for this—"I had nothing to do with that. You brought her here, Ryet. *You* did this."

"Because a demon took over my body and was about to rape her!"

"Don't forget the part where he got me pregnant," Syrsee adds.

I roll my eyes. Children. "Regardless. Half of you is here, half of you is there. It has been done. It *is* done. You are split. And here's what happens next. I'm going to leave you for a short while, during which time neither of you will come up with any stupid ideas to… escape, or whatever." I pause to give them both a stern I-will-fucking-kill-you-both look. "I need to go bury Ryet's soul-body in the earth under the house. Then I will come back here." I point at Syrsee now. "You will release me from the spell you put on me. I will leave again, because my spirit is back in the compound tower bedroom where Ryet was third-born, and then I will finish up some other important work out west. After which I will return to the cabin, collect your soul-body, Syrsee, and take it back with me to Montana."

"What's going on in Montana?" This is Ryet. "Where the hell is Josep?"

"He's taking care of other things. In Montana."

"He doesn't know about this, does he? You didn't tell him, did you? Whatever you did tell him, it was an empty promise, wasn't it?"

"Ryet, I'm trying my best here. And it wasn't an empty promise. It was—"

Syrsee interrupts. "What was the promise?"

"We're in the middle of a rather long and complicated revenge scheme. The baby is part of it. The Darkness is part of it."

"And me?" Ryet points to himself. This is when it all hits

home for me. Because we've done it. And I'm *sorry* we've done it. "What's gonna happen to me, Paul?"

"The part of you that goes to the Guild with Syrsee will… find a way to save us all." He scoffs. "But the part of you that goes into the ground, Ryet…" I shrug. "I'm doing my best. That's all I can say. I'm trying to save it."

"His soul, you mean?" Syrsee's face has gone ghost white. "That's what you're talking about here. You're trying to save his soul, right? Because if it's yours, and you just admitted it was, then you were going to use it to bargain. What did you get for it, Paul? Something good, I hope." All her words come out dripping with rage, and contempt, and loathing.

"He's the first of a new breed of vampire. It was… a long, complicated process that I've been working on with Josep for more than two hundred years."

"You didn't answer my question. You're using his soul as… payment?"

"No, Syrsee. It's really got nothing to do with the soul in Ryet's case." I don't want to look at him, but I can't help myself. And the instant I do, I regret everything. Even allowing him to be born.

"What are you doing to me, Paul?"

And this is it. The moment I've been dreading. The moment when he learns the truth. But I've told so many lies, he needs the truth for this one. "I'm turning you *into* the Darkness. A perfect copy of it. Something that can live outside the vessel. Something I can control, unlike the one that we use now."

"So I will never be back in that body again. I will spend eternity as a soulless thing. Is that what you're saying?"

I nod. "Yes, Ryet. That's exactly what I'm saying." I look at Syrsee now. "But that's not all of it." She is too stunned to spit words at me, so I just continue. "You are pregnant. And the baby is growing inside both versions of you. It will be born. But in order for that baby to have the best possible outcome you must reunite with your body before giving birth. It can exist, theoretically, at least, split in half as a fetus. But it cannot be born that way."

I'm not certain what that baby might be like if it was born split in half, but I do know that the one Syrsee would give birth to at the Guild would not be anything resembling a human.

None of us says anything for almost a minute.

Then Ryet sighs. "How do we get to the Guild, Paul? We're in a dreamwalk."

"It's not a dreamwalk, Ryet. It's just a mechanism of travel that we stay in for periods of time. To live a fantasy, to have conversations we otherwise cannot, to have sex with people and drink their blood when they are far away in distance. But we don't have to stay. We can travel anywhere we want. You know this, Syrsee. You did it back at my resort when you came into the greenhouse building and joined in on the fun Ryet and I were having." Ryet scoffs at my characterization of that particular morning. But I ignore him and look at Syrsee now. "This is all you. Ryet doesn't control the purple. You do because you control the mist. You can be in the mist and have a dreamlike experience, a magical dreamlike experience that is completely real on another level. Where you can be anything you want and see anything you want. It's part imagination, part dimensional skipping. But you can just wipe the mist away, Syrsee. And come back to reality at any time."

"But if I wipe the mist away, won't I end up as Syrsee in the tunnel?"

I hesitate.

It's the wrong move because she snaps at me. "What? What aren't you telling me?"

"That soul—*your* soul—it belongs to the Darkness now."

Ryet takes a step forward. "You're not making any sense, Paul. And that's because, as usual, you're leaving things out. What are you leaving out?" He's glaring at me with narrowed eyes. So much like the man he was just a few short weeks ago. But then again, so very different.

He's angrier, for one. He's gotten angry with me plenty of times before this new birth, but I never saw the kind of malice in his eyes that I see now.

"I didn't leave anything out." I'm angrier now too. I think it's the stress. We're all under a lot of stress. "I already said she has been severed. This"—I pan my hand in the direction of Syrsee—"is the empty vessel. The soulless one."

"My question was"—even Syrsee is angrier now—"if I can leave the dreamwalk any time I want, as you just said I could, why wouldn't I just slip back into being Syrsee who has my soul?"

She's smarter now too. Because this question of hers hit the bullseye. "I don't think you understand the literal meaning of the word 'severed.'" I say this to Syrsee, but then I look over at Ryet too. Just to make sure he understands as well. "The Darkness *took your soul*, Syrsee. You exist right now because you had access to the purple, which I gifted you at birth, and you're a Black witch with a lineage that goes back to the Ice Maiden herself, so the gold mist you see is your birthright. But the point I'm making here, and the only thing that matters, is you have no soul."

Ryet sighs. Rubbing both hands down his face like he's very tired. "She's dead."

"She is not dead."

"She's dead. I'm dead. You're dead. We're all fucking dead."

"Ryet—"

He puts up a hand, glaring at me. "Don't. I'm not in the mood."

"We're *not* dead. We're still in the game."

"But it's not good though, is it?" Syrsee's tone is pragmatic and reasonable. "We're in the game, but we're losing, aren't we?"

"Well, I'm not losing, Syrsee. My victory here is pretty much guaranteed. So. No. It's not good. But it's the best I could do."

Ryet grabs his hair, like he's losing his shit. "What. The fuck. Are you talking about? You did the best you could? You did *all* of this, Paul! This is your grand plan playing out! You're the one I blame, not the fucking Darkness! *You did this.*"

"I *did.*" These words come out through clenched teeth. "But. I changed my mind. OK? And now I'm trying to fucking fix it. I'm trying to keep you alive, and her alive, and me alive. And, I might add, I'm betraying the one vampire I have counted on for centuries to do this. *So calm the fuck down.*"

Ryet and I stare at each other for many long seconds. Both sets of eyes seething red with rage.

Syrsee interrupts. "You still haven't told me where I would end up if I left the dreamwalk, Paul."

I take a deep breath, count to three, let it out, and look at Syrsee. "Nowhere. You will end up nowhere. There." I look at Ryet. "Happy now?"

"At least you're starting to tell the truth."

"You want the truth? Fine. Here's the fucking truth. Syrsee"—I look at her now—"you are a soulless creature, a wraith. A remnant."

She squints her eyes at me. "A ghost? I'm a ghost?"

"As good a term as any. But not entirely accurate. You exist, Syrsee. You are real. You're just..." I have to stop here because the word I'm about to say is heavy with truth. I say it anyway. It is the truth, after all. "Hollow."

"Hollow?" She lets out a sigh with the word.

"Empty. *But*. You won't feel hollow. There are many, many hundreds of thousands of humans who exist in this world as wraiths and they never know the difference. This is how it will be for you as well. They have no idea at all that they entered the life they're living without a soul. And if I didn't tell you, you would not know either. It all felt real, didn't it? When we were together inside the greenhouse back at the resort? Did it feel like a dream, Syrsee?"

She shakes her head. "No. It didn't."

"That's what your life is now. When it's time for us all to leave here you will wake up wherever you want to wake up because you command the dreamwalk. Both the purple and the gold."

"What about me?"

I exhale as I turn to Ryet. "You never had a soul, Ryet. You have always been a wraith. I'm going to bury the vampire Ryet in the earth under your cabin and you—*this* you, this *remnant* of you—it will go with Syrsee."

"But... *who am I*, Paul?"

"You're no different now than you were when you were born. A slave to the Darkness. Just like me. Just like Josep. Just like every vampire on Earth. This is why I'm doing this." I look at Syrsee now. "I'm tired of being a slave. And I want control over the copy of the Darkness that is living inside the vampire Ryet. It's going to mature, it's going to leave the vessel, and I'm going to make it *my* slave. And in doing so, I will free you both."

"How?" Syrsee's anger is gone now, her voice much softer than it was. "How will you save us?"

"There are many factors—"

"He doesn't know." Ryet's anger, on the other hand, is still building. "He's full of shit. He's lying. He's cheating. He's... full of fucking shit." Ryet is glaring at me. Staring straight into my eyes. "You have no idea how to save anyone but yourself."

He's not wrong. "You're not wrong. But if there is a way, I will find a way. Because..." I hesitate, letting out a breath. But I might as well just say it. "Because I love you, Ryet." I've said this to him so many times before, but never, *ever* have I said it like this. "I love you. I'm going to save you and I'm going to save Syrsee too."

"Because you love me as well?"

I'm shaking my head, even as I turn it to meet her gaze. "No, Syrsee. I don't love you. But Ryet loves you, so I'm saving you for him." I look back at Ryet now. "So one day, maybe he will love me back."

He closes his eyes, refusing to meet my gaze.

But that's fine. All in good time.

"Now." I let out a long breath. "If you'll excuse me, I have to leave you for a short time so I can bury Dark Ryet in the earth."

23 - Josep

The miraculous first breath.

*T*raveling **through the dirt** is like being in the only place you've ever known.

It's like going home. And once you're inside it again, it's like you never left.

It's an overwhelming feeling of belonging.

So it makes perfect sense that coming out of the dirt is the exact opposite. It feels like death and hopelessness. The Darkness wants us to remember where we come from and where we belong.

This time, when I appear inside my bunker cave, naked and covered in dirt, and as the hopelessness washes over me, wrapping around me like a cloak, I temper it with a secret that brings me a bit of compensation.

It's just enough to keep me focused on what comes next.

Which is a whole list of things—the scions, the ritual, the burial—but before all that happens, I have one more thing to do down here.

I don't bother washing myself before I set back down the tunnel that leads to the hole that will take me to the darkness. I just get to the hole in the ground as quick as I can and jump, unfurling my wings to slow down my descent. Still, my feet land hard, causing a rumble through the earth.

I pause here, taking in every detail with my vampire eyes.

Little Baby is a tattered mess. Bloody and almost nothing left of her. But not *quite* nothing.

I walk forward until I am standing over her body. She is unrecognizable and in pieces. But I bend down, slide my hands under what's left of her spine, and pick her up.

A foot is left behind. A few ribs. And a hand.

But it won't matter. What I have is enough.

I turn and go back, standing under the hole in the earth I just came down, and with one strong wingbeat, I am ascending again.

A minute later I'm walking back down the tunnel to my cavern and seconds after that I am walking into the pool of black water, Little Baby still in my arms.

I settle on a ledge of rock and breathe a sigh of relief.

It's lonely being me and I'm tired of it.

Transforming the girl called Echo into the sacrifice named Little Baby is the only opportunity I will ever get to have a partner who is not Paul.

To have something that is all mine. Made by me, sacrificed by me, resurrected by me.

The scions are not loyal to me because I wasn't the one who fed them as they grew. I wasn't the one who had conversations with them, or took them to bed, or gave them the blood kiss. They don't even know I exist.

Paul has them. And he can tell me all day long that they don't mean anything to him, but he's lying. Especially about Ryet.

I am not stupid. I know he's going to try to save Ryet. He won't betray me—not completely. He will sacrifice Ryet to complete our mission, but some way, somehow, he will find a way to work around his obligations to me in order to save Ryet.

He's in the process of putting it all in motion right now. That's why he wanted to be alone at the end.

But I don't care.

Because I'm going to work the same magic with Little Baby.

And like Paul, I too have been planning.

I bite the palm of my hand, letting my fangs seep deep into the flesh. Then I drip my blood all over Little Baby's remnants.

What happens next is just... a bit of science. As is most of what's happening down here in the earth. Coulomb's Law, which is unnecessarily wordy, can be broken into this: opposites attract. I gave her blood when I left her last. Just a little bit to get her through the pain. But it's also a marker. One that will attract new blood. My new blood, specifically. Which is so charged with magic—from Paul, from Ryet, from Syrsee, and, of course, from the Darkness itself—that it can do wondrous things.

Even make a tattered halfbreed whole again.

I close my eyes and get comfortable in the pool of black water with only the sound of the trickling waterfall to keep me company. Time passes. It is not important how much time. This will take as long as it takes and I am prepared to wait for my reward.

Slowly the remnants of Little Baby in my arms become more solid. Muscles grow back. Bones mend. Skin reforms. And the parts of her that were missing—the foot, the ribs, the hand—are restored.

Then... the miraculous first breath. It comes out as a gasp and she sits up. Coughing, and sputtering, and crying.

She turns in my arms, then pushes off me, splashing backwards into the black water. Trying to get away from me.

I just smile. I smile, and smile, and smile as she grabs on to the ledge of rock and struggles to haul herself out of the pool.

She gets one leg over, then one arm, then she's out. But exhaustion takes over and she collapses into the loose dirt that lines the rocks.

I stand up in the water and wade over to her. She cries harder when I reach for her, but she has used up all her energy, so she must stay where she is.

My words are whispered right into her ear. "Rest now, Little Baby. I'll be back for you soon. And then you'll see, all the pain and trauma will be worth it. I promise."

I kiss her head, then wade back over to the front of the pool and walk out of the water.

Clean and feeling more complete—more *myself*—than I have in two thousand years.

I make the journey back up to Paul's bedroom alone, leaving Little Baby in the pool of water. And after I close the door, I program a new code into the keypad.

She will be safe down there.

She will go insane, but it's nothing that I won't be able to fix with a good long drink of blood once the New Darkness is born.

Then I go downstairs with heavy, drooping wings and skin the color of a fresh bruise to finish the job we started.

24 - Syrsee

He made us him.

*P*aul *doesn't wait for Ryet*, or me, to give him permission to leave. He simply disappears.

Ryet lets out a breath, his eyes lingering on the empty space that once contained Paul. It takes a few seconds for that spell to be broken and for him to redirect his gaze and attention to me. "Are you all right?"

I scoff. "Am I all right?" But it doesn't come out mean. Because... actually, I think I am all right. "I... feel hungry, but other than that?" I shrug. "I don't know Ryet. Some crazy shit just happened to us and I don't even remember it all."

"Right?" He scoffs too, then takes my hand and pulls me down to the ground, our backs resting against a library stack. He guides me into his lap. We're naked, and sweaty, and bloody.

Also, not real?

"Ryet?"

"Hmm?" He's looking up at me with a blank expression.

"What's it all mean?"

He chuckles a little. "Well, my guess is..." He nods his head. "We're..."

"Fucked?" We both laugh. It's not funny, not even a little bit, but it's more of a hysterical laugh than anything amusing.

"Yeah, Syrsee. I think 'fucked' is the right word."

"So what do we do?"

He blows out a breath. "I'm not sure we have much of a

choice. I don't understand what this is, either." He motions to the library. It's not real. It's in the magic... whatever the purple and gold is. "But here's my takeaway from that whole word salad Paul just spewed at us—we're something between alive and dead, but with powers to act like we're alive."

"Yeah. I caught that too. It just doesn't make sense."

"I don't think we need to worry about that. Yet. I think we just go to the Guild and bide our time. Read the books." I smile at him when he says this. "You'll read the books, at least. Remember? This was our plan before everything went sideways with the blood. I'll give myself to them, you'll get the books, and we'll... figure it out. It's really the only choice we have."

I lean into him and rest my head on his shoulder. I don't do this to get closer to the blood flowing through his jugular, but I'm, actually, very close. So close I can smell the blood. And suddenly I am so hungry, I have an urge to bite him.

Ryet pulls away, like he senses this. "Are you OK, Syrsee?"

"I don't know. I'm hungry again. For you."

"You need a drink?"

"I think so." He raises his palm to his mouth, but I grab it. "No. Not the palm."

"My neck?" He doesn't even try to hide his surprise. "But you don't have fangs, Syrsee."

I know this. What I'm asking is gross. I want to bite his neck with blunt human teeth. But I don't say anything. I just... let him try the idea out.

So it's his decision when he says, "Fine. If that's what you need, then do it."

I'm already leaning in, ready to take that bite out of his neck, when I hear, "No."

And when I look up Paul is back. I meet his gaze,

embarrassed for some reason. And then pull back, away from Ryet, ashamed.

Paul bends down to us. But he's only looking at me, not Ryet. I'm about to start apologizing for being a sick, disgusting monster when he says, "I'll do it." We stare at each other for a moment. Then he directs his gaze to Ryet. "If that's OK with you."

Ryet goes tense beneath me. Paul made his feelings for Ryet pretty clear in that little speech of his before he left us alone, but I'm not sure what Ryet's feelings actually are for Paul. It's not hate, even though I think Ryet wishes it were. But it's not love, either. At least, he doesn't look at Paul the way he looks at me. There *is* a difference between us.

But I know he feels something for Paul. Something he probably can't quite explain, either.

"She needs it," Paul says, still looking at Ryet. "She's addicted. She's going to keep needing it." His eyes shift over to mine. "At least for a while." Which implies that there will come a day when I won't.

And even though I'm in the midst of a blood-addiction craving that makes me feel dirty, and sinful, and vile—I'm already missing the future me who will never want this blood again. Which makes me feel even more wicked.

The weird thing, though, is that I don't care. It doesn't bother me in the least if I'm a vile, sinful, dirty blood whore. I. Just. Want more blood.

"Fine," Ryet says. "Do it."

Paul sits down on the ground next to Ryet, turning his body in to him. Ryet tilts his head towards Paul, exposing his neck, just as Paul lowers his mouth down. Teeth appear, sharp and pointy, and then, in one quick motion, so fast I barely see it, he bites Ryet. Leaving two puncture marks behind, dripping blood.

I'm just staring at this blood, craving it so hard, but lost in the beauty of just looking at it. Paul's hand is on my head, guiding my mouth down to Ryet's neck. And the moment his blood touches my lips, I lose myself. With eyes open I watch as the purple swirls up and the gold mist falls down like rain.

The three of us are somewhere else. All tangled up on a bed. Naked.

Ryet's bleeding, I'm drinking, and Paul is leaning to me, whispering. "Set me free, Syrsee. Let me go so I can save him for you. Release me."

I don't want to pull back from my drink. I don't know when I'll get another one. I don't even know how to release Paul. I don't even know how I trapped him in the first place.

But then Paul's whispers are there, his mouth right up next to my ear. "Let me drink you while you drink him. That's how you release me."

It doesn't really add up, but I barely know where I am, so maybe it's OK to be confused?

Even if I objected, it probably wouldn't stop him. Because he doesn't wait for my understanding and I don't even give him verbal permission, but since when did Paul ever need words? He's inside me. He's inside Ryet. This much I know.

And then he's pulling blood from me and I'm back in that bliss, the blood lust growing stronger and more insistent even though I'm in the middle of getting my hit. Ryet's hand is on my breast, and every time I take a pull from him, he squeezes it, sending a flood of sensations that get all mixed up with the feeling of Paul taking his own pull from me.

Then Ryet leans to Paul, practically ripping his neck open. Blood suddenly pours down Paul's neck. I slip my fingers into it, dragging it over to my lips. And then I stop drinking from the meager puncture wounds, and join Ryet as we both drink Paul's blood from the gaping wound.

Paul pulls off me, digging his fangs into Ryet. But only long enough to get a taste. Not long enough for me to protest. Because before I can object, he's drinking me again. And we're drinking him. And then we're drinking Ryet. And then they're drinking me.

It's a blood orgy. Ryet, me, and Paul.

And there's something inside me that knows... this is exactly how Paul planned it.

He made us for this.

He made us *him*.

And even though, in the back of my head, all those painful feelings of shame are still there and I know, even if I know nothing else, that this is evil—I don't want him to ever stop.

I want to stay here and get lost in the blood lust.

Which is, of course, the moment when Paul pulls back and starts whispering again. "Release me, Syrsee. Right now."

I don't want to. I want to keep him in this moment forever. And for sure, I do not want to move forward into the dark, depressing, empty future in front of me.

But since when did what I want ever matter to Paul?

"I release you." I don't even mean to say it, it just comes out.

And then he's gone.

And the moment he leaves, the mist begins to fade...

This is the dream.

𝒲 *hen I open my eyes*, I'm home.

I sit up, catching the scent of old, dried blood. Then I see Lucia's head on the floor, near the armoire filled with medical supplies.

It's a rotting piece of bone and remnant flesh and her formally green eyes are now a gross shade of yellow gray. But a smile creeps across my face. Then a laugh.

This laugh is interrupted by the resounding chime of the lodge doorbell coming from the floors below. I walk to the door, then turn, wanting to take one last look at the room where it all happened. What happened in this tower is the defining moment of my long life and I want to burn it all into my memory.

The bloodstained floor. The dirty IV needle and the tubing attached that used to drain those first drops of Black blood out of Syrsee. The rumpled bedsheets where the three of us consummated the union. And, of course, the lingering gold mist.

A present from Syrsee that she didn't even know she gave me.

Voices below. But not Josep's.

Then I remember what's actually going on here and leave the room. Naked, but fully clothed in my vampire skin. Wings so heavy, the muscles in my back tremble with the effort to hold them upright. I'm out of practice, but I'll get used to it soon enough.

I hit the floor below, travel the hallway until I reach the stairs that will take me down to the grand foyer, and then descend slowly, as I take in the scene. The gorgeous wood-planked floor that Ryet so painstakingly laid with his own hands is covered in a layer of halfbreed dust that is inches thick.

But it's the large group of scions who have my attention. One of them, Nioh, is standing at the open front door, talking to someone.

I nod my head with satisfaction, pleased that it all worked out, as I continue my descent.

Two more scions enter, each carrying one end of a coffin. Then another pair with a second coffin.

"Put them in the dining room." My voice booms through the foyer, echoing off the ceiling.

Everything in the room stops. Even the scions bringing in the coffins. Every face turns up to me. They immediately bow their heads and go down on one knee. "My lord," they say, nearly in unison.

None of them were the chosen one. That was Ryet.

But they are still alive and Ryet isn't.

He's not back in the dirt under his house, either.

He's in one of those coffins. Because we are not done with him yet.

Or sweet little Syrsee, who is in the second coffin, though for different reasons. She is carrying the new Darkness inside her and it's just easier to transport bodies all the way across the country using a commercial transport if said body is in a coffin.

"Good." Josep's voice booms the way mine did just a

moment ago. He's in his vampire form too. And it's been quite a while since I've seen him in the flesh like that. "You're back. How did it go?"

"Scions." They all look up at me with their full attention. Eyes filled with adoration, ready to be told what to do. "Resume your duties. Those of you with no assigned duties, please go find yourself a place to stay on the compound."

There's about thirty seconds of bustle as the scions get out of our way, and then it's just Josep and me, standing opposite each other in the foyer, right under a massive chandelier made of moose antlers.

He starts first, repeating his last question. "Did you have any problems?"

"Not a single one. The coffins are here and we're good to go. How about you? Did you run into any trouble?"

"None at all. I'm ready."

We're both lying. But neither of us cares. Because regardless of what comes after the ritual we're about to do, the ritual itself will be flawless.

"Then by all means, blood brother." I smile at him, then pan my hand in the direction of the dining room. "Let's eat. We have a lot of hungry scions to feed."

Josep leads us into the dining room where Ryet's and Syrsee's bodies have been laid out on the long table, their heads positioned on either end for easy access, their feet touching in the middle.

The room of scions is quiet as we enter and take up our positions at the head of the room where two massive golden wingback chairs have sat since the day this place was complete.

Maybe Lucia sat in them, over the years. Or a halfbreed.

But these chairs belong to Josep and me.

And when we sit it all becomes real.

He and I look at each other, smirking.

Because while we might both be in the middle of betraying each other, teamwork makes the dream work.

This *is* the dream.

I raise my right hand in the air, commanding my scions to give me all their attention. "There will be no frenzy, do you all understand?"

Some of them are licking their lips in anticipation, but all of them nod out an affirmative.

I let Ryet do whatever he wanted for the most part. Because he only plays a small part in my ascension to Dark Lord.

Not only is he the first third-born vampire in hundreds of years, he is the one who will save us all. But just because he's the one we've been waiting for—and the start of a brand-new vampire bloodline— this doesn't mean he's the one who gets to see it all through. Because, realistically, when it all comes down to it, he is just food.

These men—well, these men are a whole other breed of scion.

And when I pull the new Darkness out of Ryet when that baby is born, they will be my Dark Army.

I lower my hand and command them to, "Proceed!"

They start drinking. One at Syrsee's neck, one at Ryet's. And then they move on, following the men in front of them, until they have had their drink of my two blood lovers.

When they have gotten both sides of the Darkness inside them, one by one, they come up to Josep and me and we begin a new version of the long drink.

A death that isn't death, but a revival.

Not a drink to kill, but one to renew.

And when we have drained them to the point where they are almost unable to stand, we lead them out into the back woods where the dirt is loose, and rich, and wet. Where they dig their own shallow graves, lie down inside, and cover themselves with the earth.

Josep and I wait until every one of them has been concealed and is protected.

Then we dig our graves, sit down in them, take one last look at each other. Then lie back and sink into the Darkness.

26 - Ryet

Two very rare creatures indeed.

*I*t's only when I slowly begin coming back that I realize I was gone. Lost in some kind of soulless monster stage or something. And I only know this because when I open my eyes the purple-gold mist is still kinda there and I catch it at just the right moment to watch it fade, withdrawing back into Syrsee like she is the source of all that magic.

And she is, I guess.

This is when I remember what happened to us. I don't understand it, but I remember.

This is also when I realize that we're sitting in the truck, in the town of Mount Royal, right in front of the general store. It's the middle of the night so the part of the sign that says 'General Store' is lit up, but flickering. More off than on, so that the horse and rider symbols on either side are sometimes the only thing visible in the dark.

It takes several more moments for me to actually care about all this because I am lost in my head. Thinking about road trips, and wing buds, and little witch girls who put a spell on you. Thinking about root cellars, and jars of magic, and bacon. Then Paul and Josep, who I can't even picture in my head. I know he was there. I know he was drinking me, and me him. But what he looks like, I can't recall. Maybe I don't remember. Maybe I never saw him. Maybe he was never really there.

Maybe none of this is happening?

"Ryet?" It's almost a whisper. And when I look at Syrsee, I see why. The purple and the gold is all gone now. There is no more mist in this truck. But it took something of her with it. Because she is very pale and looks very weak.

I reach over and put my hand on her face. "Are you OK? Do you need to feed?"

Her eyes brighten with the invitation to drink, but only a little.

"You do need to feed." I bite my palm, then hold it up to her lips. She grimaces. Like the blood is making her sick, even though she hasn't started drinking yet.

She pushes my hand away, shaking her head. "I don't want it."

I'm not sure it matters if she wants it. In fact, I'm positive it doesn't. "It's got nothing to do with wanting it, Syrsee. You need it. You don't look good."

She scoffs, her eyes finding mine. "Well, I've been through a lot, so sorry I look like shit."

It comes out defensive, and I don't blame her. I'm not even sure there are words that explain what happened to her.

"Sorry." She blows out a breath. "I didn't mean it to come out like that. I'm not feeling quite myself."

Even though I'm worried about this—how she looks so sick right now—it feels... right. Maybe right is the wrong word. But at the very least, it feels... real. Whatever happened to us in that dream walk didn't feel real. Didn't feel like anything, actually.

But we were *severed from our souls.*

That is such a big deal I'm not sure I'll ever grasp the full meaning or consequences. But I do know one thing—when you lose you soul, you should *feel* it.

I didn't feel it when it happened. I don't even feel it now. But I see it. I see it in Syrsee's eyes, in her pale skin, and in the way she's slumped in the seat. Like she's exhausted.

Like she's… sick. Like she's a person dying. Someone you know is fading fast so you go to them. To say a final goodbye.

She looks like that. Like she's only half here now. Like she might fade right before my eyes.

"It's fine," I say. "I understand."

My understanding makes her attempt a smile. "Yeah. You do. You're the only one, Ryet. The only person I have on this whole planet who understands what happened to me. And I hate that you do. I hate that you were there. That you saw it all. And that when you look at me now, you know. And you'll be thinking—"

"I'll be thinking… about how much I crave kissing you."

She's looking at me in confusion.

"I'll be thinking about how much I crave complimenting you."

"Complimenting me?"

"Isn't that what we decided? In the beginning there was Ryet and Syrsee. She was pretty and he couldn't stop himself from telling her so. He drank her blood, but what he really craved was her kisses. Isn't that what we decided?"

She lets out a long breath, like she was holding it in. Then she nods. "We did decide that. But that decision feels like a very long time ago. And our situation was decidedly simpler."

I reach over and take her hand, lacing our fingers together. "Actually… it's all been pretty fucked up since the beginning, Syrsee. And I'm not talking about that night in White River when all you wanted was a cheeseburger and found yourself a vampire instead."

"Ham sandwich."

"What?"

"I think I was craving a ham sandwich that night."

I smile, shaking my head at her. "The point is, it was never OK. It was always a lie. And I'm only speaking for me here, but I'd rather know the truth than live a lie." I nod my head at the general store. Sitting right there in front of us. Waiting for a decision. "I'd rather face it head on than hide away, pretending."

Syrsee blinks at me. "We don't have *souls*, Ryet."

"I don't think we ever had souls, Syrsee. And if we did, they certainly never belonged to us. So as far as I see it, nothing's changed. We're here. Not back in the dirt. And I don't know if we're alive or what this really is, but it's real enough for me. So we're not gonna give up. We're gonna live. Because we're gonna go in there"—I nod my head to the store again—"and we're gonna tell whoever's in charge that I will cooperate. And we're gonna go to that Guild place and you're gonna read the books and find us a cure."

She's not convinced, and neither am I. But part of this new reality we're living in is faith, I think.

Because faith that this is possible is the only way we win.

Belief is a powerful motivator.

"OK?" I ask her.

She thinks about things for a few more moments. There are only two choices. Go inside and face the truth so we might beat it. Or drive away and live in ignorance, sure to fail. So it wasn't a real question I was asking, just a way for her to see the two paths clearly. And she does. Because she says, "OK."

I give her hand one more squeeze, kiss it as I look her in the eyes, then we let go of each other and get out of the truck.

We spend a few more seconds looking up at that flickering sign, then we walk forward to the door and I pull it open.

There was never any doubt in my mind that the door was unlocked. And it is. A bell jingles as we pass through. Then Syrsee leads me through the back and into a hallway. We turn a corner and at the end of the hall there is a door made of frosted glass and a shadow can be seen pacing on the other side of it.

Suddenly the shadow turns towards us, then the door is opening.

A man. Tristin, I think. But I've never met him, so I can't be sure until Syrsee introduces him.

"Tristin, this is Ryet." She looks at me and smiles. "This is Tristin. He's on our side." Then she directs her gaze to him again. "You said if we come together, we'll be safe and I will be allowed to read the books."

"That's correct." Tristin says this very seriously, looking Syrsee directly in the eyes. "Come home, Syrsee, and we will protect you." Now he adjusts his gaze to me. "You as well, if you need it. But just so we're all clear here—nothing is free as far as you're concerned. They want to study you. So if you come and accept our protection, you're agreeing to that. Do you understand?"

This is the proper place to stop and gather up all the details, thoroughly sort through them, and make informed decisions. But there's no other way forward. So whatever the Guild wants from me in exchange for Syrsee's safety, I will give it to them. So I nod my head. "I understand."

Tristin exhales. Like he was holding his breath. And his smile is immediate and big. Like he just won a prize.

And I guess he did.

A Black witch and a vampire—two very rare creatures indeed.

He opens the door wider, inviting us into the lounge. We

enter and follow him through another door, down a hallway, and then we stop at the end in front of a blank wall.

He says some words in a language I don't speak, and then the wall turns into a mist. Not purple, not gold, but silver. And slowly, the mist is replaced with an entrance to a massive room, empty of people, but filled with books. Hundreds of thousands of books.

He brought us right to the library.

Tristin walks through and I start to follow, but Syrsee pulls on my hand, stopping me. "What the hell is this?" She's looking up at Tristin.

"You want the books? The books are yours. And you've got a lot to learn, Syrsee. So let's get started."

Epilogue - Paul

It was worth it.

Going into the dirt is like going home. It's like being in the only place you've ever known, and once you're back inside its soothing embrace, it's like you never left.

To be in the ground is to belong. To know oneself. To understand your place in the universe.

It's almost as addicting as the blood.

It can be a place of travel, since the dirt is a medium. You can leave the physical body behind and be anywhere, be anything, be anyone.

It's a realm of endless possibilities. Like… a video game with cheat codes.

I like this analogy. I got it from Tristin, since I, obviously, don't spend time in spaces that offer up video games.

It's also a really nice place to have a good long think about your choices.

And I'm thinking about Tristin. Not just the video game analogy, but the whole conversation we had when he and I met up the last time we were both in the dirt, just before the old witch died and Syrsee was revealed to me.

"*Why* am I doing this?" Tristin was looking at me with a look of confusion. "You mean, why am I helping you?" His scoff was real. "Why the fuck do you think, Paul? I'm a rogue. They cut off my fucking wings. Do you think… what, that I just let them cut my wings off so I could come to America and fuck around with a bunch of Guardians? No." His eyes were darting back and forth, searching my own. "*No.* I was sent here to help you. How many times do I have to tell you that before you believe me?" He scoffs again. "It doesn't matter what you think, actually. I'm here to help. If you want me to deliver Syrsee's and Ryet's bodies to your Montana compound after the Darkness claims Ryet and impregnates Syrsee, then I'll do it. You don't have to believe me." He leaned forward, right into my space. We were the same height—eye to eye. And he spit the last few words out at me. "You don't have to believe anything. All you have to do is *watch*."

I didn't put much faith in him. I didn't put any faith in him, actually. When I left Ryet and Syrsee in the purple-gold mist to bury the vessel of Darkness that used to be Ryet's body, I was fully expecting to be arranging logistics for transporting coffins using that kitchen phone he has.

But when I got upstairs, Tristin was waiting on the porch. Like we'd been planning it down to the very last detail, when in truth, we hadn't discussed any of it in months.

He stood up when I opened the door. Kinda... looked me up and down. The purple mist was clinging to me that evening. It was so thick, I was probably glowing. But I was too surprised at Tristin's *reliability* to really notice how strange I looked.

Tristin must've read my expression because he smirked at me. It was a lovely smirk. So full of confidence. Overflowing with self-assurance. Almost boastful of the fact that he was *faithful*.

"You showed."

"Told ya." Then he winked at me. "I did not let those old fuckers cut off my wings just so I could come to America and be a good little Guardian, neutered and loyal to the enemy. I came here to help you, Paul."

"Why? And don't say the Obscurati told you to. Because we both know that's bullshit."

"Of course they didn't. They hate you." He took a step forward, placing a hand on my cheek. Staring right into my eyes. The *nerve* of this boy. He was either very competent or very stupid. "But I am an opportunist, Paul. I know where all this is going."

"Do you?"

He nodded. "The Obscurati? They end with you. You, Paul, are the new vampire. A vampire for the next age. One who will outlast the ones who came before you. And wings were a small price to pay for the opportunity to serve *you*, my lord."

Then he dropped to one knee and bowed to me like a scion.

It's a literal gesture of offering. A pledge of devotion.

He didn't move. I didn't move, either. He bowed to me for three minutes and seventeen seconds before I finally released him and he stood once more.

"I've made all the arrangements. Two coffins delivered to the Montana compound. All I need from you are two of your scions to accompany them. I have to wait in town, for obvious reasons. Did Syrsee agree?"

I didn't answer right away. It's not often that one is presented with a new ally.

He could've been lying, but even if he was, as long as he delivered the coffins to Montana, it didn't matter.

From that point on, the process was unstoppable.

And he did deliver.

I close my mind in the dirt, putting the memory of that meeting to rest, and allow myself to belong to the new Darkness incubating inside Ryet's body.

Because Tristin is right.

This is the dawn of a new age of vampire.

And every sacrifice I had to make to get here was worth it.

Epilogue - Syrsee

It's me.

The Guild Headquarters in New Hampshire encompasses nearly a thousand acres and spans across a wide valley and several entire mountains. I didn't see most of it as a kid. And I don't think that was due to me being a charity case, it's just everything but the school was off limits to anyone but Guild Citizens. Which is different than being a Guardian, even though the two separate statuses are related.

You can be a Guardian and not a Citizen, but all Citizens were Guardians at one point in their lives.

The first few years I went to school here I thought being a Guardian was the pinnacle of aspirations. I saw the headquarters that night I arrived with my grandma at age seven but it was dark, and mostly empty, and I was too frightened to take notice of anything of consequence.

It was also a quick visit. Maybe two hours total to sort things out. And then I was put into a gondola and sent up the mountain to the Guild school campus. This was a mostly self-contained community that had shops, and restaurants, and local services like a market, laundromat, and health center. There were other things to do on the school campus as well. Entertainment things. There was a lake with access to small boats, a campground and hiking trails, and a movie theatre.

So once I arrived at the school there was almost no reason for me to ever leave it.

The other kids did go home for semester and summer breaks, but I never did. Not even as a guest with one of the other students. Not even with Zusi.

At the time I didn't think about this very much. Kinda like I never thought about the books. I just accepted the fact that I was an outsider. I accepted the idea that I should expect *less* because no one had ever bothered to teach me to expect *more*.

I didn't feel worthy of the things other students took for granted like trips home to see family and reading the books in the library.

I felt like… like this incomplete existence was all that I deserved. Not that anyone ever said something like that to me —no one ever did. I always just felt… lucky? And that when given a gift, one should not look at that horse's mouth too closely?

But lucky is the wrong word.

I didn't feel lucky. I felt… indebted. Like I was getting something that I didn't earn.

A loan. It felt like a loan. One I didn't put up collateral for and would never be able to pay back.

Of course, it took a while for this feeling to fully bloom. I lived in the Community building with all the other younger kids until I was eleven and didn't move over to the Merchant building until middle school. That's when the differences between myself and the others really started to show.

All the other kids lived on floors two through nine. But I was put up on the fifteenth floor. The attic, as it was called by the other kids. I wasn't given a roommate but Zusi volunteered to move in with me.

Looking back now, I guess it's pretty clear that she didn't volunteer.

She was assigned to me.

But even this realization isn't enough to foul my mood today.

Ryet and I were not given some after-thought attic bedroom. We aren't even on the same mountain as the Guild school.

We live with all the other Citizens. In a nice one-bedroom apartment inside a charming A-frame house that looks like something right out of a Swiss fairytale. The whole village that we're staying in looks like that. A cross between a chalet and a ski resort—though most of the snow is gone now.

The village is vertical. Going up and down the side of the mountain. And I get the feeling that it's a coveted spot because everything is close by. The research center—where Ryet reports every morning—is about a quarter mile down a little path that is so picturesque I can't help but bliss-out out at the view when we walk that way.

And the library—not the same library where we came in through the mist—is another quarter-mile walk in the opposite direction.

I've only been gone a couple of months, so I don't know why I was expecting everything to feel foreign and strange, but I *was* expecting that.

And it's not. Like... at all. There are familiar faces from the Guild school campus all around me. They smile at me, greet me, and Ryet and I have even gotten invitations to weekend gatherings.

Each morning he and I say goodbye outside our little chalet house and go our separate ways until lunch when we meet up for an hour at one of the restaurants in our village. Then we say goodbye again, go back to work—or... whatever it is—and meet up at home around six.

We are both hungry at that point, and not for food.

We drank each other at lunch that first day we were here,

but the blood makes us tired and lazy. So we've decided to eat food at lunch and save the drinking for dinner.

I never imagined a life where I drank my boyfriend's blood for dinner every night, or a life where I was carrying a wraith-like demon of the Darkness inside me, or a life where everything was so... temporary.

Because of course, nothing about this life we're living is permanent. I don't even have a soul.

But there's no way to change any of that.

Either I find a way through it or I give up.

And I have decided that Ryet, and the Guild, and the library are my way through it.

***

This is our fifth day here.

I step through the doors of the library and walk in just far enough to get out of the way of people behind me. But then I pause, like I've done every morning for the past few days, to take it all in. I just can't believe I never knew about this place.

Even though Tristin brought us back to the Guild using the mist that led to the school library, that's not where I was told to report on the second day. This library is everything you picture in your head when you think of a place called the Guild Library. Old, and Gothic, and ornate. The one for the school kids—the one I worked in (the only one I knew existed four days ago)—would be considered utilitarian in comparison.

I've been reporting to a private first-floor reading room that is more like a small office than the study rooms I was used to from school. It's comfy with golden velvet-tufted couches facing each other and a round wooden table between them. Every single inch of wall space is filled with bookshelves.

I have yet to be allowed to read a book. Which is funny— but not in a funny way—since upon arrival with Tristin five days ago, I was told to get started.

I haven't even been allowed to touch a book yet.

The brass plate on the outside of this door calls this room 'Level One'.

I'm starting at the beginning, I guess.

I've been in kind of an orientation with the Guild Archivist—a middle-aged man called Jaedon. He is tall, and handsome, and wears a cliché robe that gives off a high-ranking priest vibe.

But that's not who's waiting for me when I enter the 'Level One' room today.

I recognize his face, but can't immediately place his name. His robes give off a similar priest vibe, though not a high-ranking one like Jaedon's.

He extends his hand. "Syrsee. Hi. It's…" He pauses here to just stare at me.

And that's when I realize why he's familiar. *"Myer?"*

He was already smiling but it grows bigger now. "You remembered. I wasn't sure you would."

I let out a long breath but don't say anything. Because the last time I talked to Myer I was fourteen years old and we were about to have ourselves a kiss out by the Guild school lake.

This kiss was preempted by my bodyguard.

To save him, Myer the Guardian, from me, Syrsee the Black witch. Not the other way around.

"What are you doing here?" I glance around, looking for

the Guild Archivist, acting like there is any possible way another person might be hidden from view in this small room.

"I'm your guide. From now on, anyway. I was assigned to you last night."

I meet his gaze again. Unsure what this is all about. "Guide for what? I know how to read, I know how to find books in a library, and I know what I'm looking for. I'm pretty sure I don't need a guide."

"Well." He sighs this word out. "You *think* you know. But." He pauses to frown. Then his tone becomes more serious. "There's actually a lot more to reading the Guild books than… well, *reading* them. So they—the Archivists—they want me to…" He shrugs. Almost bashfully. "They want me to take you through it." He leans forward when he says this last part. And his voice lowers. Like he's telling me a secret. "I'm the youngest Archival apprentice and I guess they figured, since we knew each other, that it would be…" He shrugs again. "Funner?"

"Funner?" I'm confused.

"I mean, more enjoyable. Since funner isn't even a word."

I smile, then chuckle unexpectedly. "What are you talking about?"

"Why don't I just show you?" He walks over to the book shelf, pulls on the spine of a thin, colorful book, and then turns back to me and walks over to one of the couches. He sits down, and beckons me to take a seat next to him.

I hesitate. Feeling exasperated, and tired, and a little bit like a fool. Because all I want is to read the fucking books and every time I feel like I'm getting closer to doing that, something gets in the way.

But he pats the couch again and, well, I think throwing a fit over this right now would probably be the wrong move.

So I sit and Myer places the book on the table in front of us.

I glance down and read the title out loud. "Good. Dog. Good?" I look back up at Myer. "What the hell? I didn't come here to read a picture book about a dog, Myer. I'm looking for secrets, and history, and... and... *illumination*."

He raises a single finger. "Hold that thought." Then he reaches for the book and with that one single finger, he opens the front cover.

In this same instant the brightest, most glorious gold light spills out of the book. Illuminating the room in a brilliant glow—like the sun just rose inside the room with us.

It takes me several seconds of open-mouthed staring to actually look back up at Myer. "What is that?"

But before he can answer, the light becomes a mist and the room is gone.

We are somewhere else.

In front of us is a cartoon dog, white with black spots, wagging his tail and looking up at me with a goofy cartoon smile.

Myer shifts closer to me until we are bumping shoulders. Then he pans a hand down at the dog. "We don't *read* books, Syrsee. We go *inside* them."

He says more, but I'm lost now. Lost in the possibilities before me.

Lost in all the ways in which my life just changed.

Lost in all the ways in which I was misled, as well.

But none of that matters. Because I suddenly realize I've done this before. I've been inside the story before. And then

I'm there. Back, under the water with Lucia, watching the aquis equī in all its tentacled glory, and I shiver.

Not from the lingering memory of the ice and cold, but from the sudden realization that the Guild *is* going to keep their promise and that I *am* going to learn things. And that I will *finally* understand my place in this world.

And all this understanding will come to me, not by reading about it, but by *living it*.

In this moment I forget.

I forget about the unfairness of my time here at the Guild the way a mother forgets the pain of childbirth. Every complaint I had about my life before this moment with Myer is wiped away.

I let out a breath and meet Myer's gaze straight on. "Does every book do this? Does every book in the library contain the light?"

Myer is shaking his head before I finish. "No, Syrsee. It's not the books who have the light. It's… *you*."

And just as he says this, the light disappears and we're back on the couch.

He closed the cover.

Myer gets up, walks over to the bookshelf, and chooses another book. Then another. And another. Until there is a stack of them on the coffee table in front of us. They are all children's books, simple things meant to ease me into the world of living stories, but I don't even care that I am starting out at Level One.

I don't even care because finally, I'm *starting*.

I forget about Zusi's betrayal, and Paul's obsession, and Josep, and the Darkness, and how I am carrying its demon seed inside me, and all the ways in which my life fell apart over the last two months.

I even forget about my addiction to the blood, and how I drink my boyfriend for dinner, and how none of this is going to save my doomed, severed soul.

I forget because even though the price was high, it was *worth it*.

End of Book Shit

Welcome to the End of Book Shit. This is the part of the book where I get to say anything I want about the story you just read or listened to. It's not edited and always written last minute.

So. First let me say that I really did not see this book coming. I'm not sure how it completely took over what I thought I had planned, but it definitely did. I'm pretty sure it's Josep's fault. I just never know what these characters are gonna be like until I start writing them. And then, all of a sudden, there they are. Real as real can be (at lease while locked up inside my head) and this vampire really surprised me.

Because I had no idea he was gonna turn out the way he did.

I have to remember here that this is only book 2 and you haven't read book 3 yet. But I finished writing these books a long time ago. This book, Blood Brothers, was completed in July 2023. And when it was done I just kinda sat here in front of my computer and had a meme moment.

That whole 'escalated quickly' one.

Because almost none of this was in my plot. And I'm telling you, it was Josep. I think if he had stayed under the ground in that container this would've been a lot less "Stephen King".

But we all know what happens to 'the best laid plans'.

Anyway, I guess this is just part of being a writer. And it's not like I haven't had characters take over before. There's always one who won't behave and insists on more attention. Ford comes to mind. Spencer. Sasha was persistent. Jordan from Taking Turns series. Irina from Sick Heart. I'm sure there's a bunch of them that I can't think of right now.

But we liked them. Right? Spencer and Ford were all possessive and controlling in the best loyal-alpha away possible, Sasha was badass and cute, we were curious about Jordan, and who doesn't like Irina?

Josep, on the other hand... yeah. I'm never getting involved with this guy. He's not BFF material, he's not boyfriend material, and any deal he offers me is getting an instant rejection. Nope. Never gonna happen.

So it kinda pissed me off that he was so charismatic and insisted on jumping off the page. I feel like he hijacked my story. I really did kind of imagine American Vampires as... not sweet, or anything, but somewhat romantic.

And Josep just fucked up all my plans. He is evil! And I know that in the EOBS for book one I told you guys these vampires were evil, but I don't think I was prepared. I used to think that Meet Me in the Dark was the darkest book I ever wrote but I'm pretty sure it's now American Vampires. Book 2. I think book 2 is definitely darker than book 3 BUT ONLY because I tried my very best to control Josep in book 3. If he had his way, it would've been a horror show.

And basically, this is a 'horror romance'. I would not call it 'gore romance' – I don't know why that's so popular in romance, but it IS a thing and it gets a lot of attention. But I don't think this is gore. But it's definitely horror and I really didn't plan it that way.

And this is the reason I never released this book back in 2023. I didn't know how I felt about it. Not the story, or the characters, or the blood and sex.

Just... the message, ya know?

It's looking evil right in the face. Being eye-to-eye with it. And I don't know about you, but I'm not in to the evil. I like dark romance for the feels. I like the angst. That's what I show up for. I'm not there for the shock. I'm really not.

And what Josep does to Echo by turning her into Little Baby kind of horrified me. In fact that whole name—Little Baby—horrifies me still. And I will say this, part of the way I wrangled Josep in for book 3 was to make Echo a main character. We get her point of view in the next book. She gets a say.

I'm not gonna go into details about book 3 and that's really all I have to say about Josep because he's NOT the main character in this book.

But... neither are Syrsee and Ryet.

This is another thing I realized after finishing book 2. Everything I thought this story was, isn't. So yes, this is a romance about Ryet, the emergent vampire, feeding on Syrsee, the Black Magic witch—which in and of itself, should be a BIG red flag. All the real angst in this book is between them. The love story, the push and the pull, they are the literal definition of The Black Moment.

But their story doesn't even belong to them. Because it belongs to Paul. He created them. He's the puppet master. It is his plan that we're watching unfold.

We didn't see very much of Paul in this book but trust me, he's back with a literal vengeance in book 3.

These books are the story of Paul the Vampire. It's all about him. And once you realize that, a lot more of what's happening makes sense.

That was my conclusion after I finished this book and let it sit for a year, trying to figure it out. It took me a while to understand what this story was trying to tell me. Because I do firmly believe that every story I tell is a message to me. It's really got nothing to do with you guys, the readers.

Sometimes readers (especially 'influencers' who think their opinions should matter to everyone) hate when I say stuff like that. But if you've been reading me since the beginning, you know I don't write books for money. I don't write books for fans, either. I've always said that I write books for me.

So in this case, after I was done with Blood Brothers, I had to decipher the message. Because the whole fuckin' story is disturbing. And I don't know what else to say about that except, this is just the story. I don't really write them guys, they just appear in my head and I copy them down.

I could no more make Josep redeemable than I could stop Mr. Romantic from presenting Ivy with that 'contract'. Because I didn't write Mr. Romantic. It appeared in my head and I copied it down.

This is what happened with Blood Brothers. So it what it is. I almost didn't release the second and third books, and if the audiobook for Blood Brothers wasn't so fucking amazing (holy shit, did Oliver Clarke nail Josep, or what? I'm dead over that performance.) – If I didn't have the audiobook for this one, I would've put them all on the shelf. But it was too good of a performance by all the narrators to let it die that way.

And while I do not have book 3 back from audiobook production yet, it's gonna be even better. I'm actually looking forward to listening.

Anyway, I think my horror was in this message that the story was sending me. I'm not sure who this message is from, but it's a disturbing one. Because my takeaway is that we're not in control of anything in this life. Not a single piece of it. We can do our best to influence our tiny lives in this massive universe, but in the end it doesn't matter.

Because there is a game being played out all around us. And we've got nothing to do with it. Not a single fucking thing.

There are no humans in these books for a reason. Because we're not in their game. We're not players, we're not chess pieces, we're not dice. We simply don't exist.

And to be honest, I'm relieved about that message. Because I don't want to play their game. I want the vampires of this world to stay in their own fucking lane and leave me the hell alone.

Thank you for reading, thank you for reviewing, and I'll see you in the next book.

Julie
JA Huss
March 5, 2025

ABOUT THE AUTHOR

JA Huss is a New York Times Bestselling author and has been on the USA Today Bestseller's list 21 times. She writes characters with heart, plots with twists, and perfect endings.

Her books have sold millions of copies all over the world. Her book, Eighteen, was nominated for a Voice Arts Award and an Audie Award in 2016 and 2017 respectively. Her audiobook, Mr. Perfect, was nominated for a Voice Arts Award in 2017. Her audiobook, Taking Turns, was nominated for an Audie Award in 2018. Her book, Total Exposure, was nominated for a RITA Award in 2019.